LAYING DOWN THE LAW

"Listen to you," Jake Bass sneered. "Who in hell do you think you are?"

"I've already told you."

"Mister, you have sand," Crusty said. "Not much brains but a lot of sand. We'll give Mr. Knox and Bull your message. And then you'd best be ready for when we come ridin' in to settle your hash."

"You misunderstood," Asa said. "I didn't say I want you to deliver the message. I said I need to send one. I'll hire a boy to ride out to the ranch for me."

"Why, when we can do it?" Crusty said.

"You won't be able to."

"Why in hell not?"

Asa Delaware always liked this part. He liked the looks on their faces when it sank in. "Because," he said matter-of-factly, "both of you will be dead."

Also by David Robbins

Thunder Valley
Blood Feud
Ride to Valor

TOWN TAMERS

DAVID ROBBINS

A SIGNET BOOK

SIGNET
Published by the Penguin Group
Penguin Group (USA) LLC, 375 Hudson Street,
New York, New York 10014

USA | Canada | UK | Ireland | Australia | New Zealand | India | South Africa | China
penguin.com
A Penguin Random House Company

First published by Signet, an imprint of New American Library,
a division of Penguin Group (USA) LLC

First Printing, December 2013

 REGISTERED TRADEMARK—MARCA REGISTRADA

ISBN 978-0-451-46575-7

Printed in the United States of America
10 9 8 7 6 5 4 3 2 1

To Judy, Joshua, and Shane

Part One

1

———

It was Saturday night, and the Circle K cowhands thundered into town whooping and hollering and firing their pistols, as they always did.

The few townsfolk foolish enough to be abroad quickly scattered to home and hearth or to the back rooms of their businesses, as they always did.

This night the Circle K's ranny, Bull Cumberland, was with them, and he was the first to see the new bartender when he slammed through the batwings of the the Whiskey Mill. New barkeeps weren't unusual. They tended to suffer a lot of "accidents" and often lit out for healthier climes after only a couple of months.

Bull hooked his thick thumbs in his gun belt and bellied up to the bar. He pounded it hard enough to be heard a block away and only then noticed that glasses had been set out in a long row. His blow caused them to rattle and jump.

The young bartender smiled at him and said, "What will it be, Childe Harold?"

Bull barely heard him over the ruckus his fellow cow nurses were raising as they jangled and clattered in, and he raised a huge hand and bellowed, "Quiet!"

It was as if the Almighty Himself had spoken. Every puncher stopped cold and fell silent. Several put their hands on their six-shooters.

Bull looked the new barkeep up and down and gruffly demanded, "What in hell did you just call me?"

"Not 'what,' but 'who,'" the young man said. "Childe Harold is a name."

"Who in hell is he?"

The young bartender smiled. He was handsomer than most, had broader shoulders than most, and had dark eyes that seemed to sparkle with amusement. He was also clean-shaven and wore a white shirt with a string tie and a spotless apron. "I'd imagine you haven't read it, then."

"Read?" Bull said. "Did you say *read*?"

"The poem."

"The what?"

"*Childe Harold's Pilgrimage*. It's by Lord Byron."

Then, to Bull's astonishment, the young bartender put a hand to his chest and raised his other hand aloft. "'Childe Harold was hight—but whence his name and lineage long, it suits me not to say. Suffice it that perchance they were of fame, and had been glorious in another day.'"

"God in heaven," Bill said.

"I was quoting from the poem," the young bartender said. "Isn't it glorious?"

Bull looked at the other punches and they were as stupefied as he was. Some of them had their mouths open and a couple had cocked their heads as if they couldn't quite believe what they were seeing.

"I ask you again," the young bartender said. "What will it be for you and your fine company?"

Bull shook his head to get his brain to work and leaned

over the bar to study the newcomer much as he might a new kind of snake. "What *are* you?"

The young man touched his apron. "Isn't it obvious?"

Jake Bass came up next to Bull and let out a snort. "A whistle, is what he is."

Old Tom stepped up on the other side and said in wonderment, "Whistle, hell. This feller is educated."

"Educated how?" Jake Bass said. "Doesn't look to me like he knows the hind end of a cow from a fiddle."

"You heard him the same as me," Old Tom said. "Ain't it plain? He's got more book learnin' than all of us put together."

"Is that so?" Bull said.

"One of those." Jake Bass said.

Crusty joined them, his cheek bulging with chaw, and said simply, "Hell."

The young bartender took a full bottle from a shelf and held it for all of them to see. "Who wants some ambrosia of the gods?"

"You shouldn't ought to talk like that," Bull told him.

"I beg your pardon?"

"Do you have a handle, sonny?"

"Who doesn't? In fact, I bear the same name as the man who wrote the poem. To my great delight and pleasure, I am proud to bear the moniker of Byron."

"God, how you talk," Jake Bass said.

"Well, By-ron," Bull said, practically making two words of it as he hitched at his gun belt. "I reckon you haven't long to live."

2

Usually when Bull Cumberland threatened someone they had the good sense to show fear. But the young bartender went on smiling as if it were of no account that he was the lone mouse in a room full of angry cats.

"Let me have him," Jake Bass said. "The only thing I hate more than a gent who thinks he knows everything is redskins."

"I don't know everything," Byron said, "but I do know my namesake. I've been reading him since I was knee-high to a calf."

"Don't think you can talk cows and save yourself," Crusty said.

Jake Bass slowly drew his Colt and pointed it at Byron. "How about I start with his ears? Then a finger or three. Then we can make him dance and I'll work on the toes."

To Bull's surprise, Byron ignored Jake and turned to him.

"That's why I thought of *Childe Harold's Pilgrimage* when I saw you."

"What?" Bull said, and was annoyed at himself for saying it so much. To his consternation, the young barkeep touched his chest again and raised his hand.

"'Sudden he stops—his eye is fixed—away—Away, thou heedless boy! Prepare the spear.'"

Jake Bass cocked his Colt. "I've listened to enough of this."

"Wait," Bull said. "What was that about a spear?"

"'Now is thy time, to perish, or display the skill that may yet check his mad career!'" Byron quoted. "'With well-timed croupe the nimble coursers veer. On foams the Bull, but not unscathed he goes; streams from his flank the crimson torrent clear.'"

"Did you say Bull?" Bull said.

Byron nodded. "You can see why I thought of you, can't you?"

Bull couldn't see any such thing but he didn't want to admit it.

"Mr. Tandy told me about the Circle K when he hired me," Byron went on. "He said you're the cocks of the walk in these parts."

"Ain't that the truth," Crusty said.

Byron went on addressing Bull. "He described you and said I'm to treat you special. That you're to be respected. That what you say goes."

"George Tandy said all that?" Bull said.

"And more."

"Can I shoot his ear off or not?" Jake Bass asked.

"Not," Bull said.

"Why in hell can't I?"

"Because I said so."

"Damn it. Look at him. Standin' there all dandified and spoutin' that stuff."

"Holster your smoke wagon."

Jake's jaw muscles twitched. He glared at Byron, glanced at Bull, and reluctantly let down the hammer on his revolver and thrust it into his holster. "If this don't beat all," he grumbled.

Bull held out his hand to Byron. "You get to go on breathin', boy."

Crusty spit into the dented spittoon caked brown with misses and wiped his mouth with his sleeve. "I don't like it nohow."

"You buckin' me?" Bull asked.

"Not so long as I'm in my right mind," Crusty replied. "But a saloon ain't no place for Nancy talk."

"I sort of like it," Bull said.

Old Tom shook his head. "Just when I reckon I've heard everything."

Byron began filling glasses, tilting the bottle expertly and not spilling so much as a drop. He went down the row so fast that the cowhands were impressed. Righting the bottle with a flourish, he announced, "Wet your throats and let the fun commence."

In no time the saloon filled with raucous laughter, ribald jokes, and the tinkle of poker chips. Everyone forgot about the new bartender. They paid him no mind when he mentioned that he was going into the back room for more bottles.

Byron whistled as he went down the hall and opened a door.

A small man in a rust-colored suit perched on a stool in a corner gave a start. His bald pate was sprinkled with sweat, and he anxiously said, "I didn't hear shots."

"You see me, don't you?" Whistling, Byron moved to a shelf and selected a couple of bottles of Monongahela. "You should go home, Mr. Tandy. Try to relax and get some sleep."

"How can I, with what we've done? If they find out—" Tandy stopped and his throat bobbed.

"They won't," Byron assured him and flashed another of his smiles. "The Circle K outfit doesn't know it yet, but hell is coming to call."

3

Along about midnight, things turned ugly.

By then the punchers had guzzled a river of liquor, those who had money to lose at poker had lost it, and the jokes and the boasts had worn thin.

Old Tom started things by saying to no one in particular, "Well, this has gotten dull."

Crusty missed a spittoon and wiped his mouth with his other sleeve. "Watchin' grass grow would be more excitin'."

"It's Tandy's fault," Jake Bass said. "He should hire a new dove. Hell, he should hire five or six."

"You shot the last one," Old Tom reminded him.

"Only in the leg," Jake Bass said. "And only because she poked fun at me."

"What did she say, again?" Crusty said and scratched his chin as if he was trying to remember. "Now I recollect. She said your pecker was the size of a pencil."

Many of the cowboys laughed but not Jake Bass. He reared out of his chair with his hand poised over his Colt. "On your feet, you son of a bitch. I'll blow out your wick for that."

Crusty was drunk enough that he put his hands on the table to stand.

"No," Bull Cumberland said from over at the bar.

Jake Bass swore a mean streak, then snapped, "Why are you buttin' in? You heard him insult me."

His back to the room, Bull raised his glass and swallowed before he answered. "Lavender wouldn't have called you a pencil, except you were smackin' her for refusin' to take you to bed, and she got mad."

"She was a dove, damn it."

"Not all doves sell themselves," Bull remarked. "And she had the right to say no if she wanted."

"Why are you takin' her side all of a sudden?" Jake Bass asked. "You've been pickin' on me all night. You wouldn't let me shoot that no-account poet, and now this."

Bull set down his glass and turned. His right hand was close to a Smith & Wesson he wore high on his hip and when he spoke, his voice had a timbre that caused every man in the place to stiffen. "You're commencin' to rile me."

Old Tom quickly said, "He don't mean nothin', Bull. He's had too much to drink, is all."

"We all have," Tyree Lucas said.

Bull moved a couple of steps to one side so no one was between him and Jake Bass. "I'm waitin'," he said.

Jake Bass looked around him, apparently expecting someone to say something. When no one did, he elevated his arms out from his sides and offered a sickly grin. "Tom is right. I didn't mean nothin'."

"Your problem, Jake, is that you let your mouth get ahead of your brain."

"I do," Jake agreed. "I truly do."

"You're always ready to sharpen your horns at the drop of a feather, and you drop the feather."

"I am," Jake said. "I surely am."

"One of these days you're goin' to sharpen them at the wrong time and someone will put windows in your skull." Bull's mouth split in an icy smile. "Maybe me. Maybe here and now."

"I have a notion," Old Tom piped up. "Why don't we tree the town and have us some fun?"

"Tree the town?" Crusty repeated. "You don't tree towns, you old goat. You tree law dogs."

"Same thing," Old Tom insisted.

All eyes swung to Bull Cumberland, who hadn't taken his off of Jake Bass. Now he did, to gaze thoughtfully at the batwings.

In the act of wiping a glass, Byron said, "Most folks are in bed by now. You'd wake them up."

"So?" Bull Cumberland said.

Old Tom, Crusty, and several others stood up, and Old Tom said, "Let's do 'er. Let's rouse 'em and pass out some booze and have us a frolic."

"Let's," Bull Cumberland said.

Just like that, the saloon emptied. Yipping and laughing and unlimbering their hardware, the punchers bustled out into the night and spread up and down the main street.

Bull went out last, taking his time. He paused at the batwings to say, "Bring me a couple of bottles."

"Sure thing." Byron came around the end of the bar. "I hope no one gets hurt."

"Why would they? We're only havin' fun." Bull took the bottles and said, "Keep things like that to yourself from here on out. You'll last longer."

Byron watched the man-mountain stride off, then hurried to the hall to the storeroom.

Tandy was still on the stool in the corner, looking as glum as a human being could look. "You're running out of whiskey again?"

"They're fixing to rouse the town," Byron said. "Figured you'd want to know."

"Oh God." Tandy came off the stool as if shot from it. "You have to stop them. All kinds of things can happen."

"Not me by myself I can't," Byron said. "I have to stick to the plan."

Tandy nervously rubbed his hands together and bit his bottom lip. "You can see why we sent for him, can't you? You can see how it is?"

"So far I haven't seen much," Byron said. "Some prodding and tempers, but no blood has been spilled. I'd hate to think I came all this way for nothing."

"Just you wait," Tandy said. "You don't know them like I do. They're animals. They fooled you by acting tame but it won't last. Their true natures will come out and innocent people will suffer."

"Do you always expect the worst?"

"I know them, I tell you," Tandy declared. "There have been seven killings in two years, one of them our last marshal, plus the stage robberies and that drummer who was found dead. They're bad men, the whole bunch."

"The man you sent for is worse," Byron said.

4

At the second house they came to, Crusty pounded on the door and hollered, "Open up in there. We're invitin' you to a town social."

The windows were dark. No life showed within until Crusty pounded harder. A glow lit an upstairs window, and a few moments later it slid open and a head poked out.

"What in tarnation is going on down there?"

"Open up, Ed," Crusty said.

"What are you loco cowpokes up to now?" Ed demanded. "Do you have any idea what time it is?"

"Come on down and bring the missus."

Other punchers were pounding on other doors and other lamps and candles were being lit, other windows brightening.

Crusty stepped back from the door and looked up. "Didn't you hear me, Ed?"

Ed was gaping at the state of events in amazement. "You can't do this. We're decent, law-abiding folk."

"There hasn't been any law since Bull shot that tin star," Crusty said. "And drinkin' and dancin' is only a little bit indecent."

"You're loco, the whole bunch of you," Ed said.

Crusty and Tyree Lucas swapped scowls.

"Ed," Crusty said, "I like you. I've been in your store more times then I have fingers and toes and you've always treated me kindly."

"You and everyone else," Ed said.

"But we want a frolic. And what we want, we will by-God have."

"My wife and I aren't coming out for no silly frolic, and that's final."

"You're a poor excuse for a friend," Crusty said.

Tyree Lucas moved to a patch of flowers ringed by rocks and hefted a big rock. "This will do," he said, and let it fly at the nearest ground-floor window. The glass shattered with a tremendous crash.

"No!" Ed cried. "What are you doing?"

Tyree bent and picked up another rock.

"He'll stop chuckin' when you open this door," Crusty said.

Ed's head disappeared.

"That did the trick," Crusty said, and he and Tyree chuckled.

It wasn't twenty seconds more that the busted window glowed and they heard the rasp of a bolt and the front door was flung open.

In the doorway stood Ed in his nightshirt. He was short and portly—and holding a doubled-barreled shotgun.

"Well, hell," Crusty said.

Ed was so mad, his whole body shook as he pointed the shotgun at them and placed his thumb on a hammer. "You broke my window, damn you. You'll pay for it, you hear? For the glass and the cost of putting it in."

"Lower that cannon," Tyree Lucas said.

"I will not."

"Where's that missus of yours?" Crusty said. "She always struck me as havin' more sense than you."

"Leave Myrtle out of this," Ed said.

"I was hopin' to have a dance with her."

"Over my dead body."

Bull Cumberland appeared out of the darkness with his Smith & Wesson in his hand. He fired, and the impact of the slug when it smashed into Ed's chest staggered Ed back against the jamb.

Ed stared in disbelief at a spreading scarlet stain on his nightshirt and then at Bull Cumberland. "You've done killed me."

"You shouldn't ought to point shotguns at Circle K riders," Bull said, and shot him a second time.

A hole blossomed in Ed's temple, and his legs melted out from under him.

"Well, hell," Crusty said a second time. "Did you have to?"

"What's the rule?" Bull asked as he calmly set to reloading.

"We stand up for each other," Crusty said.

"We ride for the brand above all else," Tyree Lucas threw in.

"That we do," Bull said. "Anyone points a gun at us, they die. Doesn't matter who they are, they die. Male, female, young, old, they die."

Crusty sadly shook his head. "We've all of us known Ed Sykes for years. He always treated us decent at the general store. I doubt he'd have shot me."

"You can't ever take anything for granted," Bull Cumberland said.

As if to prove him right, Myrtle Sykes stepped out the front door. She had on a bulky blue robe and blue slippers, and her hair was in a bun. She also held a pocket pistol.

"What do you think you're doin'?" Bull demanded.

"Killing you," Myrtle said, and trained her pocket pistol on him.

5

---·-·---

Crusty was nearest to her, and he thrust out both hands and said, "Just you hold on there, Mrs. Sykes."

"You murdered my man," Myrtle said, her cheeks flushed with fury. She closed one eye and squinted down the short barrel with the other eye at Bull Cumberland's broad face. "Someone should have done this a long time ago."

"Why, Myrtle," Bull said. "I never knew you didn't like me."

"No one does, you dumb ox. You act like you're God Almighty, doing as you please and the rest of the world be damned. You've shot how many people? Robbed how many?" Myrtle glanced at her husband's body, and a tear trickled from her eye. "Now my poor Ed."

Bull hadn't finished reloading. He was holding his pistol with the barrel pointed at the ground and had a cartridge in his other hand. "Maybe we should talk this out."

"Talk?" Myrtle said, and more tears flowed. "You want to *talk* when you've just done murdered my man? The only talk you deserve is this." She stopped shaking and curled her finger around the trigger.

"Ma'am—" Crusty tried to intervene.

"Shut up, you jug head."

That was when Tyree Lucas threw the rock he still held. It hit Myrtle on the shoulder, and she swung toward him just as Jake Bass appeared out of nowhere, his six-shooter in front of him, fanning three swift shots.

The slugs smashed into her chest and jolted her onto her heels. Her teary eyes widened, and she fell across her husband, convulsed a few times, and was still.

"Damn," Crusty said. "Now I won't get that dance."

Jake Bass stood over Myrtle and nudged her with his boot. "She had spunk. She and her rooster, both. Ain't many folks will stand up to us like that."

"You saw the whole thing?" Bull asked.

"I did."

"You took your sweet time shootin' her."

"I wanted to be sure," Jake Bass said. "I needed to be in close." He chuckled. "You're alive, aren't you?"

Bull inserted the cartridge into the cylinder of his Smith & Wesson, stepped over to the bodies, pressed his revolver to the back of Myrtle's head, and shot her again.

"What in hell was that for?" Crusty said. "She was already dead."

"She pointed a gun at me."

People were gathering. A woman wailed. A man quietly swore. A little girl was among them, and she pressed against her mother's nightgown and set to sobbing.

"So much for a frolic," Crusty said.

Bull glared at the half ring of scared and hateful faces. "I have half a mind to burn this town down."

"Where would we drink?" Old Tom asked.

"There's not another town for a hundred miles," Crusty said.

Bull Cumberland slid his Smith & Wesson into his holster and put his big hands on his hips. "Listen, you folks. They shouldn't have done what they did. All we wanted was to have some fun, and they came out loaded for bear."

From among the crowd a woman timidly said, "You shot them both down like dogs."

"It was me shot the old hen," Jake Bass said.

Bull scowled and motioned. "All of you might as well go back to bed. No one's in the mood now."

"I am," Crusty said.

Bull pushed him aside and made for the saloon but had only taken a couple of steps when he saw the new bartender in the shadows, staring at the bodies. "You have somethin' to say?"

"No," Byron said.

"You don't look like you like it."

"Who would?" Byron replied.

"Things happen. They lost their heads and did what they shouldn't."

Byron lifted his gaze from the sprawled forms. "You want me to set up a round for your outfit?"

"No," Bull said. "We're headin' back to the Circle K."

"We are?" Old Tom said.

"Mr. Knox will want to know," Bull said, with a nod at the Sykeses. "In case anyone gets the notion to go skulkin' to the law."

"Who would?" Crusty said. "They'd be as good as dead and know it."

Bull walked on with the rest of the Circle K riders trailing after him. They mounted their horses, reined from the hitch rails, and rode off with the air of men whom life had treated unfairly by spoiling their frolic.

"Scum," a townswoman said.

"Someone fetch Sam," a man said, referring to the undertaker. "He'll see to the bodies."

Tandy emerged from the saloon and walked over to stand next to Byron. "I told you."

"You did," Byron said.

"You've seen this before, I take it?"

"Too many times."

"You'll get word to him?"

"Don't need to. He'll be here in three days."

"That soon?"

"Once he takes a job, he doesn't waste time," Byron said.

"Does he always send you on ahead?"

"Usually. I scout the lay of the land, so to speak." Byron looked around them. " 'And sunk are the voices that sounded in mirth, and empty the goblet, and dreary the hearth.' "

"What was that? More of that poet fellow?"

"Lord Byron."

"How many poets do you know?"

"A few, but I know the most about him."

"I don't know any." Tandy let out a loud sigh. "I can't believe I'm talking poets with those bodies lying there. They were good, sweet people."

Byron didn't say anything.

"Once he's here, how long, do you reckon, before he gets the job done?"

"Before he kills everybody?" Byron let out a sigh of his own. "Not long at all."

Part Two

6

———— · • · ————

Asa Delaware winced when the wheels hit a rut. His back didn't take long stagecoach rides well anymore. A cloud of dust swirled in, and he breathed shallow and pulled his derby lower against the glare of the afternoon sun.

"Let me guess, friend," said the passenger across from him who had been trying to engage Asa in conversation. "You're a drummer, like me."

"No," Asa said.

"We dress the same."

Asa looked at him. The man was heavyset with sagging jowls and a suit that had seen better days, worn slovenly. Asa's was new and had been freshly pressed before he got on the stage in Austin. The other man's derby was dirty. Asa's was spotless save for the dust. On the seat beside Asa was his slicker, neatly folded, while propped against his leg was a custom-made soft leather case with ties at both ends.

"Yes, sir," the slovenly drummer said. "You sure look like a drummer, even if you're not."

"We all look like something," Asa said.

"If you don't mind my saying," the drummer said, "you also look part Injun."

"Do I?" Asa said coldly.

The drummer blinked and sat up. "I didn't mean any insult, friend. Your face. Your skin. That black hair, even with the gray streaks."

"I know what I look like."

For a while the drummer was silent, and Asa was grateful.

The only other passenger was a woman in her twenties who sat with her hands folded in her lap and must have gnawed on her lip a hundred times. Brown curls poked from under her bonnet. Her eyes were brown, too. She hadn't uttered a word in hours, but now she cleared her throat.

"Both of you gentlemen are bound for Ludlow, I take it?"

The drummer brightened and smoothed his jacket, as if that would help his appearance. "Why, yes, my dear. I am. I believe I told you earlier that I sell ladies' corsets."

"You did, Mr. Finch."

"And your name is Sykes, wasn't it?"

"Madeline Sykes. I'm on my way home to visit my mother and father."

"Ah, well." Finch did more smoothing and somehow contrived to slide closer to her. "Perhaps you'll permit me to interest you in one? They're made of the finest cotton, and the busk is ivory. Two-piece, not one, for the comfort of the wearer. When we reach Ludlow, if you'd like, you can try one on and—"

Madeline Sykes held up a hand. "I don't wear corsets, Mr. Finch."

"Why not? They're all the fashion."

"For some," Madeline said.

Finch winked at her. "A small waist, my dear, draws the male eye. It accents the bosom and the thighs, and—"

"That's enough about thighs," Asa said.

"I beg your pardon, sir?" Finch said.

"You heard me."

Finch coughed, opened and closed his mouth a couple of times, and finally said, "I'm only trying to make a living. If you were knowledgeable about the fine art of salesmanship, you'd know that a product's selling points are important."

"Make all the points you want," Asa said, "without talking about her thighs."

Madeline gave him a warm smile. "I thank you for your kindness."

"All I was saying—" Finch began, and was again interrupted when Madeline raised her hand a second time.

"Mr. Finch, I'll be frank. I hate corsets. I hate what they do to women. I hate that women think they must wear them to be attractive. I hate that men use them as a way to control us."

Finch's expression was almost comical. "Just hold on, young lady. This is my livelihood we're talking about."

"Are you aware that your livelihood has caused a lot of women to lose their babies? That those ivory busks you boast about can cause internal bleeding?"

"So *some* claim," Finch said defensively.

"Are you also aware that a woman's normal blood pressure in pounds per square inch without a corset is 3.5 but that with a corset the pressure is reduced to only 1.65?"

"How in the world would you know that?"

"And that in many instances, the pressure your corsets apply to internal organs has been measured at over seventy pounds."

"I ask you again, madam," Finch said, "how do you know all that?"

"I'm studying to be a physician."

"Excuse me?"

"A doctor, Mr. Finch. You have heard of them?"

"A *lady* doctor?" Finch said incredulously.

"It surprises you?"

"A woman's place is in the home. Everyone knows that."

Madeline Sykes had her dander up, and jabbed a finger at him. "Your corsets, sir, are an abomination. Women have been fed the lie that if they wear them, men will fall over themselves to woo them. No mention is ever made of the potential harm to a woman's health. Were it up to me, I would have a law passed to ban them."

"Now see here, young lady," Finch said.

That was when he placed his hand on her knee.

7

Asa Delaware snapped his right arm up, and a black-handled Remington derringer filled his hand. With lightning speed he pressed it to the drummer's forehead. "Take your hand off her, or die."

Finch's eyes nearly crossed as he gawked at the derringer, and then he jerked his fleshy hand off Madeline Sykes's leg. "Here, now," he bleated. "There's no call for that."

Asa sat back. He slid the derringer up his sleeve and deftly fitted it into the wrist rig he'd had made to his specifications.

"Thank you," Madeline said.

Finch had turned pale. "I resent your behavior, sir. I resent it very much."

"Don't take liberties, then," Asa said.

"Who do you think you are, shoving a gun in people's faces? I have half a mind to report you to the marshal when we get to Ludlow."

"There isn't one," Madeline said.

"Well, I still resent it." Anger had smothered Finch's fear. "You saw what he did," he said to Madeline. "And all I did was touch you. Where's the harm in that?"

"I didn't ask to be touched," Madeline said.

Finch focused his ire on Asa. "I ask you again, who do you think you are? If you're not a drummer, what are you? A gambler? Is that why you have a hideout?"

"I don't gamble . . . with cards," Asa said.

"Do you have a name? Or is it presumptuous of me to ask? I wouldn't want that gun shoved in my face again."

"There is a name I use."

"How do you 'use' a name? Or are you on the dodge and afraid to say?"

"It's Asa Delaware."

"Well, Mr. Delaware, let me tell you a thing or two about—" Finch stopped again, and blinked. "Wait. Did you say Asa *Delaware*?"

"You're sitting right there," Asa said.

Finch became paler still. He glanced at the leather case with the ties at both ends, and beads of sweat formed on his upper lip. "Is that what I think it is?"

"I can take it out and we can see."

"No," Finch said. "No, that's all right." He moved away from Madeline until he was against the side. "Asa Delaware, by God."

"I'm sorry," Madeline said to Asa. "I know you wanted to keep it a secret and I was to pretend I don't know you."

"For your own safety," Asa said.

"Wait," Finch said. "You two are acquainted?"

Madeline Sykes nodded.

"Ah," Finch said, looking confused. His eyes narrowed, a lecherous cast marked his face, and he said again, louder, "Ah."

Asa placed the leather case on his lap. He untied one end then the other, slid his hand inside, and brought out the shotgun. It was a beautiful weapon, a Winchester lever-action altered to meet his special needs. The wood was black walnut, the stock shortened to half its original length. The barrel had been sawed off to where it was barely an inch longer than the tube magazine. Every piece of metal, from the barrel to the magazine to the receiver and the lever, were bright black, not blued, and without a scratch or nick. Jacking the lever to feed a 12-gauge shell into the chamber, Asa pointed it at the drummer's head. "Say 'ah' one more time."

Finch tried to wilt into the seat. "Here, now! You can't keep shoving guns in people's faces."

"Only yours," Asa said. He shifted the shotgun so the barrel rested on his shoulder. "That's twice you've insulted her. One more time will be the last."

"Damn it, man," Finch blustered. "I don't care who you are. You don't have the right to threaten a person."

"I can do more than threaten."

Finch went to respond, and Madeline quickly said, "I'd hush up, were I you. I've only known Mr. Delaware a short while, but I've learned he's a man of principle."

"High-handed, is what he is," Finch grumbled.

Madeline stared at the shotgun. "The newspaper said you use a scattergun."

"Used to, I did," Asa said. "But they only hold two shots." He touched his cheek to the Winchester. "This can hold five."

"Why not use a rifle? I don't know a lot about guns, but I know they can hold a lot more."

"A rifle puts a hole in a man," Asa said. "A shotgun blows him in half."

"But a rifle can shoot a lot farther," Madeline persisted. "Wouldn't that be better?"

"Most of my work is close-up."

"Work," Finch said, and snorted. "Is that what you call it? You kill people for a living, for God's sake."

"No," Asa said. "I tame towns."

8

The driver liked to put on a show when he arrived any-where. He cracked his whip, let out a "yip," and sat as if he were on a throne instead of balanced on a bouncing seat.

Several people were waiting, among them George Tandy. The portrait of sorrow, Tandy seemed reluctant to step out from under the overhang.

The driver jumped down, opened the door, and dipped in a bow. "We're here, lady and gents."

Madeline Sykes carefully placed her foot on the step. When the driver offered his arm, she alighted and saw George Tandy and smiled. But the smile promptly faded, and she went up to him and asked, "What's wrong?"

"I don't know how else to say it, so I'll come right out with it," Tandy said. "Your parents—"

Madeline didn't wait to hear the rest. She whirled and ran down the street, heedless of the looks cast her way.

Asa Delaware stepped down and watched her hurry off. He had donned his slicker, and his shotgun was in its soft leather case, the ends tied, under his left arm. He stood watching her until she reached a house and went in.

"Are you going to get out of my way or stand there all day?" Finch demanded.

Asa looked over his shoulder and said in utter contempt, "Slug." Then he collected his carpetbag and moved around the stage and across the street to a building with a sign that read ETHEL'S BOARDINGHOUSE. He'd never been to Ludlow before, but he knew the town as well as he knew the lines in his own face, thanks to the information provided by those who had hired him. He opened the door and found himself in a comfortable foyer with a counter to one side and a gray-haired woman knitting in a chair behind it.

"May I help you, sir?"

"Are you Ethel?"

"I am."

"Looks more like a hotel than a boardinghouse," Asa commented.

"This?" Ethel rose and tapped the top of the counter with a knitting needle. "Bought it cheap when the Tumbleweed Hotel went out of business. Makes thing easier when folks sign the register." She set her knitting down. "Would you like a room by the day or the week?"

"Week," Asa said.

"I have rules," Ethel said. "No liquor. No gambling. No tobacco spitting. No women unless she's your wife. No loud noises. By that I mean no hollering. No stomping. No cussing. No slamming of doors. No treating the other guests with disrespect." She stopped.

"That's a heap of rules."

"I like quiet and order in my establishment," Ethel said.

"I'm fond of order myself," Asa said. "And I have some rules of my own."

"Rules about what?"

Asa didn't answer. Instead he asked, "How many guests are here at the moment?"

"Five, not counting you," Ethel said. "There's Mr. Gattersby, who works at the feed and grain. He takes his room by the month. There's Miss Marple, a 'spinster,' some call her, and a dear friend of mine. There's a nice young fellow by the name of Byron Gordon. He works at a whiskey fountain over at the saloon, but he's as polite as anything."

"Good upbringing," Asa said.

"There's a young lady who showed up just two days ago.

Noona, she calls herself. Noona Not. Now I ask you, is that a peculiar name or is that a peculiar name? She took a job at the saloon, too. I warned her she shouldn't, but she took it anyway."

"Some people never listen."

"Ain't that the truth." Ethel studied him. "You're part Indian."

"Is that a problem?"

"Not in the least. I'm not one of those who looks down their noses at inferiors. Mind telling me which tribe?"

"Is it important?"

"Only if you're part Apache. I'm sorry, but I don't trust Apaches worth a lick. My pa was killed by them nigh on forty years ago."

"That's a long time to hold a grudge," Asa remarked.

"Grudge, nothing. I hate them, pure and true." Ethel paused. "Now which tribe are you?"

"The last name I use is Delaware."

Ethel's face scrunched in thought. "I seem to recollect a tribe by that name. Aren't they from back east somewhere?"

"They were. The government moved them."

"Did the government move you, too?"

"I have nothing to do with them. My grandmother was a Delaware, and she married a white. She left the tribe to live with him and never went back. She had two sons and a daughter and all three looked white. The daughter married and had two sons by the white she married and one of them is me. And you can see how I look."

"I'll be," Ethel said. "So both your parents are white but you look Indian? How did that happen, do you reckon?"

"I was told it's in the blood," Asa said. "I was told it sometimes skips a generation."

"Who told you that?"

"A doctor."

"Well, a doctor should know. It must be strange, you being raised white and looking so redskin."

"It's something," Asa said.

9

Madeline Sykes was in the parlor on the settee, quietly crying. George Tandy and his wife and a dozen other townspeople stood in the hall or were seated in the kitchen. The knock on the front door seemed to startle them.

George Tandy answered it. He opened the door and said, "*You.*"

"Me," Asa Delaware said.

"Now might not be a good time. Her parents were murdered by the Circle K hands three days ago. We couldn't get word to her because she was on her way here."

"Move," Asa said.

Tandy stepped aside, and Asa walked down the hall to the parlor. He took his derby off and went to the settee.

"I'm sorry to hear about your folks."

Madeline looked up, her eyes brimming. She sniffled and shook her head and lowered it again. "I can't talk right now."

"It might help."

"We should have sent for you sooner. If I had, they'd be alive right now."

"You don't know that."

Madeline sniffled some more and dabbed at her nose with a handkerchief. "Why do you think I contacted you after I read that newspaper account? I've lived in constant fear for their lives ever since that Knox took over the Circle K and hired that Bull Cumberland and his bunch."

Asa waited.

"It was me who persuaded my father and Mr. Tandy and the others to hire you. I told them they had to do something. That if they didn't, more good people would die."

"The dying is about over," Asa said.

Madeline looked up again. Anger had stopped her tears but not the dribbling from her nose. She dabbed and said, "You'll kill them? Every last one?"

"Those as don't run."

"Good," she said, and then, more forcefully, "*Good*."

"The woman at the boardinghouse told me about your parents when I asked her about the latest goings-on," Asa said. "I came to pay my respects. But after this, I don't know you until it's finished."

"That's all right. I understand."

"I probably shouldn't have come to your home."

"I'm glad you did."

"If any of them saw me, they might wonder."

"I don't care if any of them did." Madeline stood and touched his arm. "I appreciate the gesture. You're not anything like the newspapers say you are."

"Yes," Asa said, "I am." He put his derby on, nodded, and retraced his steps to the front door. Halfway there, George Tandy stopped him.

"A word, if you please."

"Make it short."

"I just want you to know that the town council backs you one hundred percent."

"Do they?"

"Need you ask, especially after this?" Tandy gestured at the parlor. "Ed and Myrtle were well-liked. He was the one brought us the idea of hiring you after Madeline wrote to him."

"All of you agreed then and there?"

"Well, no," Tandy admitted. "Some of us balked. You ask an exorbitant fee, or so we felt at the time."

"And now?"

"I just told you. We back you one hundred percent."

Asa regarded him a few moments. "Make it clear to them. There's no backing out. Make sure they understand that I always finish what I start, no matter how much they might complain."

"Why would they complain? We sent for you. We paid you half in advance. We want the job done as much as you do."

"I doubt that."

"It's our town, Mr. Delaware. We've had to live with those curly wolves running roughshod over us for far too long. They shot our marshal and do as they damn well please, and they have to be stopped."

"I'll stop them."

"You're one man against many." Tandy glanced at the soft leather case. "Even with that, I don't see how you can do it."

"I have a secret."

"Care to share it?"

"No." Asa moved to the door and gripped the latch. "One last thing. This town have an undertaker?"

"Sure. His name is Sam Wannamaker."

"Have him send word to the Circle K. Have him tell them that he wants them to come in so he can fit them for coffins."

"Do what now?"

"You heard me." Asa opened the door.

"Hold on," Tandy said. "If Sam does that, they'll want to know why. What should he tell them?"

"He's to say that Asa Delaware asked him to."

"Sam is to say who you are?"

"He is."

"Is that wise? They're not stupid. Some of them will have heard of you and will put two and two together."

"That's the idea."

"You *want* them to come looking for you?"

Ada nodded. "Saves me the trouble of going to them."

"And then you'll kill them?"

"When the time comes," Asa said, "I'll kill them as dead as can be."

10

The evening's festivities were in full swing for the middle of the week when Noona Not came out of the back of the Whiskey Mill and sashayed to the bar. The men lining it and those at the tables stopped what they were doing to gape. She was an eyeful, and she knew it.

Lustrous black hair hung to the small of her back. Her eyes were a lovely hazel, her body an hourglass. Her red lips formed a perpetual pout and made her all the more enticing. Grinning in amusement, she turned in a circle and airily asked, "What do you think, barkeep?"

"You look like a whore," Byron Gordon said.

Noona laughed. "That was poetical."

"I don't like it, and you know it."

"You never do."

A townsman half in his cups sobered enough to ask, "What are you two talkin' about?"

"Nothing," Byron snapped. "Go back to drinking."

"Bite a man's head off, why don't you."

"Careful," Noona said.

"I always am," Byron replied irritably, and moved down the bar to pour for another customer.

"He's a mite prickly tonight," the townsman said to Noona.

"Not just tonight." Noona smiled sweetly, clapped the man on the arm, and moved to a table where four others were playing poker. She leaned on the table and said, "Having fun, gents?"

"We are now," a husky said.

"We're awful glad that Tandy brought you in, ma'am," remarked another.

"You're just what this place needs," commented the third.

"I bet you say that to all the gals," Noona said.

"I wish," the man said. "My wife would kill me if she heard me compliment another female."

Noona laughed and moved to the next table. Out of the corner of her eye she saw Byron glowering at her, and she shot him a glance to warn him. She would have thought by now he was used to it but he always was too protective.

She made small talk and did more teasing, and when she returned to the bar, he was waiting. Careful not to be overheard, she quietly said, "You'll give it away, consarn you."

"Look at you," Byron said. "Prancing around like you give it away."

"Now, now," Noona said. "The smart doves sell it. They never do it for free."

"That's not even a little bit funny."

"To me it is."

Someone bellowed for Scotch, and Byron turned to the shelves and selected a bottle. When he turned back, he said, "You never take this seriously enough."

"Not that again." Noona grinned mischievously. "Besides, you're here, aren't you? What do I have to worry about?"

"I'm not him."

"He's arrived, you know, today on the stage. I saw him get off."

"Then it could start tonight."

"Could," Noona said.

Byron went to say something but glanced sharply at the batwings and visibly tensed. "Watch yourself," he said.

Noona turned.

Two cowboys had entered. Dusty from their long ride,

they both wore Stetsons, chaps, and spurs. One was short and flinty-eyed and had a Colt high on his hip. The other was a rake handle whose upper lip drooped over the lower as if about to fall off. .

"Circle K?" Noona said.

Byron nodded. "The rooster is Jake Bass. He shot the last girl who worked here in the leg and shot a townswoman dead the other night."

"And you wonder why I do this?"

"The other one is called Crusty. He looks harmless, but I've asked around and they say he does his share of the killing, rustling, and robbing."

"They've seen me." Noona casually placed a hand on her hip and contrived to thrust out her bosom. "Look at them. Their eyes are fit to bug out."

"Be careful," Byron said. "Be very careful."

"He taught me, didn't he?"

The man who had bellowed for a Scotch bellowed again, and Byron reluctantly moved around the end of the bar and went over to a poker table.

Noona leaned her elbow on the counter and bestowed her most charming smile as the punchers approached. Jake Bass was ogling her, but Crusty hung back a step, acting nervous. "What have we here?" she greeted them.

"I was about to ask the same thing, gorgeous," Jake Bass said. He came uncomfortably close and raked her up and down with pure lust in his eyes. "Ain't you a sight."

"I am?" Noona said innocently.

"You're right pretty, ma'am," Crusty said.

"Where did you come from?" Jake Bass asked.

"My ma's womb."

Jake Bass cackled and Crusty giggled and Jake said, "How much for a poke?"

"You get right to it," Noona said.

"Gal, it's been a coon's age, and I ain't one to beat around the bush."

"From what I hear tell," Noona said, "you put lead in them, too."

Jake's cheeks colored. "Someone has been talkin' out of school."

"Well, you did shoot Lavender," Crusty said. "This new one was bound to hear."

Jake Bass glared at him, and Crusty took a step back. Then Jake gripped Noona's arm and said, "I asked how much. And I don't mean tomorrow."

"Take your hand off."

"Don't prod me, bitch. You make me mad and you won't like what happens."

Noona knew she shouldn't provoke him, but she swatted his hand off her arm and jabbed him in the chest. "*I* decide who does and who doesn't, and they have to be a gentleman about it."

"Is there a problem here?"

Byron had come up unnoticed and was holding an empty bottle by the neck.

"Butt out, poet boy," Jake Bass said.

"Yeah, butt out," Crusty said.

"Mr. Tandy left specific instructions," Byron said. "I'm to look after her and see that she doesn't come to harm like the last one did."

Jake Bass faced him, and his hand moved to within a whisker's width of his Colt. "When I tell someone to butt out, they damn well better."

"It's my job," Byron said.

"It can be your funeral, too."

"Tend to the drinks and leave us be," Crusty said. "Or else."

Noona was afraid that Byron wouldn't back down as he should. She was about to motion him away when the batwings parted. It took a bit for what the drinkers and the card players were seeing to register, and then the place fell as quiet as a cemetery at midnight.

Asa Delaware had that effect.

11

The Winchester lever-action shotgun in his right hand with the barrel on his shoulder, Asa surveyed the saloon. Instead of making straight for the bar, he circled and came up on the four people in the middle so that no one was between him and them.

The two punchers had been alerted by the sudden silence. They were more curious than anything.

"What's with the artillery, mister?" Crusty asked.

"The pair of you ride for the Circle K," Asa said. He'd been given descriptions of the hands, especially the most notorious. "You're Crusty Wilkins and this other is Jake Bass."

"What's it to you?" Jake Bass said.

"I'm Asa Delaware," Asa said.

"So?" Jake responded.

"You look part Injun," Crusty said.

"I am."

"Which tribe?"

"Why does everyone ask that?"

Crusty shrugged. "Probably because a lot of folks, me included, don't like redskins much. Which tribe is it?"

"Guess," Asa said.

"Comanche?"

"No."

"Kiowa?"

"No."

"Lipan Apache, maybe? Or Caddo?"

"No and no."

"Wichita?"

Asa shook his head.

"You don't look Pueblo."

"I'm not."

"Damn. You must be from one of those faraway tribes. Which is it?"

Jake Bass growled, "What the hell difference does it make? A breed is a breed."

"I was only askin'," Crusty said.

Asa looked at Byron and Noona. "You two might want to go over by the wall. Blood tends to splatter."

"Blood?" Crusty said.

Noona plucked at Byron and when he didn't move, she grabbed him and pulled him away.

Only when they were out of the spread of the buckshot did Asa fix his complete attention on the cowboys. "I take it you've never heard of me."

"Mister," Jake Bass said, "we don't know you from Adam. But I've commenced to take a powerful dislike to you."

"You shouldn't be in here," Crusty said. "This ain't a breed-friendly town."

"Friendly enough to hire me," Asa said.

"How's that again?"

"The Circle K blew out the wick of the last lawman and they haven't been able to hire a replacement, so they brought me in."

"You're a lawman?" Jake Bass said.

"No," Asa said. "I tame towns."

"You what?" Crusty said.

"That's what the newspapers call it. I don't much like being wrote about, but the important thing is that I've been hired to put an end to your outfit."

"Put an end to the Circle K?" Crusty asked, and laughed.

"All by your lonesome?" Jake Bass said.

"I need to send a message to your employer, Knox, and to his ramrod, Bull Cumberland."

"This should be good," Jake Bass said.

"What's the message?" Crusty asked.

"I'm serving notice. Every Circle K hand with sense has one week from today to pack their war-bag and light a shuck. If they're still around after that, I put them on the list."

"What list?" Crusty asked.

"I call it my Boot Hill list."

"Listen to you," Jake Bass sneered. "Who in hell do you think you are?"

"I've already told you."

"Mister, you have sand," Crusty said. "Not much brains but a lot of sand. We'll give Mr. Knox and Bull your message. And then you'd best be ready for when we come ridin' in to settle your hash."

"You misunderstood," Asa said. "I didn't say I want you to deliver the message. I said I need to send one. I'll hire a boy to ride out to the ranch for me."

"Why, when we can do it?" Crusty said.

"You won't be able to."

"Why in hell not?"

Asa Delaware always liked this part. He liked the looks on their faces when it sank in. "Because," he said matter-of-factly, "both of you will be dead."

12

Crusty chuckled as if it were a joke, but Jake Bass didn't. He glanced at the Winchester shotgun and started to move his hand toward his Colt. He did it so slowly that he probably figured Asa wouldn't notice.

"Hold on," Crusty said. "You're not joshin'?"

"I never josh about killing," Asa said. "It's my work, and I take it serious."

"You come in here, you threaten us, and then you kill us?"

"If it wasn't me it would be a lawman, sooner or later," Asa said. "You can't go around murdering folks and stealing and expect to live forever."

"Mister, you beat all."

As he always did when he was about to be in a shooting affray, Asa fixed his entire attention on the men he was about to buck out in gore, which was why he didn't notice a townsman about to step between them until Byron called out, "Floyd, you might not want to do that. Turn around and hunt cover."

Floyd bore the stamp of a clerk, teller, or any job fit for a mouse. He stopped, an empty glass in his hand, and said, "I need a refill."

"Back off, mister," Noona warned.

Floyd's red nose showed he was into his cups. His brain probably didn't work too fast under the best of circumstances, and with booze in him, he was a turtle. He looked at the cowhands and at Asa and his eyebrows tried to meet over his nose. "What's going on here?"

Crusty wasn't as dumb as Asa thought. Slipping behind Floyd, he grinned at Asa. "We're on our way out, and we'd like you to escort us."

"Do what?"

"You heard me," Crusty said, putting a hand on Floyd's arm. "Tell us how your missus is. And the kids if you have any." He backed away, pulling a befuddled Floyd after him.

"Where's your big talk now, mister?" Jake Bass taunted as he, too, backed out. He stood close to Floyd so that if Asa cut loose with the 12-gauge, Floyd was bound to take some of the buckshot.

Asa stood there and let them go. He had a rule. He had a lot of rules, actually. But the one that applied here was that no innocents were to ever be harmed, not if he could help it.

At the batwings, Crusty gave a little wave and went out, pulling Floyd after him.

Jake Bass paused. "When we come back it will be all of us . . . or pretty near."

"I'll be here," Asa said.

A lot of the patrons had stopped what they were doing to stare. They'd sensed violence in the air, and more than a few had sidled toward the far walls.

"Bull Cumberland will want to have words with you," Jake Bass said, "and his words are always final."

"Makes two of us."

Bass shouldered the batwings open.

Asa moved to the front window. Careful not to show himself, he peered out. The cowboys were already mounted and had used their spurs. He frowned and cradled the shotgun in the crook of his left elbow.

Byron came up on his right, Noona on his left.

"That didn't go well," Byron said.

"What will you do?" Noona asked.

"Don't talk to me yet," Asa said. He wheeled and walked out.

Floyd was coming back in but staring after the Circle K hard cases, and almost collided with him. "Say. What was that about, anyhow?"

"They used you as a shield," Asa said.

"Are you saying there might have been gunplay?"

"No might about it."

"My word. I could have ended up like poor Ed and Myrtle Sykes."

"Just like them."

The man swallowed and quaked. "Those cowboys are the bane of our lives. I wish someone would put an end to their reign of terror."

"Someone will," Asa said.

"Who?"

"You're looking at him."

13

Asa Delaware left Floyd with his bewilderment and walked down the street to the Sykes house. He hesitated, then knocked lightly. He was about convinced no one would answer when the door opened and lamp light spilled over him. "You're still here?"

"We all are," George Tandy replied. "Come on in, please."

"I was hoping to pay my respects to Miss Sykes."

"She's in the kitchen with the rest. Follow me."

To Asa's surprise, Madeline was at the counter cracking eggs into a bowl.

Four men were at the table, two in chairs over by a pot-bellied stove. Middle-aged or older, their clothes marked them as more prosperous than most.

"Gentlemen," George Tandy said. "I'd like you to meet the famous Town Tamer, Asa Delaware."

"The one we hired?" a portly man at the table said.

"The very same, Horace," Tandy said.

At the stove, a bespectacled man with sharp features adjusted his spectacles and said with barely concealed disapproval, "You didn't tell us he was an Indian."

"Be nice, Thaddeus," Tandy said. "He's doing us a favor."

"Favor, hell," Thaddeus said. "We're paying him more than I earn in two months."

"You can afford your share," Tandy said. "You're the banker."

"Even so," Thaddeus said. "You know how I feel about Indians."

"Doesn't everybody?" Horace said.

Madeline stopped breaking eggs and glared at them. "I'll thank you to show more respect to my guest. You're in my house, after all."

"My apologies, my dear," Horace said glibly. "I meant no disrespect. I have only the greatest fondness for you, as I did for your parents."

The reminder caused Madeline visible hurt. She turned and came over to Asa, saying, "To what do I owe this visit?"

"I wanted to see how you were holding up."

"She's holding up fine," George Tandy interjected.

"We're holding a council session."

"Here?" Asa said.

"We came to offer our condolences," Horace said, "and figured we might as well discuss the situation since we're all here."

"I don't mind," Madeline said, although from her tone, it was plain she did.

Asa simmered. When Tandy stepped to the table, he leaned close to Madeline and said in her ear, "Say the word and I'll make them go."

Madeline wearily smiled and shook her head. "That's awful kind of you, but no. My father was on the council, and these are his friends."

"What are you two whispering about?" Thaddeus asked.

"None of your business," Asa said.

"It's most unseemly, if you ask me."

"No one did."

Madeline held up her hands in appeal. "Please, Mr. Falk. Let's be civil, shall we? This day has been horrible enough. The last thing I need is petty bickering."

"I'm never petty," the banker said in a mild huff.

"How about those eggs you offered?" Horace said. "My stomach is rumbling again."

"Coming right up, Mr. Wadpole."

Asa moved to the counter and leaned against it, the Winchester cradled in front of him, deliberately staying aloof from the townsmen.

"So tell us," Thaddeus Falk said. "How exactly do you plan to go about ridding us of our problem?"

"I thought you knew," Asa said. "I kill everybody."

They looked at one another. Horace Wadpole harrumphed and said, "Ed Sykes showed us the newspaper clippings Madeline sent. From those and your statement just now, I gather that you have no compunctions about shedding blood."

"Not a lick."

"Yes, well," said a spindly specimen with a hooked nose, "I can't say as I'm entirely comfortable with that."

"Then why did you hire me?"

"Permit me to answer that," George Tandy said. "We hired you because we're at our wit's end. We literally had nowhere else to turn. You know about our marshal being shot? What you might not know is that we sent for someone to replace him and when he showed up, Bull Cumberland beat him so severely that he took the next stage out."

The banker cleared his throat. "We contacted the Rangers. They sent a pair to investigate, but Mr. Knox swore his punchers are the salt of the earth. And since we have no evidence against them other than hearsay, there wasn't anything the Rangers could do."

Horace Wadpole took up the account. "Then Ed Sykes told us about you, how you've cleaned up a dozen towns or more and could do the same for us."

"Only, we'd like it done with as little blood spilling as possible," the spindly man said.

"How much spills is up to the other side," Asa said.

Madeline had finished cracking eggs and was carrying a bowl and a large spoon to the stove. "If I am to be so bold, gentlemen?"

"Certainly, my dear," George Tandy said. "You have every right to offer an opinion."

"Keeping in mind that you're not a member of this council," the banker said.

"And your opinion has no weight where official matters are concerned," Horace Wadpole added.

"Her opinion matters to me," Asa said.

"Let's hear what you have to say, my dear," Tandy said.

Madeline bestowed a warm smile on Asa. "Well, then. Speaking only for myself, you understand, I sincerely hope that you kill every last one of the sons of bitches."

"Count on it," Asa said.

14

Asa expected the Circle K riders to come roaring into Ludlow the next day. Since the ranch was to the west, he picked a spot at the west end of town between the feed and grain and a barber's, intending to confront them as they rode in. But the afternoon waned, the evening waxed, and stars filled the firmament, and still they didn't appear.

The next morning they would show up, Asa reckoned. He was awake at the crack of dawn and waiting at the same spot before the sun was half an hour into the sky. The morning dragged and noon came and went, and nothing happened.

Asa figured there must be a good reason they had been delayed. He anticipated that they'd ride in by sunset at the latest. But the sun sank, blazing the horizon with vivid splashes of red and orange and yellow, and once again, they failed to show.

Meanwhile, word had spread of who Asa was and why he was there.

Most of the townsfolk avoided him as if he were infected with plague. Men swung wide and wouldn't meet his eye. Women crossed the street to avoid him, tugging their sprouts after them.

Asa was used to the ill treatment. He was a man killer, and man killers were looked down on unless they toted tin badges. Worse, he had Injun blood in him, and many whites regarded half-breeds as contemptible.

It wouldn't do Asa any good to tell them that, yes, his grandmother was a Delaware, but his parents were both as white as could be, and he, himself, had been raised white. He had never set foot in an Indian village, never had dealings with the Delawares or any other tribe. He was white through and through and liked it that way.

But the whites didn't care. They couldn't see past his red skin.

Asa hated it. He hated being branded as something he wasn't. He was a white man in a red man's skin, and he hated *that* more than anything.

Early on, Asa had learned to ignore the looks and the sneers and the contempt. He couldn't change human nature. So he shut the haters out. As long as they left him alone, as long as all they did was sneer and mutter behind his back, he held his temper in check.

It wasn't easy. When he was younger, he'd sometimes have too much to drink. That always ended badly. He'd lost count of the saloon fights he was in, lost count of the bigots he'd beaten into a beer-speckled floor.

Then came his sweet Mary, and everything changed.

Now, waiting in the alley in the dark of the new night for the Circle K, Asa thought about Mary's love for him, and how happy she'd made him. How the twenty years they were together were the best of his life. To have her torn from his side and his heart by consumption was the cruelest trick life could play on him.

Suddenly hooves clomped, intruding on Asa's reverie. He looked out. A pair of riders was approaching, and while they and their mounts weren't more than silhouettes, he could tell they were cowboys.

Moving into the middle of the street, Asa barred their way. "Hold up," he commanded.

They drew rein and the younger said, "Who are you to be tellin' us what to do?"

"Are you with the Circle K?"

"We are," the young puncher said. "What's it to you?"

"Use your head, Kyle," the other cowhand said. "He must be the one."

"Oh," Kyle said. "You reckon so, Longley?"

Longley leaned on his saddle horn. "Am I right, and you're the jasper who had a run-in with Jake Bass and Crusty the other night?"

"I am," Asa said.

"Mr. Knox has heard about the council hirin' you. He sent us to invite you out to the ranch."

"And be bushwhacked along the way or be gunned down when I got there?"

"Mr. Knox gives his word you won't be harmed."

"Why should I believe him?"

"All he wants to do is talk. He'd like to have you to supper tomorrow night."

"No."

Longley sighed. "He was afraid you'd be pigheaded. He said if we couldn't persuade you, he'll ride into town by his lonesome tomorrow and talk to you here. Two in the afternoon at the Griddle House. Would you agree to that, at least?"

"Here is better than there," Asa said.

"It's settled, then." Longley raised his reins. "That's all we came to say."

"Can't we have a drink?" Kyle asked him.

"No. We're headin' back to the ranch." Longley wheeled his mount, then stopped and looked over his shoulder. "One thing, mister. Hurt Mr. Knox and we'll hunt you down and make you wish you weren't ever born."

"I'll keep that in mind," Asa said.

15

Asa had taken off his slicker and hung it on a peg on the wall and was about to sit on the bed and take off his boots when a light knock sounded. He snatched up the Winchester shotgun and moved to one side of the door, saying, "Who is it?"

"Who do you think?"

Asa opened the door. They were both there, and he frowned. "I told you we weren't to be seen together yet."

"Are we going to argue about it, or are you going to let us in?" Byron said.

"Please, Pa," Noona said.

Asa motioned, and when they stepped past, he poked his head out and looked both ways. The hallway was empty. He quickly shut the door. "Doesn't appear you were seen."

"We were careful," Noona said. "Just like you taught us." She spread her arms. "Do I get a hug or not?"

Asa hugged her and turned to Byron, who had plopped down on the bed in the same spot where he had just been fixing to sit. "This your idea?"

"It's always me," Byron said.

"You're the one who listens less," Asa said. "I have rules for a reason."

"We know, we know," Noona said. "So we get to go on breathing."

"Hypocritical, if you ask me," Byron said.

"Don't start on him," Noona said. "We didn't come here for that."

"Hypocritical how?" Asa asked.

"You have all these rules to keep us alive," Byron said. "Rules we wouldn't need if you didn't send us into situations where our lives were at risk. I call that hypocritical."

"Damn it, Byron," Noona said.

"Don't swear," Asa said. "Ladies don't swear. Your mother never did."

"Sis isn't her, and I'm not you," Byron said. "And we're full grown, in case you haven't noticed."

"I notice a lot," Asa said.

"Have you noticed me getting tired of this?" Byron said. "When I was sixteen it was exciting. Go into a town ahead of you, scout it out, and be ready to back your play when you made your move. I'm twenty-four now, and it's lost its luster. It's not exciting anymore. It's just dangerous."

"Always has been," Asa said.

"You're not listening, *Paw*," Byron said, drawling the "Pa" so it sounded hillbilly, because he knew it would annoy him. "We're tired of the deceit and play-acting, and neither of us wants to take lead for you or have a blade shoved in our guts."

"Speak for yourself," Noona said. "I'll take lead for him anytime."

"So he doesn't speak for both of you?" Asa needed to know.

Noona placed her hand on his arm. "I'm twenty-two now. I suppose I should be getting on with my life. Maybe find a husband and settle down and have a nice house and kids, like Ma did."

"That's what normal people do," Byron said.

"We're not normal," Noona said.

"I want to be," Byron said to Noona. "And I've put it off long enough. Hell, I started giving him hints two years ago, but he wouldn't take them."

"What hints?" Asa asked.

"How many times have I told you I'm tired of the killing? How many times have I said I'm sick of all the traveling around? If they aren't hints, I don't know what is."

Asa didn't say anything.

"I thought as much," Byron said. "You only notice when it suits you."

"Byron," Noona said.

"I'm not holding back anymore." Byron stood. "You listen, Pa, and you listen good. This is the last one. When it's over, I'm going back east. I'll take what I have saved and live like ordinary folks for a change. You can go on making the world suffer for what it did to Ma, but count me out."

"Suffer?" Asa said.

"As if you don't know," Byron said. "You didn't take this town-tamer business up until after she died."

"I still don't savvy," Asa said.

"Sure you do. You hated how she was treated when she was alive, how no one would have anything to do with her because she was married to a breed. Or that's what they take you for, anyhow. So you get back at them by killing as many of them as you can."

"That's not it at all."

"Oh, really?" Byron said. "Explain it to me, then. Explain it so I'll finally understand why one human being makes his living exterminating other human beings." Byron paused, then quoted, "'Yet this was not the end I did pursue, surely I once beheld a nobler aim.'"

"You and your poetry," Asa said.

"That's another thing you hate, isn't it? That the fruit of your loins has the soul of a poet?"

"Don't talk about loins in front of your sister."

"And don't change the subject. Explain it to me. I'm waiting." Byron folded his arms.

Asa looked at each of them and at his son and felt a knife pierce his heart. They didn't know how much it meant to him, working together as a family. He'd always known this day would come, though. That one or both of them would have enough. "I don't justify myself to anyone."

"Not even me, your own son?" Byron said in mock surprise.

"I have to admit," Noona said quietly, "that there are occasions when the ugly parts bother me."

"Sometimes the 'ugly parts,' as you call them, are the only way to settle it," Asa said.

"Sometimes?" Byron said, and snorted. "Name one town you've tamed where you haven't had to kill somebody."

"*We've* tamed," Asa corrected him.

"There you go again," Byron said. "You avoid answering when you don't like the question." He stood and stepped to the door. "This is getting me nowhere, sis, as I knew it would. Let's go."

Noona looked into Asa's eyes. "I'm sorry."

"What for? He's the one who's quitting on us."

Noona pecked him on the cheek. Byron cracked the door and glanced both ways, and they slipped out and were gone.

Asa shut the door after them, leaned his brow against it, and closed his eyes. "Oh, Mary," he said.

16

The Griddle House was popular. The woman who ran it made some of the best flapjacks this side of the Mississippi River, and her other food was equally delicious. Breakfast and supper were her busiest hours, but the middle of the afternoon still saw a lot of people at different tables.

"After you, Mr. Delaware," Weldon Knox said, holding the door open.

"No. You first," Asa said. He'd waited at the end of town, and when a half dozen riders appeared, he figured he'd been lied to. But they'd stopped a ways out and Knox came on alone, true to his word.

Now Knox entered, saying, "You don't trust anyone, do you?"

"It's how I stay alive."

Knox made for a table near a mother and her young girl, but Asa said, "Over here," and chose one in a corner where he could sit with his back to the wall and watch the door and the window, both.

"Yes, sir," Weldon Knox said. "Not a sliver of trust in you." He removed his bowler and placed it beside him. Nattily dressed, he wasn't much over five feet tall and had a thin mustache and no chin. His eyes were ferretlike and his jaw twitched a lot.

Asa chalked that up to nerves. He leaned the Winchester against his chair and folded his hands. "They said you wanted to talk."

"I do, indeed." Knox glanced at the front door. "I can't believe I got away with it."

"With what?"

Before Knox could answer, the lady who owned the eatery came over. Knox asked for soup. Asa settled for coffee. Nothing more was said until after she returned with their order and walked off.

Knox cleared his throat. "What do you know about me, Mr. Delaware?"

"You came here to talk about you?"

"Humor me, if you would."

Asa shrugged. "You're from back east somewhere. You bought the Circle K about seven years ago. For a while you and the town got along well, and then you hired Bull Cumberland."

"'Hired' isn't how I would put it, but go on."

"You brought in more like him—border trash. Gunmen and rustlers and road agents . . . so now you have your very own wild bunch."

"Did you ever think they might have me?"

"You're the big sugar," Asa said.

"I own the ranch, yes, but I haven't run it in a long while." Knox seemed to wither in on himself and placed both hands on the table and bowed his head. "God help me."

Asa waited.

"I didn't *hire* Bull Cumberland. He showed up at the ranch one day and informed me that he was going to work there, and that was that. I was a little put off, but to my sorrow I didn't have the gumption to tell him no—even when my foreman objected. And the very next day, my foreman was dead." Knox looked up. "Kicked by a horse, Cumberland claimed. Fool that I was, I believed him. And when he offered to take my foreman's place, I let him."

Asa stayed silent.

"I was stupid, I know. But Bull Cumberland has a way of intimidating people. Part of it has to do with his eyes."

"Say again?"

"There's nothing in them. No emotion, no feeling. They're as flat as I hear the eyes of sharks are supposed to be. They're killer eyes, Mr. Delaware, if there is such a thing. I confess that when he looks at me, my legs turn to water."

"Folks say he's snake-mean," Asa mentioned when the rancher didn't go on.

"They don't know the half of it. Anyway, he wasted no time bringing in more of his kind—that vile Jake Bass, the gunman; Old Tom, the stage robber; Crusty, who's an expert at changing brands with a running iron; Tyree Lucas and Chadwell and the rest. And before I knew it, they'd taken over."

At moments like these, Asa wished he could peer into a person's soul. "You expect me to believe that?"

"As God is my witness," Knox said solemnly, "I'm telling you the truth."

"You didn't go to the marshal?"

"I have a wife, Mr. Delaware. Bull made it plain what would befall her if I opposed him. And besides, he murdered the marshal not long after."

"Why didn't you say something to the Rangers when they came?"

"Same reason. When they showed up at my ranch, Bull stood behind me on the porch with his hand on his revolver while I talked to them. He'd already told me what to say."

"I see," Asa said. But did he? "This could well be a trick."

"I'm not that devious."

"So you say."

Weldon Knox glanced at the front door and wrung his hands. "What can I do to make you believe me?"

Asa debated with himself. If the man was shamming, he was good at it. "You never once thought to slip word to friends in town?"

"I haven't been allowed to come here alone until now," Knox said, "and I wouldn't feel right putting another's life in peril. If Bull Cumberland were to find out—"

"He let you come in alone today."

Knox nodded. "To deal with you on his behalf. I've been meekly doing as he wants for so long, maybe he believes I wouldn't dare do what I'm doing."

"Deal with me?"

Knox did more nodding. "He's heard of you. How or where I don't know. Some of the others wanted to kill you, but he told them no. I thought that maybe he's afraid of you."

"Your story is stretching thin," Asa said. "I've met his kind before. They're a lot of things, but yellow isn't one of them."

"You didn't let me finish. I thought he might be afraid but I learned different. He says that if they kill you, word might get around. A town marshal is no big thing, because no one much cares except the town. But for someone famous like you, the newspapers might write it up. And the Rangers or the federal law might investigate. You were a federal marshal once, I've been told."

"Deputy U.S. marshal," Asa said.

"Same thing, more or less. Bull Cumberland thinks you might have friends who are federal law, and he doesn't want them nosing around."

"Smart of him," Asa said. Truth was, he didn't know if any of the men toting badges back when he did were still at it. He'd resigned pretty near eleven years ago, shortly after Mary took sick. He was by her side every day and night until the consumption claimed her. He didn't regret it. Not one bit.

"Anyway, that's why I'm here," Weldon Knox was saying. "Cumberland wants me to buy you off."

Asa sat back. "You don't say."

"He's heard that your standard fee is a thousand dollars. Is that true?"

"Whatever it is, it's my business."

"Rightly so," Knox said quickly. "He instructed me to offer you five thousand on his behalf if you'll pack up and go pester someone else. His very words."

Asa whistled.

"Five thousand is a lot of money. I wouldn't blame you if you took it."

When Asa didn't say anything, Knox drummed his fingers on the table.

"Well? What will you do?"

Asa stared at those drumming fingers and an icy wind seemed to blow through him. "Tell him I'll think about it."

"He figured you'd leap at his offer."

"He figured wrong."

"What's there to think about? We're talking five thousand dollars. That's forty times more than the average person earns in a year."

"I'm not much at arithmetic," Asa said.

"Be serious, man. I don't see how you can refuse."

It took all of Asa's self-control not to reach across the table, grab Knox by the throat, and throttle him. "I need a couple of days to think about it."

"To think about five thousand dollars?"

Asa tested his hunch with, "You keep mentioning how much as if you're offering it yourself."

Weldon Knox blinked and shook his head. "It's Bull Cumberland."

"Two days," Asa said. "Ask him to give me that much."

"Very well," Knox said, and stood. "I guess I've said all I need to. I'll report back to him. Two days it is." He donned his bowler and hustled out.

The cold feeling in Asa became an iceberg. "That was another mistake you made."

17

Asa took a stroll about the town. He could use the exercise. He didn't get nearly as much as he used to. Not that he was flabby or overweight. But the gray hair at his temples was a sign he wasn't as spry as he used to be. He wasn't quite as quick or accurate with a pistol, either, which was why he favored the shotgun. Just point and fire and he could blow a man pretty near in half.

Most of the townspeople avoided him, as they'd done before. But more than a few nodded in greeting and several smiled. One man actually said, "Good afternoon to you, Mr. Delaware." It surprised Asa so much, he almost forgot to respond, "Afternoon to you."

On an impulse Asa went into the Whiskey Mill. Byron was behind the bar and Noona was joshing with some men at a table. Both glanced his way, and then ignored him as they were supposed to do.

Asa crossed to the bar and when Byron came over, said, "Whiskey."

Byron made no attempt to hide his surprise. "A little early in the day, isn't it?"

"I'm celebrating," Asa said.

"You've heard that your son is going off on his own and you're happy for him?" Byron baited as he poured.

"No," Asa said. "I'm celebrating lasting as long as I have."

"Lucky you," Byron said.

Just then the batwings creaked and in strode a pair of Circle K hands. Asa recognized them from the descriptions he'd been given. They were Old Tom and Tyree Lucas. He sipped and let them come to the bar. At close range he could sometimes down two birds with one stone, as it were. "Gents," he said when they looked at him.

"Town Tamer," Tyree Lucas said. His scorn was as obvious as his sneer.

Old Tom had more sense. "Mr. Delaware," he said.

"Surprised to see you here," Asa said.

"What in hell for?" Tyree Lucas said. "It's a free country."

"Freer for some than for others," Asa said.

"We don't want no trouble," Old Tom said. "I'm hankerin' after some coffin varnish, is all, and Tyree, here, tagged along."

"We hear it takes two days to make up your mind," Tyree Lucas said.

"Tyree, don't," Old Tom said.

"That's all right," Asa said. "I've already made it up."

Old Tom cocked his head. "Awful quick."

"It was made up before Knox asked me."

Old Tom lowered his arm so his hand was near his revolver. "So that's how it is."

"How what is?" Tryee Lucas asked. To Asa he said, "Why in hell did you ask for two days if you already knew what you'd say?"

"To do some whittling," Asa said.

"Hold on, now," Old Tom said.

"My grandpappy liked to whittle," Tyree Lucas said. "He'd sit in his rocking chair for hours, just whittlin' away. Carved me a horse when I was little. Not a bad horse, either, except he forgot the tail."

Without taking his eyes off Asa, Old Tom said, "That's

not the kind of whittlin' he's talkin' about, you jug head. He's talkin' about whittlin' on us."

"We're not made of wood," Tyree Lucas said.

"You might as well be," Asa said, and took a step back. The Winchester was in his right hand, pointed down.

"Why us?" Old Tom asked.

"Have to start somewhere," Asa said. "The more now, the fewer Knox can send when he realizes I was stringing him along."

"Bull Cumberland, you mean," Old Tom said.

"I mean Weldon Knox."

"So much for his great brain," Old Tom said. "Bull told him it wouldn't work."

Tyree Lucas was growing more exasperated by the moment. "Will one of you tell me what this whittlin' and stringin' is about?"

"It's about gophers," Asa said.

"You're loco," Tyree Lucas declared.

"When a man has gophers, he can sit in a chair and wait for one to poke its head out of its hole so he can blow it off. Or he can cover all their holes except one and smoke them out. Or he can drop castor beans down in their burrows and poison them."

"What do gophers have to do with whittlin'?"

"Whittling can be easy or hard depending on how you go about it."

Old Tom did the unexpected. He held his hands out from his sides. "I refuse to draw on you. I refuse to even touch my hardware. You want me dead, it'll have to be in cold blood, with witnesses."

"Bull Cumberland had witnesses when he shot Ed Sykes," Asa said. "Jake Bass had witnesses when he gunned down Myrtle Sykes."

"They've told you about that?" Old Tom took a slow step toward the batwings. "But that's Bull and Jake, and you're not them. You have to abide by the law."

"Who says?"

"You tame towns for a livin'. You can't do that by goin' against the law."

"Who says?" Asa asked a second time.

"You're supposed to be on the side of law and order."

"The only side I'm on," Asa said, "is mine."

Byron laughed. "Imagine that."

Asa had forgotten he was standing behind the bar. "You might want to move."

"No one has explained this to me yet," Tyree Lucas said.

"The Town Tamer, here," Byron said, "is fixing to shoot the two of you."

"What? Why?"

"It's what he does."

"You're serious, boy?" Tyree said.

"I am," Byron said, and nodded at Asa. "And so is he."

18

Experience had taught Asa that Tyree Lucas would be the one to throw common sense to the wind and he was right.

Lucas swore and clawed for his six-gun. He was fast, although not as fast as some Asa had gone up against.

Unfortunately for him, all Asa had to do was whip the Winchester's muzzle up and cut loose. He fired one-handed. Where the recoil might have torn the shotgun from the hand of most men, it didn't with him. He practiced firing one-handed every chance he got, and knew to hold firm and to move his arm with the force of the recoil.

It caught Tyree Lucas square in the chest. The impact lifted him off his boots and flung him a good five feet. He crashed down on his back with blood squirting from some of the holes the buckshot had made. He'd never cleared leather, and his limp fingers waved wildly while his mouth opened and closed as he gurgled blood.

Old Tom had his hands in the air and was gaping at his pard. "No," he bleated.

Asa jacked the lever, feeding another shell into the chamber, and pointed the Winchester at him.

Tyree Lucas tried to speak. His words consisted of bubbles of blood, but the look in his eyes was meaning enough. Then he thrust his legs out, convulsed, and was gone.

Old Tom swallowed and regarded Asa and the shotgun. "Hold on, now. I ain't goin' for my smoke wagon. My hands are empty, as everyone here can plainly see."

"Doesn't matter to him," Byron said.

"Byron, please," Noona said from somewhere slightly behind Asa.

"How is it you know him so well?" Old Tom asked Byron.

"He's been my nightmare since I realized snuffing wicks isn't a profession—it's vengeance."

"You dream about him?" Old Tom said in confusion.

"Not if I can help it," Byron said.

Old Tom seemed to think that by talking to Byron he could somehow keep Asa from shooting. He said, "Explain that to me, if you would."

Byron pointed. "He's my pa." Again he used the exaggerated, hill-folk way of saying it.

Old Tom's eyes widened. "Wait until the others hear this."

"They won't hear it from you," Asa said. By then he had tucked the stock to his shoulder and he shot the old outlaw full in the face.

Anyone who had ever shot melons with a shotgun could have predicted what would happen. Old Tom's head exploded in a shower of bits and chunks and larger pieces including one with an eye and half of Old Tom's nose. Deprived of its brain, the body swayed and the fingers twitched, and it melted into a heap.

Someone somewhere gasped out, "God Almighty."

"You didn't have to do that," Byron said.

"I did once you told him," Asa said.

"Don't blame it on me."

"Who said anything about blame? When you exterminate vermin, you don't feel sorry for it." Asa worked the lever and turned to the stunned onlookers. None acted disposed to object to the killings. To make sure they understood, he said, "These men and their friends murdered Ed

Sykes and his wife. They murdered your marshal. They've robbed and rustled."

"You don't need to tell us, mister," said a man holding a cigar. "We live here."

"You did right," said another.

"Listen to them," Byron said. "Maybe they'll erect a statue in your honor when it's over."

"Byron," Noona said.

"It's come to this, has it, son?" Asa said. "Very well." He wasn't angry at Byron, just disappointed. "From here on out we stick together."

The batwings slammed open, and in rushed George Tandy. He lurched to a stop in horror at the sight of the bodies. "I was down the street and heard shots."

"Half the town must have heard them," another man said.

Tandy coughed, collected himself, and advanced a few halfhearted steps. "What a mess."

"Have some of these men tie what's left of them on their horses," Asa instructed. "Then point the animals at the Circle K and slap them on the rump."

"You killed them," Tandy said. "You should do it."

"Hear, hear," Byron said.

"Until this is over, this shotgun doesn't leave my hands," Asa said.

"Not even in the outhouse?" Byron taunted.

"Byron, consarn you," Noona said.

George Tandy was shaking his head. "We send those bodies back, it'll make Bull Cumberland mad as hell. He's liable to swoop in here with his whole bunch to wipe you out."

"That's the idea," Asa said.

19

---·---

Ludlow was abuzz. Word of the killings had spread like a prairie fire.

As Asa, Byron, and Noona made their way to the boardinghouse, people pointed and whispered.

"Must make you feel important," Byron said.

Noona made a hissing sound. "For God's sake, what's the matter with you? Why won't you let it drop?"

"Because I'm sick to death of it, sis. Not just a little bit, but to the very depths of my heart and my soul."

"You even talk poetical," Asa said.

Byron stopped and his jaw jutted like an anvil. "I've put up with a lot, but no more of that. You leave my poetry alone."

"It's never bothered you this much before," Noona said to Byron.

"There comes a point when you have to say enough is enough."

"I say it in every town I tame," Asa said.

"Oh really? Is that how you justify it?"

"I told you in the saloon," Asa said. "You don't have to justify doing right."

"I am so sick of you."

"Byron!" Noona exclaimed.

Asa walked on and they followed, but Byron dragged his heels.

Ethel was outside her boardinghouse, her knitting needles and the shawl she was working on in her hands. "Those were shots I heard."

"They were," Asa said.

"Was it you?"

"It was."

"How many?"

"Just two to start."

"Good," Ethel said.

"Brotherly love," Byron said, "where art thou?"

"What's the matter with him?" Ethel asked. "Is he one of those weak-sister kind of Christians?"

"He's a poet," Asa said.

"Ah," Ethel said.

"Someone shoot me," Byron said.

Asa held it in until they were in his room and he'd closed the door. Forcing himself to keep his voice calm, he said, "Not another carp out of you when we're in public." Byron opened his mouth, but Asa held up a hand. "Families should air their differences in private, boy."

"Another of your rules?" Byron said.

"Without rules, we'd treat each other the same as animals do."

"That applies to laws, too," Byron said. "And what you just did is against the law, to say nothing of hardly being civilized. 'Thou shalt not kill,' remember?"

"Since when did you start quoting the Bible? All you ever quote is that dandy with a limp."

"What a way to describe a man of Lord Byron's genius."

"How would you describe him?"

"As he described himself," Byron said. "As a degenerate modern wretch."

"Degenerate," Asa said. "And you admire him?"

"More than I admire you."

"No insults," Noona said.

"Go to your rooms and fetch your things," Asa said. "We're staying together until this is over."

"I can take care of myself," Byron said.

"Not in the state you're in," Asa said.

"And what state would that be, Father? The state of dis-illusion brought on by my sire?"

Asa opened the door and moved aside. "Don't dawdle. There might be more of them in town."

Byron stalked out, his fists clenched.

"My poor brother," Noona said softly. She stopped and touched Asa's hand. "I'm sorry he's treating you this way."

"It's him doing it, not you."

"He does care for you, you know."

"I wonder."

"He's always been the smartest of us."

"Too smart," Asa said.

"Do you remember when he first heard there was a poet who had his name, how excited he was when you bought him his first book on Lord Byron?"

"I thought I was doing him a favor," Asa said.

"You did. He loved that book more than anything and went out and got everything he could find on Lord Byron."

"Look at where it's brought us."

"You should be proud. How many fathers can say they have a son with the heart of a poet?"

Asa adored her for trying to smooth things over, but there was too much at stake. "He's gone soft. Too soft. If I could I'd put him on the next stage east, like he wants. As it is, I don't know as I want him backing me when the Circle K rides in."

"He'll do what needs doing. You can count on him for that."

"I hope you're right," Asa said. "If you're not, all of us could be goners."

Part Three

20

Weldon Knox liked his brandy. He always had one exactly at noon and once an hour thereafter until he retired. His wife didn't like it, but she knew better than to complain. The only time she had, he'd slapped her from the parlor to the kitchen and back again, with her caterwauling for him to stop. He liked the feeling it gave him, liked the power he had over her, liked the fear he inspired.

Weldon hadn't inspired much fear in anyone when he was growing up. Fate had dealt him a cruel blow in that he was so short. It's hard to inspire fear when you're no taller than a heifer. You have to be muscular, or tough, and Weldon was neither.

But he did like inspiring fear.

Which was partly why when he took a wife, he made sure she was shorter than he was. Esther fit the bill, and was frail, to boot, so he could smack her around to his heart's content and she couldn't do a thing.

Esther didn't like it when he brought in Bull Cumberland, either, but she kept her mouth shut except to mention that she couldn't understand why he'd hired "a man like that."

Weldon chuckled at the memory. The silly woman didn't see that Bull and him were the same. They both liked doing as they damn well pleased. They both liked making money any way they could. And they both liked hurting people.

But then, how was Esther to know? When they met, he'd fed her a cock-and-bull story about being from back east and raised religious and impressed her as being a gentleman in all his ways.

She'd be shocked, Weldon reckoned, if she learned he was Texas born and bred. That he'd lived on a small ranch over San Antonio way until his father died and left him the place. For most that would suffice, but Weldon always hankered after a bigger spread, a ranch with thousands upon thousands of acres, his very own empire that he could rule with an iron fist. One day he'd heard that the Circle K was up for sale and sold the ranch his pa had sweated and near broken his back to build up for the down payment.

Esther never suspected the rest of it, either. That he'd been running rustled stock on the sly for years. That he let wanted men hide out at his place—for a price. That for all his seeming respectability, he was as much a cutthroat as the worst of them.

And a far better actor.

It had amused him, riding into town and duping the famous Asa Delaware. It rankled a bit, though, treating the breed as if he mattered. He despised mixed-bloods almost as much as he despised redskins.

Still, things had gone "swimmingly," as a Brit he knew might say. He sipped his brandy, gazed out the big parlor window over his domain, and was content.

Then someone pounded on the front door, and Weldon yelled for Esther to answer it. Presently boots clomped, spurs jangled, and in strode Bull Cumberland with a frown as deep as the Grand Canyon.

"That damn jaguar has been at our cattle again?" Weldon guessed. Jaguars were rare this far north, but a big male had taken to filling its belly with Circle K cows.

"Old Tom and Tyree Lucas are back," Bull Cumberland said.

"This early?" Weldon said. The sun wouldn't set for an hour yet. They had the night off, and he wouldn't have expected them until past midnight.

"What's left of them."

"Say that again?"

"Old Tom is missin' most of his head and Tyree has a great big hole where half his chest used to be."

Weldon came out of his chair so quickly, he spilled some of his brandy. "What the hell?"

"You said you had Asa Delaware hoodwinked."

"I did."

"You said he'd never refuse five thousand dollars."

Weldon swore.

"You said we could get rid of him easy and go on as before."

"Quit reminding me of what I said."

Bull Cumberland walked to the bar, and without being invited to, commenced to help himself to some whiskey. "I figure him sendin' them back blown to hell is his way of tellin' you to shove your five thousand up your ass."

"Damn him," Weldon said.

"We have to do it now. If we don't, folks will say we're paperbacked. They'll get up the grit to stand up to us. We can't have that."

"No," Weldon said, "we can't."

"So how? Just me by my lonesome? Or can I take Jake and Crusty and a few others?"

"All of you not out on the range."

About to tilt the glass to his mouth, Bull Cumberland arched a bushy eyebrow. "Sort of overdoin' it, ain't you? He's just one man."

"You do it my way," Weldon said. "You ride in together. You confront him together. You cut loose on him together. That way, witnesses can't pin the blame on just one or two."

"Mighty clever," Bull said with a grin. "The law can't arrest all of us."

"They might," Weldon said. "They might even prosecute. But a good law wrangler will tie a jury into knots over which man fired the fatal shot. Likely as not, you'd all get off."

"This is why I stay on with you," Bull said. "You're always one step ahead of everybody."

Flattered by the compliment, Weldon said, "I try to be."

"After we're done, we'll head right back."

"Bring the body."

"You want proof we did it?"

"I want to feed him to my hogs," Weldon said. "Without a corpse, it's that much harder for the law to prove its case."

"Don't you beat all?" Bull raised his glass in admiration. "Here's to thinkin' ahead."

"And to dead town tamers," Weldon said.

21

A plague had swept through Ludlow—the plague of fear. Every business closed, save for the saloon. The children were sent home from the one-room schoolhouse. The streets were deserted, the hitch rails empty.

It's like having the town to myself, Asa thought. Although that wasn't entirely true.

As he walked down the middle of Main Street, curtains and shades moved and faces peered out. No one shouted encouragement. No one hollered, "We're with you, Asa!"

Asa didn't expect them to. It was their town, but he wasn't part of it. He had been hired, was all. And he was—in their eyes if not his own—a breed.

Asa came to the end of Main. Far across the prairie, the setting sun blazed on the horizon.

He couldn't predict when the Circle K boys would come, but he doubted they'd wait very long. He'd thrown down the gauntlet, and they had to come after him quick or be branded cowards. That would never do.

Asa went back up the street four blocks and stopped. To his right was the bank, the tallest building in town. It had a steeple at the top. Why, he couldn't say. Maybe the banker, Thaddeus Falk, was fond of churches. Or maybe he just wanted to have the highest building in Ludlow.

On Asa's left was a dress shop. It was only one story high but had a flat roof.

He didn't look at the steeple or the roof after that, in case unfriendly eyes were watching.

Asa cradled the Winchester and waited. He was good at that. Patience was his prime virtue, as Mary used to say. A legacy of his Indian blood, he reckoned, since Indians were noted for theirs.

The sky darkened and night fell, bringing with it a cool wind out of the west and the ululating wail of coyotes.

Asa didn't move. He could stand there all night if he had to. Once, he could mimic a statue for days. His sinews weren't what they once were, but they were still better than most.

Few lights came on, and that wasn't good. Fortunately, just when he had made up his mind to hunt George Tandy down, who should come walking up the street but Tandy and Thaddeus Falk.

"Ask and you shall receive," Asa said.

"What?" Tandy said.

"We demand you desist." Falk got right to it. "We'll pay you the full amount but pack up and go before they get here."

"Can't," Asa said.

"It's not a request," Falk said.

"Still can't."

George Tandy was less arrogant. He tried being reasonable. "Please, Mr. Delaware. We've changed our minds. We realize a lot more blood will be spilled, and we don't want that."

"You knew there would be blood going in," Asa said.

"Yes," Tandy admitted, "your reputation preceded you. We anticipated violence. But imagining violence and experiencing it aren't the same thing, we've discovered."

"Is that right?"

"The bloodbath in the saloon taught us we're not as bloodthirsty as we thought we were."

"Few are."

"You seem to be," the banker said.

"Part of the job."

"We want you to go," the banker demanded.

"No."

"Damn it, you pigheaded—"

"Be careful," Asa said before Falk said something worse. "You don't want to go too far."

"Or what? You'll blow my head off like you did that puncher's?"

"He was a rustler and a kiler and you know it." Asa didn't have time for a lot of talk, so he got to what mattered by saying to Tandy, "Have everyone along Main Street light their lamps as usual."

"I beg your pardon?"

"But no lights at the bank or the millinery," Asa amended.

"People are scared," Tandy said. "They're hiding in their homes. They don't want lights to draw attention to them."

"I need the edge."

"And what if we don't?" Falk asked. "Will you give in and leave?"

"Get it through your head I'm staying. I run now, and I won't ever be asked to tame a town again. And Knox and his hellions will take that 'bloodbath,' as you call it, out on all of you."

"I'll be damned if I'll help you by having the lights turned on," Falk said.

"If you don't and I live, the first thing I'll do is come find you."

"Was that a threat?"

"No," Asa said. "A promise."

George Tandy broke in with, "Let's be mature about this, shall we?"

"The lights," Asa said. "As quickly as you can have it done."

Tandy gazed up and down Main and reluctantly nodded. "Very well. I'll see to it personally." He was about to turn when his eyes narrowed and he bent toward Asa. "What are those things you're wearing under your slicker?"

"Bandoleers," Asa said.

"Good Lord. They must hold fifty shells or better."

"Fifty is right," Asa said. More were in his pockets. Every pocket.

"That might not be enough," the banker said, sounding as if he hoped it wasn't.

"I'll save one for you if those lights aren't on."

Falk turned on his heel and stomped off muttering to himself.

"You shouldn't antagonize him like that," Tandy said.

"It's good for a man to be reminded he's not God now and then."

"That applies to you, too."

"If I were God, my wife would still be alive," Asa said. It came out before he could stop it.

"I heard about her. I'm sorry."

Of all of them, Asa liked this one the most. "The lights, George."

"Right away. I only wish you'd reconsider. Next to Ed Sykes, I was most responsible for sending for you. I wouldn't want your death on my conscience."

"Be sure to tell the folks who live along Main to stay away from their front windows," Asa instructed him. "Better yet, have them move to the back of their houses." Bystanders were notorious for taking stray lead.

Tandy surprised Asa by holding out his hand. "Since you refuse to listen to reason, I wish you the best."

Asa shook, and lowered his voice. "If something should happen to me, see to it that my son and my daughter make it out safe."

"I have children of my own," Tandy said. "I couldn't do what you do and involve them in something like this."

"The lights," Asa said again.

"Certainly." Tandy hurried off.

Asa hoped there was time. He gazed at the stars and thought of Mary. "Maybe I'll get to join you at last." It wasn't in his nature, though, to just let it happen. She'd clung to life for as long as she could, and he was the same. "Damn me, anyhow," he said.

22

My own little army.

That was how Bull Cumberland thought of the twelve men at his back as he galloped the last mile to town. Sure, they were Weldon Knox's men, but he was Knox's right hand—Knox's lieutenant, some might say—and that made them his little army.

Bull was the one who always gave them their orders. Bull was the one who rustled with them, robbed stages with them, killed with them. Some days, he wondered why they needed Weldon Knox at all.

The answer was obvious. Knox had something Bull didn't have, not to any excess, anyway. Weldon Knox had brains. Knox was as clever as a fox and always knew the right thing to do to keep them from ending up behind bars or at the hemp end of a strangulation jig.

Bull didn't mind so much that he had to do as Knox told him. After years of riding the high-lines, of sleeping countless nights on the hard ground and eating countless meals of nothing but beans and coffee, it was nice to have a roof over his head, a bunk of his own to bed down in, and three squares a day if he wanted them.

No, Bull didn't miss the owlhoot trail. He did miss not

being able to bust people up as often as he used to. He missed bucking them out in gore on a whim. Nowadays, he only ever killed when he had to.

Holding back was a nuisance. But as Knox liked to say, why draw tin stars when he didn't really have to?

Bull thought of the Town Tamer and smiled. He wouldn't have to hold back with him. They were going to shoot Asa Delaware to ribbons.

Lights appeared in the distance, and Bull slowed his sorrel to a walk. Jake Bass promptly came up on one side and Crusty on the other.

"Can't wait to do him," Jake Bass said, expressing Bull's own sentiments.

"He has to pay for Old Tom and Tyree," Crusty said.

They were a quarter mile out when Jake Bass remarked, "That's peculiar."

Bull didn't like Bass much. Jake was quick on the shoot, but he was also quick with his temper and that made for a troublesome combination. But Jake did have good instincts about other things, so Bull asked, "What is?"

"The lights."

Bull looked and couldn't see anything strange about them. "The town always has lights at night."

"Only on Main Street?"

Bull drew rein. Damned if Jake Bass wasn't right. Main was lit from end to end except for a space in the middle. None of the other streets showed a lick of light anywhere.

"Say, that is strange," Crusty chimed in. "What do you reckon it means?"

Bull wasn't about to admit he didn't know. "Ride ahead and find out."

"Me?" Crusty said.

"Take Charley and Slim."

"And if we see Asa Delaware? Do we put windows in his noggin or save him for you?"

Bull would like to do in the Town Tamer personally, but he replied, "Bed him down permanent if you have to, but otherwise go careful."

"We'll be careful as hell."

Jake Bass chuckled. "Scared of that old breed, are you?"

"A bona fide"—Crusty pronounced it "bona fidee"—
"man killer ain't to be taken lightly."

"Hell," Jake said. "He bleeds like everyone else."

"So do we," Crusty said.

"Get goin'," Bull commanded. Shifting in the saddle, he
called out to the rest, "Dismount if you want. We'll be
waitin' here a spell."

"Hell," Jake Bass said, swinging down. "I say we ride on
in and do it."

"You buckin' me, Jake?"

"Not ever," Jake instantly replied. "But you know me. I
ain't much for twiddlin' my thumbs when killin' needs to be
done."

"That's why Knox relies on me more than he relies on
you."

"You ever hear me squawk about that? I agree you've
got more sense than me. I try to rein myself in, but I can't
help bein' me."

Some of the others were climbing down, but Bull stayed
on the sorrel. He could sit a saddle forever. His brother
used to josh that he had an iron ass. Then a lawman went
and put a slug through his brother's brain.

Bull stopped thinking about his brother. It always upset
him, and he needed a clear head. This Town Tamer, Delaware, was supposed to be living hell and not apt to go down
easy.

Time passed, and Jake Bass said out of the blue, "What
I'd like to know is why us."

"Us who? The Circle K?"

Jake nodded. "Why did Delaware come here when
there's towns that need tamin' a lot worse than Ludlow?"

"Someone sent for him." Bull stated the obvious. "The
town council, most likely. That's how it's usually done."

"When we're done with the half-breed, we should pay
each of them a visit."

"You know," Bull said. "That's not a bad idea."

Jake suddenly stiffened and stared toward town. "Do
you hear that?"

"I ain't deaf."

The quiet of the night had been shattered by pistol shots

and the unmistakable blasts of a shotgun. There were several more shots and the shotgun blasted a second time and after a bit once more.

"What are we waitin' for?"

Bull raised his reins. "Back on your critters, boys. Crusty is in trouble."

"Do we ride in with guns blazin'?" Jake Bass eagerly asked.

"We ride in with our guns out," Bull said, "and blaze away the moment we set eyes on Asa Delaware."

"Let the fun commence," Jake Bass said, and whooped for bloodthirsty joy.

23

They thought they were being smart, but Asa had the eyes of a hawk. It came from his grandmother, one of the few things her legacy was good for.

Three riders had appeared. Two broke one way and one another. They were swinging wide to go up the streets that paralleled Main.

Asa moved into the murk along the side of the bank and sprinted to the rear. He reached it when the two riders were still a couple of blocks away. They were no more than black silhouettes, but that was enough. One of the advantages of a shotgun was that you only had to point it in the general direction of your target. The spread took care of the rest.

The street was narrower than Main, another factor in his favor.

They came on slowly and Asa heard one of them whisper, "I don't see hide nor hair of anybody, Slim."

"Me neither, Charley."

Asa's impulse was to shoot without warning, but he had to be sure, however slim the chance they were strangers passing through. "You Circle K punchers were warned to leave the country."

They reined up and one blurted, "It's by-God him, Charley! What do we do?"

Charley was already doing it. In the dark Asa didn't see his hand move, but suddenly the night flared with a firefly and a six-shooter cracked. "Fill him with lead!" Charley cried.

Asa fired.

The force of it lifted Charley from his saddle and sprawled him catawampus in the street.

Slim banged off a shot and hauled on his reins. He was trying to get out of there, and as his mount turned, Asa let him have it, broadside. Slim screamed and toppled, and his horse ran off.

Asa ran to them to make certain. It was another of his rules: Always be sure.

Pale ribs poked from Slim's chest. Charley had a hole where his stomach should be.

Working the Winchester's lever, Asa turned and sprinted toward Main. The third one had heard and was coming at a gallop.

It was the one called Crusty. His eyes were almost as good as Asa's, because he triggered several shots that sizzled lead uncomfortably close.

Asa dived and fired. The Winchester kicked but his aim was true and Crusty imitated a crow shot on the fly.

No shots at all came from the bank or the millinery, and Asa was pleased they were doing as they were supposed to.

Covering the stricken rustler, he moved closer.

Crusty was breathing in great gasps that sent a scarlet mist spraying from holes in his throat. "You've done me in, you son of a bitch."

"Buckshot usually means burying," Asa said.

Struggling to stay conscious, Crusty rasped, "Bull will get you. Him and Jake and the rest."

"The more the merrier."

Crusty sagged and froth filmed his lips. "Think you're funny."

"Did Weldon Knox come?"

"He doesn't do his own killin'."

"Shame," Asa said. He pointed the Winchester.

"Can't you see I'm almost gone? Why waste it?"

"Need to be sure."

"Miserable stinkin' breed."

Asa stroked the trigger.

24

---·-·---

Asa left the body lying there and retreated to the doorway of the bank where the outlaws wouldn't see him until they were right on top of him. He quickly replaced the spent shells, sliding new ones from loops in a bandoleer.

The town might as well be a cemetery. Nothing moved, except for him.

No one came to help, either. Not that he blamed them. Yes, this was their home, but they were clerks and tellers and a butcher and a barber and others who'd hardly ever held a gun, let alone fired one.

Thanks to the lurid accounts of so-called journalists, folks who lived east of the Mississippi River believed that every man who lived west of it never stepped out the door without artillery strapped to their waist. But the journalists, as usual, were full of cow droppings. Most Westerners lived peaceable lives and went about unarmed except when they hunted or traveled through hostile territory.

Outlaws were usually heeled, but most couldn't hit the broad side of a barn when sober, let alone when under the influence. Expert shootists were as rare as hen's teeth. Wild Bill Hickok was justly famous for once shooting a man through the heart at seventy-five yards, a feat no one had duplicated and likely ever would.

Asa wasn't Wild Bill. He was content to blow them apart at five yards. For him, skill didn't count for much. But surviving did.

Hooves pounded, and soon the west end of Main Street filled with riders. Bull Cumberland and Jake Bass were in the lead, Cumberland a mountain on horseback, Bass coiled like the snake he was.

They didn't slow. That was their first mistake. They stayed bunched together, too. That was their second. Bathed in the light from the houses they passed, they didn't draw rein until they reached Crusty. That was their third mistake.

Asa stayed in the doorway. It was up to him to start the blood flowing, and he had to choose the right moment.

Bull Cumberland glared at the body, his hand on his revolver. "I told him to be careful."

"Why, half his head is gone!" another man exclaimed.

"And the brains that were in it," said a third.

Jake Bass was scouring Main Street. "Where's that damn Town Tamer?"

"He has to be somewhere," Bull Cumberland said.

"Pair up and go door-to-door until we find him."

Asa moved into the open. None of them noticed him until he was close to Cumberland's sorrel. Cumberland was looking the other way but must have caught movement out of the corners of his eyes and jerked around. "I wouldn't," Asa said, the Winchester centered on Cumberland's broad chest. "I can't miss at this range."

"No one try anything," Cumberland said to the others without looking at them.

They obeyed. Jake Bass, though, had a wild look on his face that didn't bode well.

"You figure on droppin' all of us?" Bull Cumberland asked.

"No," Asa answered. To claim he could would be foolish.

"Set down the cannon, and maybe I'll make it quick," Bull said.

"Steers fly now, do they?"

Bull wasn't amused. "No, you're right. After what you

did to Old Tom and Tyree and now Crusty, you should beg for it to end."

"Not in this life or any other."

"You've got, what, five shots in that howitzer? There are ten of us left."

"We'll put more holes in you than there are in that foreign cheese," Jake Bass boasted.

"Hush," Bull Cumberland barked at him, again without taking his eyes off the Winchester.

"What are we waitin' for, damn it?" Jake Bass said.

"Use your head," someone snapped, "or Bull will lose his."

Jake colored with anger. "You'll answer to me later for that, Pike."

Bull Cumberland was surprisingly calm. "How do you aim to do this? Have us drop our hardware and lie down in the street so you can have us hog-tied?"

"Do you see a tin star on my shirt?" Asa said.

"So it's root, hog, or die?"

"Always has been," Asa said. "Every town I've tamed. I never take anyone alive. They either die or they skedaddle for parts unknown."

"We're none of us skedaddlers."

"You're not," Asa said. "But the rest of them aren't you. Grit comes hard for most."

"You have your share," Bull Cumberland said, "comin' out to meet us like this. You'd have been better off huntin' cover."

"I needed all of you sitting still."

"Does it matter much with a shotgun?" Bull said.

"No," Asa said, "but it does with rifles." And he threw back his head and roared, "*Now!*"

25

Surprise was key. It was why Asa always sent them on ahead. Why he insisted they avoid one another once he arrived in a town.

The odds were always against him. Never once was Asa asked to tame a town where only one bad man was giving the locals fits. It was always a lot of bad men, always a wild bunch, and they always thought he was facing them alone. They were wrong.

Asa had an ace in the hole. Or, rather, two aces, since his daughter insisted on doing her part, and truth be told, she was as good at it if not better than her rhyme-loving brother.

So now, when Asa roared, Byron reared up on the flat roof of the millinery across the street, and Noona heaved up in the steeple atop the bank.

The outlaws who had pretended to be cowpokes didn't see them. They were concentrating on Asa, which was exactly what Asa wanted them to do. He cut loose at Bull Cumberland even as he threw himself to the ground. He was sure he scored, but somehow Bull stayed in the saddle. Then the rest of the outlaws were jerking pistols, and Jake Bass, the quickest, snapped a shot that kicked up dirt practically in Asa's face.

Then the rifles of his children opened up.

They were as important as the element of surprise. Rifles had range. Rifles were man-droppers. Rifles—some—held more rounds than his shotgun.

These weren't ordinary rifles—not Winchesters or Henrys, even though both were popular.

Byron used a Colt rifle. The company was famous for their pistols, but they manufactured long guns, too, some of the finest ever crafted. Byron's was a Colt Lightning, the large-frame model with a slide action, not a lever. For long range Byron had his choice of a detachable scope or a peep sight. Or, for night work, he could rely on the front peep sight.

Noona preferred a Spencer. She loved the thing. She practiced with it every chance she got. Hers was fitted with a Blakeslee quick-loader and a removable tube magazine. Instead of loading it cartridge by cartridge, she carried seven extra tubes in a special-tailored vest. It took her mere moments to replace an empty tube with a full one. She shot faster than Byron, faster than Asa, faster than anyone Asa knew.

The first blasts of the Colt Lightning and the booms of the Spencer were drowned out by the banging of six-shooters. The Circle K riders didn't realize they were being shot at by shooters other than Asa, but they found out when four of them dropped in as many seconds.

Asa rolled, felt a sting in his side. Horses were plunging and whinnying, and he got one between him and most of his would-be killers.

"Up there!" a Circle K killer hollered. "Someone with a rifle!"

Asa didn't know if they had spotted Byron or Noona. He had a more immediate concern, and couldn't look.

Jake Bass had reined around the others and jabbed his spurs to send his mount straight at Asa. Asa did more rolling, but a hoof clipped his shoulder and pain exploded. His arm felt half-numb as he came to a stop on his back.

He fired at Bass as Bass flew by, but he rushed his shot and misjudged the angle and did something a shooter with a shotgun seldom did that close up. He missed.

By now most of the bad men were firing at the millinery and the bank. One aimed his revolver at Byron and steadied his arm, and up in the bank steeple Noona's Spencer thundered, and the man's hat and no small part of his head went flying.

Noona had saved her brother's bacon.

Asa unleashed a blast that smashed a rider from his saddle. Gaining his knees, he fired into the thick of them. Once. Twice.

A hornet buzzed his ear.

Jake Bass had reined around and was coming at him again, intent on riding him down.

Asa raised his Winchester, but he was a shade slow. The horse was almost on him. In another few moments he would be trampled and there was nothing he could do.

Then the Colt rifle on the millinery cracked and Jake Bass's temple spurted blood, and in the same heartbeat the Spencer in the steeple crashed and the head of Bass's horse did the same. The horse plunged to one side as if to escape the pain that had killed it. It didn't trample Asa but it didn't miss him, either. He was slammed to earth so hard, it was a wonder he didn't break every rib in his body.

Just like that, the shooting stopped.

Stunned, his head ringing, Asa was vaguely aware of hammering hooves. A lone outlaw was taking flight. Heading east, not west.

Asa couldn't lie there. Some might still be alive. He forced his legs to work and managed to stand.

Bodies were sprawled everywhere, and Bass's horse, besides.

Asa reloaded. His arm was still numb, and he fumbled with the shells. He got done just as Byron came from across Main and Noona emerged from the bank at a run, her long hair tied in a tail.

They surveyed the slaughter and Byron said, "Well, we've done it again. Three cheers for us."

"Not now," Asa said, searching for signs of life in the riddled forms.

Noona said, "The one who got away won't get far. I hit him solid."

"Good girl," Asa said.

Byron overheard and mockingly asked, "Am I a good boy, Pa?"

"Not now, I said."

Byron motioned at the Circle K figures. " 'Our life is a false nature—'tis not in the harmony of things.' "

"You quote poetry now?" Asa said.

Byron didn't get to answer.

Behind Asa and Noona a gun hammer clicked and a familiar voice said in vicious delight, "I've got you, you son of a bitch."

26

Asa braced for a shot and searing pain, but nothing happened.

Noona had the good sense to freeze.

Byron started to raise his rifle but caught himself. "Thought you were dead," he said.

Asa turned his head.

Bull Cumberland had risen on the elbow of his remaining good arm. The other arm and the shoulder it was attached to had been mangled by buckshot, and all that connected the arm to the shoulder was a shred of flesh. It also looked as if he'd been hit by the rifles. Yet he had life enough to clutch his six-shooter and train it on Asa. A wolfish grin curled his mouth and he snarled, "You've done me in, but now I'll do you."

Asa forced himself to stay calm. It was rare for anyone to get the drop on him. He was too cautious. It had only ever happened once before. That time, the gunman hadn't realized he'd emptied his revolver while swapping lead and when he squeezed the trigger, they both heard the click. Asa had resorted to his shotgun to end it.

He couldn't do that here. He'd have to spin and shoot, and Bull Cumberland, hurt as he was, would nail him.

"Drop your guns," the man-mountain rumbled. "All three of you."

Asa let the Winchester clatter at his feet. Noona was clearly loath to do the same with her Spencer, but did. Byron hesitated.

"I'll kill your pa before you can blink, boy," Bull Cumberland said. "So help me God."

Byron held the Colt by the barrel, set the stock down, and let gravity take over.

Bull grunted. "Good." He stared at the slain and at what was left of his other arm and shook his head. "You have shot us to ribbons."

"How are you still breathing?" Asa stalled. Judging by the pool of blood there couldn't be much left in Cumberland's body.

Bull ignored the question and said bitterly, "But then, you had help, didn't you?" He glared at Noona and Byron. "The newspapers never said anything about you havin' helpers."

"I try not to let that get out," Asa said.

"So the boy's your son."

An icy spike of fear pierced Asa.

"Is the girl his wife?"

"Marry my own brother?" Noona said, and snorted. "I'd sooner slit my throat."

Bull studied her face, his own so pale, he was the same white as a bedsheet. "They don't look anything like you, Town Tamer."

"We're the fruit of his loins, all right," Byron said. "More's the pity."

"You talk funny, boy."

"He's a poet," Asa said.

"A what?"

"He likes poetry."

Bull Cumberland did the strangest thing. He laughed. Not a short bark but a deep laugh that ended with him swearing and saying, "Don't this beat all. Shot to pieces by an old man and a girl and a poet."

"I'm not that old," Asa said.

"He had us young," Noona said.

"Shut the hell up, all of you." Bull raised his revolver higher. "Time to end you, half-breed. And then the kids."

Asa clasped his hands and put as much emotion into his voice as he could. "Not them. Please. I'm begging you."

"Are you, now?" Bull said, and smirked in sadistic pleasure. "Get on your knees, then. If you're goin' to beg, do it right."

"Gladly," Asa said. He sank down, his hands still clasped, and held them out toward Cumberland. "I'm begging you with all my heart to spare them."

"I'm glad I lived long enough for this," Bull said. "Do you want to know why?"

Asa unclasped his hands. "Why?"

"Because I'm goin' to shoot them first and then shoot you. I want you to see them die. I want to see the look on your face. Then I can go happy."

"How about if we reverse it?" Asa said.

Under different circumstances, Bull Cumberland's confusion would have been comical. "Reverse it how?"

"How about if you die first?" Asa said. He flicked his right wrist and the Remington derringer was in his hand. He cocked it as it cleared, and fired.

A hole appeared in the middle of Bull Cumberland's forehead. His head snapped back and his good arm sagged. His wide eyes fixed on Asa in surprise as life fled them, and his bulk thudded to the earth.

Noona exhaled in relief. "That was close."

Byron picked up his Colt rifle and came over and stared at Cumberland.

"Nothing to say?" Asa asked.

"Took you long enough," Byron said.

Interlude

27

Weldon Knox was worried. His men should have been back by mid-morning at the latest. But here it was late afternoon and still no sign of them.

Knox sat in a rocking chair on the front porch of his ranch house and stared to the east. He'd been sitting there for hours. When the screen door creaked he didn't look over. He knew who it was.

"No sign of them yet?" Esther asked.

"If there was," Knox said, "do you think I'd still be sitting here?"

"I was only asking," Esther said timidly.

"Well, don't." Knox gestured at the other rocking chair. "Join me."

It wasn't a request. It was a command. Esther folded her hands in her lap and perched as if she was ready to take flight if he lifted a hand to strike her. "I can understand you being upset."

"I doubt that you understand anything about me, woman," Knox said. "I doubt you understand anything at all."

"As you say, dear," Esther said.

"I should think you'd have gotten it through your head by now. You're female. Women don't think as deeply as men do. A lot of what goes through my head is beyond you."

"I do keep forgetting that, yes."

"Well, don't. I would rely on you more if you weren't so female."

Esther did something she seldom did. She looked him in the eyes. "How do I not be me?"

"That's simple. You listen to me and do as I tell you and when an idea of your own pops into your head, you ignore it."

"That does sound simple."

"Honestly," Knox said. He reached into an inside pocket and brought out his pipe and tobacco. "I can use a smoke."

"For your nerves?"

"Just to smoke. I don't have a problem with my nerves, thank you very much."

"I do. I'm worried sick. Mrs. Livingstone was telling me that this Asa Delaware is bad medicine."

"What would she know?"

"She's a friend. She wouldn't make things up."

Knox tore his gaze off the road that cut across his land to end at the miles-distant Ludlow. "Did I hear you right? You've struck up a friendship with the *cook*?"

"Why not?" Esther said defensively. "She's a person like you and me."

"Don't lump me in with the help," Knox said. "I have half a mind to fire her."

"What? Why?"

"Hirelings should know their place."

Esther squirmed in her rocking chair. "What gives you the right to put on airs?"

Knox turned toward her. "Did you just sass me?"

"No."

"You certainly did. I heard you. You talked back to me."

"I never would, Weldon."

"When this is over I think I'll take out the switch," Knox said, and had the satisfaction of seeing stark fear grip her.

"Not that. Please."

"You need to be reminded every now and then of your proper place."

Esther was quiet a while and then said softly, "I never expected this when I married you. You were nice when you courted me. You never once let on that—" She stopped.

"Finish it."

"No."

"I will by-God beat you black and blue if you don't."

"Very well. You never once let on that you'd treat me as you do and beat me as you do." Esther sadly gazed out over their ranch and gave a mild start.

"What?" Knox asked, looking in the same direction. "Do you see Bull and the rest?"

"No. I thought I saw—" A peculiar expression came over her and Esther said, "I'm not sure what I saw."

"Females," Knox spat.

Esther clasped her small fingers and unclasped them and remarked, "I remember hearing you menfolk talk once."

"Just once?" Knox said sarcastically.

"You were in the kitchen. Bull Cumberland and that awful Jake Bass and Old Tom and you."

"We talk a lot," Knox said.

"It was about riding the high-lines, as Bull Cumberland called it, and how he always had to be on the lookout for lawmen and hostiles and whatnot."

"I'm sure there's a point to this."

"He mentioned how he watched for flashes of light. He said the sun shining off a rifle barrel always gave his enemies away. Do you think that's true?"

"Of course it is."

"Did you send all the men into town?"

Knox had his full attention on the road and was annoyed by her babble. "Listen to your chatter. You bounce around all over the place."

"Did you?"

"Some of the men are out on the range with the herd."

"Can you think of any reason they would point a rifle at us?"

Knox turned his head. "Have you been drinking? I know you sneak a nip now and then."

"Every day," Esther said. "It helps get me through the nightmare of being married to you."

Knox couldn't credit his ears. "Do you *want* to be beat worse than ever?"

"What I want, what I pray," Esther said, "is for that flash to mean what I think it means. Foolish of me, I know. I don't believe in miracles."

"What flash?"

Esther jumped at the loud *thwack* that preceded by a heartbeat the crack of a far-off shot. Her husband's head smacked against the rocker and some of his hair and bits of bone and gobs of brain splattered the wall. She sat perfectly still as the husk that had just a few seconds ago been the man she'd said "I do" to oozed out of the rocker onto the porch.

"My word," was all Esther said.

She looked toward where she had seen the flash and was taken aback when a rider appeared. She gripped the chair arms to rise and was shocked to realize the gender of the rider and sank back down.

"My word," she said again.

An attractive young woman with raven hair on a fine bay and a rifle across her saddle came as casually as you please up to the porch. "How do you do," she said.

"My word," Esther replied.

"You're not in hysterics, are you?"

"Why would I be?"

The young woman nodded at Weldon.

"Oh, him," Esther said. She stood and stepped to the rail. "How about if I invite you in for tea or coffee?"

"I just shot your husband."

"And I thank you for that."

The young woman studied Esther and then said, "I should head back."

Esther pointed at the body. "For twenty-seven years I've

been married to that man, and not once in all that time did he let me have a female friend over."

"Is that a fact?"

"I would be ever so pleased if you would visit for a bit. And don't you worry. I'll never tell a soul that I saw you here. I'm Esther Weldon, by the way, but I imagine you already know that."

The young woman considered a few moments, then said, "I'm Noona Carter." She seemed to catch herself. "Sorry. Noona Delaware."

"You're kin to that Town Tamer?"

"He's my pa."

"Which is it? Carter or Delaware?"

"It's complicated," Noona said.

"I have all day," Esther said, and a slow smile brightened her haggard face. "I can do as I please now."

"The short of it is that Carter is the family name, but given what we do for a living, our enemies might track us down if they know who we really are. So Pa picked a name he hates just for town taming."

"I think I see."

Noona raised her reins. "I'm sorry I can't stay, ma'am. My pa wanted to be sure it was over. He expects me back, or he'll get worried and come after me."

"Good day to you, then. And thank you, young lady. You have made me happier than you can possibly know."

"It's nice to make someone smile for once. Usually killing someone doesn't do that." Noona wheeled her bay. "Adios."

Esther stood and watched until the attractive young woman dwindled in the distance. "What a sweet girl," she said. She started toward the screen door but stopped to look at the body. "I was wrong, Weldon. Miracles do happen. Good riddance to you, you piece of shit."

Humming to herself, Esther went inside.

28

The town council met in what they called their Municipal Chambers, a room above the general store with a high platform for the council members and chairs for everyone else.

Asa Delaware sat in the front row with Byron and Noona at his elbows. The Winchester was propped against his chair.

George Tandy rapped with a gavel and announced, "This meeting is now in session."

Over a dozen townsfolk had turned out. The other hundred or so couldn't be bothered.

"Now, then," Tandy said. "Our first order of business is to extend our appreciation to Mr. Asa Delaware for the splendid job he did cleaning up our town."

"I'd appreciate the other half of my fee," Asa said.

Thaddeus Falk wagged a bony finger at him. "You're lucky we're paying you another red cent, the mess you made. A mess, I might add, we had to clean up ourselves."

"It's your town," Asa said.

"Show a little respect," Horace Wadpole said.

"I show as much as I'm given."

Wadpole turned red and opened his mouth to respond,

but just then Asa picked up the Winchester shotgun and set it in his lap. Wadpole closed his mouth and glowered.

"As for your money," George Tandy said, "the treasurer will pay you when this meeting is adjourned." He gazed at the townspeople. "Our second order of business is a new marshal. We intend to put out the word that we're seeking a new lawman and expect to interview qualified applicants over the next month or two."

"The sooner we have a new marshal, the safer everyone will feel," Falk said.

"That leaves the last item on our agenda," Tandy said. "We'd intended to call Weldon Knox before this body and inform him that as soon as we have our new marshal, we would have him arrested on a variety of charges. But as all of you have probably heard, he committed suicide. We sent a man out to the Circle K with our demand for him to appear, and his wife informed our messenger that he shot himself after he heard that his desperados had met the fate they deserved."

Asa Delaware looked at Noona.

"So with that out of the way, and due to the long hours we've been putting in, we'll cut this meeting short and adjourn unless someone has something pressing they must bring to our attention."

No one did.

Tandy rapped the gavel, and the council rose and filed out. The townspeople trailed after them. Several smiled at the town tamers, and an older man came over to Asa and said, "I'd like to shake your hand."

Last to go was the treasurer, after giving Asa a poke with the five hundred dollars. Asa never took a bank draft or a check. It had to be real money. Jingling it, he stuck it in an inside pocket of his slicker.

"'The dragons are dead, the slayers have triumphed,'" Byron quoted.

"You slayed your share," Asa said.

"Don't remind me."

Noona changed the subject by asking, "Why do you reckon the widow did that—lie about Knox shooting himself?"

"I don't rightly know," Asa said.

"She knew it was me. She was right there. She talked to me."

"You told us," Asa said.

"She took it so calmly. I've never seen the like."

"Live to my age and you'll see a lot of strange things," Asa predicted. "People are always full of surprises."

"Coming from you," Byron said, "that's almost profound."

"Keep goading me," Asa said.

"What will you do? Hit me?"

"I've never struck you in your life, boy, and you know it. You don't hurt family, ever."

"You turned my sister and me into killers before we were mature enough to realize what you'd done."

"Keep me out of this," Noona said.

"I taught you to be town tamers," Asa said to Byron. "That's not hurt."

"In case you haven't noticed, Pa," Byron said, "I'm hurting like hell."

"What hurts is that you'd like to live in the clouds with your poems and you hate being brought down to earth."

"You are damn right I hate it."

Asa rounded on him. "Watch your tone around your sister. If you took some pride in your work, you'd be better off."

Byron laughed. "First, it's not work. It's killing. And second, you're a fine one to talk about pride. You don't even use your real name."

"And you know why."

"So the kin and friends of those we exterminate can't come after us. But that's only part of it."

"How so?"

"You could have picked any fake name. But you chose Delaware. And the reason you did is to rub your Indian half in the faces of those who hate Indians."

"I've never been a cheek-turner, boy," Asa said. "If some folks are going to hate me for something I'm not, I'm going to hate them right back."

"Your whole life has become about hate."

"That's going too far," Asa said, "and we're done talking about it." He shouldered the Winchester and strode out.

"Must you goad him so?" Noona said.

"I'm sorry, sis," Byron said. "I can't seem to help myself."

"Did you ever stop to think that he can't, either?"

Byron appeared shocked. He was slow to answer with, "No, I didn't." He stared at the empty doorway. "Hell," he said.

29

A letter was waiting for Asa at the boardinghouse. Ethel gave it to him, saying, "This came about half an hour ago."

Asa had his mail forwarded by his sister in Austin. He had post office boxes for both Asa Carter and Asa Delaware, and his sister had access and made sure any letters caught up to him.

He didn't open the envelope until he was in his room. He was supposed to pack so they could head home, but after reading it he sat on the bed and pondered until a knock on his door roused him.

"We're ready when you are," Noona said as she and Byron entered.

"I'd like my share of the money first," Byron said.

Asa always gave each of them a third. Noona was saving hers and had quite a nest egg. He didn't know what Byron did with his.

"I'll be heading east soon after we get back," Byron said, jingling his poke.

"Any chance I can interest you in one last job?" Asa said.

"No."

"What was in the letter you got?" Noona asked.

Asa unfolded it. "How about I read it to you?"

"Go ahead," Noona said.

"I don't care what its says," Byron declared. "I'm not changing my mind."

"It's from a Cecilia Preston in Ordville, Colorado," Asa revealed.

"Isn't that a mining town?" came from Noona.

"Silver," as Asa recollected. "A man by the name of Ordville struck one of the richest veins ever found. The mine produces tons of it a year."

"Colorado is a long way from Texas," Noona said.

"Let me read it." Asa wet his throat. "'Mr. Asa Delaware. Dear sir. My name is Cecilia Preston. I'm writing on behalf of Ordville. We would like for you to come and tame our town. There are bad men here. Come in person as soon as you can. Thank you. Cecilia Preston.'"

"That's it?" Byron said, and laughed.

"She sounds sort of simpleminded," Noona said.

"Postscript," Asa read. "You will be paid five thousand dollars to tame Ordville. Please come quick."

Byron whistled.

"That's more than we've earned for any job, ever," Noona said.

"It is," Asa said.

"Will you take it or not?"

"I've been sitting here thinking," Asa said. "Five thousand is a lot of money. With your brother wanting to go off on his own—"

"Don't involve me," Byron interrupted.

"—I was thinking I would take my usual three hundred and you two can split the rest."

"No," Byron said.

"That would come to over twenty-three hundred dollars for each of you," Asa calculated.

"I don't do this for the money," Noona said. "But that is an awful lot."

"Damn it," Byron said.

"We've never been to Colorado, though," Noona noted. "Wyoming, that once. And Arkansas that time. But mostly we work in Texas."

"Colorado's no different than any other place," Asa said. "A town is a town."

"It's a long way."

"Wyoming was farther."

"I'm not objecting," Noona said. "I'll do it if you do it."

"Thanks." Asa looked at his son.

"No," Byron said, with a lot less conviction than before.

"Twenty-three hundred to bankroll your new life," Noona said.

"I don't care," Byron said.

"One last taming."

"Don't do this."

"If he doesn't want to," Asa said, "leave him be. He's a grown man now, as he keeps reminding us."

Noona placed a hand on her brother's arm. "If you won't do it for him, do it for me."

"I hate you," Byron said.

"Twenty-three hundred," she said again.

"I'm not you, sis. I don't like blowing people's brains out anymore."

"I'll help Pa blow out the brains if that's what bothering you. I just want your company."

Byron stepped to the window and stared down at the street, and sighed. "'But ever and anon of griefs subdued there comes a token like a Scorpion's sting,'" he quoted.

"Is that a yes or a no?" asked Noona.

"I'll go," Byron said. "For you, not for him. But I won't kill. I am done with killing, now and forever. Whatever else I can do, I will."

Noona grinned, went over, and pecked him on the cheek. "Thank you. You won't regret it."

"That remains to be seen."

"Honestly, boy," Asa said, rising. "You are gloom itself. We've done this how many times? We'll take the usual precautions."

"Nothing will go wrong," Noona said.

"I hope not," Byron said and turned to Asa. "But if it does, I have your epitaph."

"I don't need one."

"Listen," Byron said, and quoted with, "'Thy days are

done, thy strains begun. Thy country's strains record the triumphs of her chosen Son, the slaughters of his sword. The deeds he did, the fields he won, the freedoms he restored.'"

"I just don't understand you sometimes," Asa said.

"Enough of that." Noona raised her hand as if she held a glass. "To Colorado," she said happily, "and the last hurrah of the Delawares."

30

They took a train to Denver. Or, rather, a series of trains, since they had to switch a couple of times. It was only possible because earlier that year the Fort Worth and Denver Railway had completed their line and commenced service.

Noona was delighted. Usually they rode horseback to the next town or took stagecoaches if it was far off. She liked to ride a horse but not for days at a time, and she could only take the confines of a bouncing stage for so long before she wanted to jump out.

The train cars swayed a little now and then, and there was the constant chug of the engine and the clack of the rails, but all in all, it was as comfortable as could be compared to horseback and a stage.

"This is grand," she said as they took their seats in the dining car. "This is awful grand."

"Unusual for you," Byron said to Asa, almost as if it were an accusation.

"If it's to be our last time together," Asa said, "we might as well make it special."

"No if," Byron said. "It is."

"What will you do? How will you make a living?"

"I don't know yet," Byron said, "but anything is better than blowing out brains."

"Not that again."

Noona smacked the table so hard, their glasses of water shook. "No, you don't. I won't put up with it. Byron, you keep what's eating you to yourself. Pa, don't bring up how he feels. We're going to get along if it kills us."

"Fine by me, daughter," Asa said.

"Byron?" Noona said.

" ' 'Tis a base abandonment of reason to resign our right of thought.' "

"Another of your quotes," Noona said. "Cut down on those, too. You only do it to show off."

"Oh, sis."

"Just because you can memorize more words than anybody doesn't mean you rub our noses in it."

"I recite it because I like it."

"Be that as it may. Half the time I don't know what in blazes you're saying, and more often than not it sets Pa off."

"That's not my intent."

"Besides," Noona said, "that precious poet of yours died, what, over sixty years ago? Not much he said matters today."

Byron reacted as if she had thrust a blade between his ribs. "You can't be serious. Lord Byron will be read for a thousand years. For ten thousand. For as long as romance flourishes in the human heart."

"God help us," Asa said.

"Don't belittle me for having poetry in my soul."

Asa went to reply and glanced at Noona. "Can I? You just told me not to."

Noona frowned. "I'll make this one exception but only if you give your word that you won't bring it up again the rest of the trip."

"Yes, by all means, go ahead," Byron said.

"Did this great poet you admire so much ever kill anyone?" Asa asked.

Byron stared.

"Well, did he?"

"Byron was British. They don't go around shooting each other like we do. They're civilized."

Asa swept an arm to encompass the plush interior of the dining car with its shaded windows and cushioned seats and bronze fittings. "We're not?"

"Dress an ape in a suit and it's still an ape. Lord Byron did most of his fighting with words. He used them like other men use swords."

"We're not apes," Asa said. "And why did you say 'most'?"

"Toward the end of his life he fought for Greek independence. Before he could take part in an actual engagement, he came down ill and died."

"So he didn't kill anybody."

Byron drummed his fingers on the table. "I resent what you're implying."

"I'm not implying anything, son. I'm saying that it's unfair to compare me to this poet. He scribbled rhymes for a living. I kill folks, bad folks, the kind who will shoot you as quick as look at you."

"I know that. I've helped you how many times?"

"Then you, of all people, should see that I can't afford to look at the world the way your poet does. To me, life isn't a romance. It's grim and hard, and it will kill you if you give it half a chance."

"I don't think you should be like Byron, Pa. I just wish you didn't kill, period."

"Ah," Asa said.

"Can't you see it's wrong?"

Asa looked out the window at the scenery rolling by, then said, "I had a parson say the same thing once. Went on and on about how evil I am. He quoted from the Bible, that commandment about not ever killing."

When Byron didn't respond, Noona was prompted by curiosity to ask, "What did you tell him?"

"I've never read the Bible all the way through. Your mother did. She liked to read it sometimes in the evenings after supper. You rememember?"

Noona nodded.

"One part I recollected was that not long after God gave

those commandments the parson went on about, those Jewish people got to their Promised Land, or whatever it was."

"I remember that part," Noona said.

"What was the first thing they did when they got there?" Asa said. "I'll tell you. They killed everybody. Wiped out whole towns and cities. Folks who worshipped other gods."

"Is there a point to this?" Byron asked.

"If it was all right for the Jews to go around killing all those bad folks, I reckon it's all right for me."

"I never thought of it like that," Noona said. "It's good to know the Almighty won't hold it against us."

Byron looked from her to their father and back again. "Do they serve drinks on this train?"

31

———— · ————

Later, Asa lay on his back in his berth with a hand under his head, staring at the ceiling and waiting for sleep to claim him.

He was worried about his son. He truly was.

Byron had changed. When he was younger he was bright and bushy-tailed. Then Mary took sick, and his disposition became gloomy. After she died, he fell into a sulk that lasted over a year.

The boy read more than ever. He'd always liked to, ever since he first learned how. Asa had thought it a waste of his son's time to read so much but Mary had said to let Byron be, that book-learning was a good thing and Byron would be better for it.

Not hardly, Asa thought. After her death, the boy became so caught up in books, his book world mattered more than the real one.

Especially that damn poet. For the life of him, Asa couldn't savvy what was so wonderful about Lord Byron. Unknown to his son, he'd snuck a few looks at the boy's books about him.

A lot of the poems had to do with ladies, Asa discovered.

It seemed that every time Lord Byron fell in love, he wrote
a new poem about it. And he fell in love a lot.

Asa was surprised to come across a poem Lord Byron
wrote in memory of his dog. Any man who cared for dogs
couldn't be all bad, but still.

As for the rest, it was so much Greek. Asa tried to read
Don Juan because his son liked it so much. But a lot of the
meaning, if there was any, went over his head.

Asa would be the first to admit he wasn't the smartest
gent who ever drew breath. He could count the books he'd
read on one hand and have fingers left over. And when people talked about politics and religion and the like, it put him
to sleep.

He was a simple man with simple needs, and simple
thoughts. It amazed him that any son of his could read
someone like Lord Byron and take his meaning.

He'd long suspected that no good would come of it, and
he'd been proven right.

All that highfalutin nonsense about not killing—Asa
was sure his son picked that up from books.

He hadn't found anything in his skimming of Lord Byron's works that flat-out said so, but he did remember someone telling him once that poets had gentle souls, and ever
since his son became obsessed with Lord Byron, he'd become so gentle-minded that now he couldn't abide snuffing
wicks.

Asa rolled onto his side and closed his eyes. He needed
to stop thinking about it. He needed to keep his head clear
for Ordville.

Town taming was a serious business. It was no job for
amateurs. Or for poets with gentle souls. He was glad this
was Byron's last time. If the boy kept at it, he'd wind up as
dead as that silly poet.

32

---·---

Byron listened to the *clack-clack-clack* of the car under him and the sound of the locomotive and wished he could get to sleep.

He didn't know which bothered him more. That his pa couldn't see that town taming was flat-out wrong, or his worry over the fact that sooner or later his father's luck would run out.

When he was little, Byron had looked up to him. In his eyes, his father had been the finest man alive. Devoted to his mother, caring toward his sister and him. He couldn't recall a single instance where his father raised his voice to them in anger or beat them, as some fathers did.

Back then Asa had been a marshal, and Byron had taken pride in that—in the star his father wore and how people respected him so.

Then his mother came down with consumption, and their lives changed forever. He'd seen how devastated his father was. How a lot of the joy went out of him. How he wasn't the same man he'd once been.

Proof of that was when his father gave up his badge and took to town taming.

Byron saw the change, even if his pa didn't. Where before Asa had served the law and protected folks by arresting the bad men who preyed on them, now he served no law but his own and blew the badmen to bits with that shotgun of his.

So what if towns hired him to do just that? It was nothing more nor less than sanctioned murder.

Byron had lent a hand, at first, for no other reason than that Asa was his father. But as time went on, as the killings mounted, he began to question the rightness of it.

Asa wasn't blowing those bad men apart out of any sense of right and wrong. Everyone else assumed he did it for the money, but Byron knew better.

The town taming was an excuse for Asa to kill.

What Byron didn't understand, and desperately wished to, was *why*. Why did his father feel the need to take so many lives? What satisfaction could spilling so much blood give him?

It didn't give Byron any. He was sick of it. He'd stuck it out as long as he could, and now he wanted to quit.

He wished his sister would do the same, but she still adored Asa as he once had. She also, he had to admit, didn't mind the killing one bit.

Byron would use their time in Ordville to try and persuade her to give up town taming, to live a normal life, like he was going to do.

He refused to do any killing in Ordville. He might as well start now to live as ordinary people did.

If nothing else, it should help him sleep better.

33

Noona was restless.

She couldn't get the constant quarreling between her pa and her brother out of her head.

She tried. Pressing her cheek into the soft pillow, she pulled the blanket higher and gave thanks that she was in a comfortable bunk and not sleeping on the hard ground.

She emptied her head and waited to drift off, and didn't.

Consarn Byron anyhow, she thought.

It was one thing for him to decide he was too good to kill anymore. That was his right. No one was forcing him.

But it was another for him to constantly badger their pa about it. To belittle him. To make him seem like some sort of monster for doing what so few had the grit to do.

Noona liked town taming. She had no problem with pulling the trigger on murderers and robbers and others of their unsavory ilk. It wasn't any different from, say, ridding a house of rats. Let the rats run wild, and they'd destroy it. Let bad men run wild, and they'd destroy a town.

She was proud of what their pa did, and proud that he let her take part.

Lately Byron had been going on to her about how she should live a "normal" life. To her, normal meant a husband

and kids and a house. It meant settling down. It meant doing dishes and laundry and cleaning and stitching.

She wasn't ready for that yet.

Domesticity would be a lot less exciting than town taming.

She got to travel, to meet new people! Sure, she had to put lead into a few, but only the bad ones.

She'd go on doing it as long as she could—or as long as her pa did, and he showed no signs of stopping anytime soon.

It wouldn't be the same without Byron, though. Three was better than two when it came to watching one another's backs.

Noona cared for him a lot. They weren't like some brothers and sisters who were forever spatting. They got along fine. Or had, until he climbed on his high horse about the taming.

He'd once brought up the point that females didn't do what she did. They didn't tote guns, didn't play-act in saloons, and they certainly didn't blow holes in bad men.

But the only reason more women didn't was their upbringing. They were taught that girls should behave in such-and-such a manner. Always be polite. Always be sweet. Learn to cook and learn to sew and learn to polish silverware and shoes so they could wait on their husbands mouth and foot.

None of that for her. She wasn't a homebody. And she'd as soon gag as let a man rule her life.

Town taming let her avoid all that.

So far as she knew, she was the first and only female town tamer. For her own safety, her pa hadn't let it be well known—which was a shame.

Noona felt herself drifting off. She thought of Ordville and what might be in store for them. It wouldn't be anything they hadn't seen before.

Life seldom surprised her anymore. She doubted Ordville would.

Part Four

34

Ordville, Colorado, got its start by accident.

One summer's day a grizzled prospector with the handle of Lester Ordville was leading his contrary mule, Abigail, along an unnamed creek high in the Rockies. When she balked at going on, he sat down to rest and noticed a patch of color, not in the creek but in a bluff on the other side.

Taking his pick, Ordville chipped at the rock and soon exposed a vein—not of gold, which was disappointing, but of silver. Silver didn't fetch as much, but enough of it could put a person in money for life.

Ordville filed a claim, brought in workers, and established the Stubborn Mule Mining Company. The ground under the bluff yielded over a ton of silver in the first year, and it wasn't long before a town sprang up. They named it after him even though he wanted to name the town Abigail.

Ten years went by.

In that time, Lester had a mansion built and married a

woman thirty years younger than he was. Her name was Darcy. They met one day when she bumped into him as he was coming out of his barber's. She hinted that he should ask her out and he mustered the courage to do it. One thing led to another, with most of the things Darcy's doing, and before Lester could quite collect his wits, he was wed.

Darcy spent her money so fast, it was a wonder Lester didn't go broke. She wanted so much, and he was so eager to please, that he sold his mine to a conglomerate for what he thought was enough money to last him a lifetime. It lasted a year and a half. Darcy left him for greener and younger pastures and Lester ended up in a shack at the end of town. Just him and Abigail, who was too old and worn to go prospecting, but at least she didn't spend him to death.

The conglomerate didn't just take over the mine. They took over the town. The first thing they did was change the mine's name to the Studevant Silver Lode.

Arthur Studevant was the head of the conglomerate and liked his name on everything he owned. His philosophy could be summed up in his favorite expression: "Why settle for a hundred thousand when you can make a million?"

Studevant brought in more men and expanded operations. He increased ore production by a whopping thirty-five percent. If that was all he did it would have been remarkable, but Studevant had other business interests besides mines.

The men who worked in his mines needed someplace to live. They needed clothes to wear. Needed food to eat. Most important of all, they needed a shot of whiskey at the end of a hard day's labor and a congenial atmosphere in which to enjoy it.

That was why when Arthur Studevant took over a mine, he took over the town, too. He opened boardinghouses, bought up existing properties, and rented them out. He opened eateries. More important, as far as raking in profits went, were his saloons. In Ordville he opened five within half a year of taking over the mine and made it known that men who worked for him should frequent his establishments and not others. Small wonder that most of the existing saloons and two restaurants closed for lack of business.

Ordville became a company town.

And since Studevant controlled it, he got to run it the way he pleased. And the way he pleased was wide open.

Common sense said that saloons open twenty-four hours made more money than saloons only open for twelve. So Studevant kept his open twenty-four.

Common sense said that saloons open seven days a week made more money than saloons open six. So Studevant kept his open seven.

The town had three churches. The men of the cloth who ran them complained that Studevant was breaking the Sabbath, but he silenced two of them with generous donations. The third was Catholic, and in Studevant's eyes didn't count.

His next act should have provoked howls of righteous indignation from every upright soul in Ordville, yet only a few married women raised a fuss and were ignored.

Studevant opened the Rocky Mountain Social Club. It wasn't a club in that you didn't have to buy a membership to join, and it wasn't social except that its patrons got to frolic with naked women for money.

Studevant brought in a professional madam from St. Louis to run the place, and rumor had it they were quite close.

All of this Asa Delaware learned before he even left Texas. All it took was a couple of visits to the Austin library and newspaper. Noona did the visiting since he wasn't much at reading. She always handled that part.

Now, as the Ordville Express chugged up a steep grade to the pass that would take the train over the divide, Asa gazed out the window of the dining car at a spectacular vista of miles-high snowcapped peaks, and pondered.

He'd have to be mighty careful how he went about taming a place like Ordville.

It was one thing to tangle with an outlaw rancher like Weldon Knox and another to go up against someone as rich and powerful as Arthur Studevant.

It could be that Studevant had simply let things get out of hand with his wide-open policy and would welcome a chance to rein in the rough element. But Asa couldn't count on that.

He'd learn more once he got there and talked to the mayor.

Byron would try to land a job as a bartender and Noona would do her dove act, and between the three of them, they'd know what was what in no time.

"Always get to know a town before taming it" was another of Asa's rules.

He'd ask the mayor to keep his being there a secret until he was ready to commence the taming.

And with any luck, he wouldn't have to kill as many men as he had in Ludlow.

That should make Byron happy.

35

From a distance most towns look the same: a lot of squares and rectangles, a few buildings three or four stories high at the most, arranged in neat rows.

Not Ordville.

As the Express rounded a wide curve that would bring the train to the station, Asa peered ahead and said to himself, "I never saw the like."

The buildings reared with no rhyme or reason amid rolling foothills. Five and six stories, some of them, with one, by God, that had to be ten. Brick, for the most part, with a couple that looked to be stone from a quarry. The streets — what Asa could see of them — seldom ran straight for more than a couple of blocks. Mostly they twisted and turned like so many snakes. Everywhere, people bustled. It reminded him of nothing so much as an ant hill swarming with gaily dressed ants.

A stir of excitement filled the car as the train neared its destination. Some went to collect their bags so they would be ready to get off.

Asa was in no hurry. He'd slip out when the majority did and blend into the crowd. The mayor might have let it be known he was coming, and the opposition might have sent an assassin. The prospect was slim, but Asa never left anything to chance if he could help it.

He passed Byron in the aisle and Byron ignored him. Not out of disrespect. It was part of the plan. He and Byron and Noona were to pretend they didn't know one another until the time came to confront the bad men.

The conductor was yelling that Ordville was the next stop, as if everyone didn't know.

Asa was slightly taken aback when the conductor stopped on seeing him and said, "Let me guess. You must have heard."

"Heard what?" Asa said, wondering if the conductor recognized him somehow.

"About Mr. Studevant and Indians."

Before Asa could ask what he meant, the conductor walked on, hollering, "Ordville, next stop."

The shotgun was in its leather case, his clothes and other effects in a carpetbag. With one in either hand, Asa turned to the window just as the train pulled in.

The platform was packed with folks waiting for new arrivals and others waiting to catch the train to wherever they were bound.

Asa kept his head low as he stepped down and moved over by a pillar. Only then did he realize the station was built in some sort of Greek style with arches and columns and whatnot.

Ordville didn't do things by half.

Asa glimpsed Noona threading through the throng. She caught sight of him and broke his rule by smiling. It was unlikely anyone noticed, but it annoyed him that she didn't listen.

Inside, the station was a madhouse. People yelling and scurrying and an Express company employee bellowing that the train had arrived.

The street wasn't much better. The new arrivals were dispersing to waiting carriages and hansoms. Men on horseback clomped to and fro while people on foot thronged the boardwalks.

Asa took his time. Part of reading a town, like reading a person, was to note every little thing. The small things were important. For instance, one of the first things he noticed was how well dressed everyone was. Nary a farmer or a cowboy or a town drunk in sight. Loggers, though, and lots and lots of mine workers. Plus the tony townsfolk. Derbies and bowlers were common. So were long coats and high boots.

In his derby and his slicker, Asa fit right in.

He needed to find a boardinghouse, but first he would check in with the mayor.

The municipal building, like the train station, boasted Greek architecture. Asa hadn't seen such fancy buildings since the trip he took to Washington, D.C.

The mayor's office was on the top floor. Brass fittings sparkled, and the hardwood floor was clean enough to eat off of.

The waiting room was full. Asa stepped to the secretary's desk and had to clear his throat before she looked up from a ledger she was scribbling in.

"Yes?" she said with an air of boredom.

"Asa Delaware to see the mayor."

She was pretty, not much over twenty, with her hair worn in a new fashion and a dress that in some small towns would be considered scandalous. "Do you have an appointment?"

"No. But I believe he's expecting me."

"I'm sorry," she said. "You'll have to wait for the first available opening."

"Are you sure he won't see me right away?"

"Appointments always take precedence unless it's an emergency."

"No," Asa admitted. "It's not that."

"Well, then. Take a seat and I'll call your name when the time comes."

Asa supposed he shouldn't be bothered about it but he was. He'd come a long way. Then again, the mayor didn't know when he was arriving. "Would you at least let him know I'm here, in case he wants to see me sooner?"

"I will."

Asa claimed an empty space on a bench along a wall, set down the carpetbag, and placed the shotgun across his lap. He figured it wouldn't be long. But a half hour went by and then an hour. The secretary called out names and people went in. Most weren't in there long.

The mayor was a busy man.

Asa like to pride himself on his patience, but after two hours his was wearing thin, and after three he'd had enough. He stood, shouldered the shotgun, and was bending to pick up the carpetbag when his name was called.

A bronze nameplate on the door read TOM OLIVER. Like everything else in Ordville, the office oozed money.

From the mahogany desk to the paneling to the glass bookcase and globe lamps, it was an office fit for a governor or a president.

Tom Oliver smiled, rose, and offered his hand. In his forties, he was balding and well-fed and, of course, well-clothed. "Mr. Delaware, is it?"

Asa set the shotgun on an empty chair and his carpetbag on the floor, and shook. "I came as quick as I could."

"That's nice." Oliver indicated another chair. "Have a seat, why don't you."

Asa sank down and sat back. He'd no sooner made himself comfortable than he received a shock.

"Now then," Mayor Oliver said, "my secretary informs me that your business is urgent. So let's get right to it." He paused. "Who are you? And why have you come to see me?"

36

Noona was near breathless with excitement. She'd never been anywhere like Ordville. Most towns they went to were small. Cattle towns, with a main street and two or three saloons and drab frame houses.

She'd been to St. Louis, a growing city on the edge of the frontier. But few of the buildings there were anywhere near as grand, and the people were downright sleepy compared to the thriving swarm of humanity that buzzed about here.

Ordville was . . . intoxicating.

She stood on a street corner, deeply breathed in the cool mountain air, and swore she could feel a pulse of vitality, as if the town had a giant heart that beat to the rhythm of its riches.

And rich it was. From the ornate buildings to the costly clothes people wore to the flamboyant trappings of the carriages and wagons, the signs of money were everywhere.

Noona loved it. When she was growing up, their family never had a lot. Back then her pa was a deputy marshal, and lawmen didn't make much. They got by well enough, thanks mainly to her mother doing seamstress work to help out.

But this?

"Oh my," Noona said in amazement.

"It's something, isn't it?" said a man's voice behind her.

Noona turned and was near breathless.

He was young and exceedingly handsome with hair as black as hers and eyes as blue as the sky. His suit was impeccable, his hat tilted at a rakish angle. He had a square jaw and the nicest teeth this side of anywhere, which he displayed in a dazzling smile. "Forgive me for being so forward, but I couldn't help myself," he said. "You're something, too."

"I beg your pardon?"

"I saw you get off the train. I've been following you."

Noona's instincts kicked in. "You have, have you?" she said suspiciously. That she hadn't noticed him disturbed her. She'd been so drunk on the town's opulence, she'd let down her guard.

"Before you take a swing at me," he said with another dazzling smile, "it's my job."

"To follow women?"

"To find beautiful ones like yourself."

Noona was flustered but hid it. He seemed sincere, but she well knew how men were. "I'm not interested."

"You haven't heard my proposition yet."

Noona laughed. "Trust me. I have. At least you're keeping your hands to yourself."

"Oh, no." He laughed and shook his head. "As much as it would flatter me to have you want to, I'm afraid this is strictly a business proposition."

"What is?"

He glanced at the stream of pedestrians. "This is hardly the proper place. How about if you let me treat you to a bite to eat or something to drink and I explain?"

"I don't know," Noona hesitated. She was supposed to find the nearest saloon, apply for work, and then meet up with her father and brother.

"What can half an hour hurt? I promise to be a perfect gentleman."

"Did your folks give you a name, or do I just say, 'Hey, handsome'?"

"Listen to you," he said, and grinned. "James Tharber, at your service." He held out his hand.

Noona had to lean her rifle against her leg. It was in a long case that didn't look anything like a typical rifle case. His hand was warm, and he didn't try to crush hers. "Noona." She didn't give a last name.

"Very pleased to meet you."

Before Noona could stop him, he scooped up the case and blinked in surprise.

"Say, this thing is heavy. What do you have in here, anyway? I took it for a musical instrument."

"It is," Noona said, snatching it back. "It's a trumpet."

"A woman who plays the trumpet? Now I've heard everything."

His laugh was infectious. Noona let him carry her bag but she held on to her rifle as they walked a block or so to a restaurant called the Blue Spruce. He held the door for her. Inside was positively elegant, with booths and globe lamps and the waitresses in uniforms.

"Looks pricey," Noona said.

"What in Ordville isn't?"

"I wouldn't know," Noona said. "This is my first visit."

A waitress led them to a booth, set down menus, and left.

"So what is this about?" Noona got right to the point.

James Tharber slid his hand across and touched hers. "How would you like to make a very lot of money?"

37

——— · ———

Byron thought he had died and gone to heaven, a heaven of pure culture.

He'd never been anywhere like Ordville. The way the people dressed, their hustle and bustle and sense of purpose, the elegance of the buildings—it was like stepping into a whole new world.

Byron passed two theaters within ten blocks of the train station. Then he came to the downtown district, and he was like a child in a candy store.

There were four more theaters. Four! And an opera house so elegant on the outside, it made him eager to view the no doubt lavish interior. There were dance halls and a concert hall. Saloons, of course, and a tavern or three, but even they were far and away superior to the shabby variety of Ludlow and other cattle towns.

He went into one. It was called Pike's Peak or Bust. A crescent mahogany bar gleamed in the light of a chandelier.

The floor was polished, the tables covered with felt, the spittoons and rails gleamed, and the dealers were impeccable in their uniforms.

Byron set down his bag and the long case with his rifle,

and one of the three bartenders came over and politely asked what he wanted. "Scotch, if you have it."

"We have everything," the man said. He had seen Byron set down the bag and as he poured he said, "Just in to town, I take it?"

Byron nodded.

"If you don't mind my saying so, you seem to be in a daze."

Byron laughed. "It's that obvious?"

"A lot of small-town folks are dazzled by the glitter," the barman observed.

"I'm from Austin," Byron said.

"Down Texas way? That's a fair-sized city, I seem to recall."

"Nothing like here."

"Nowhere is like here," the bartender said matter-of-factly. "Unless maybe Leadville. But they attract a rowdier lot."

"I've never seen so many theaters and the like," Byron mentioned.

"That's Mr. Studevant's doing. I've never met him, but they say he's a cultured fellow. He likes to attend plays and the opera and take in a concert. He's also fond of poetry, if you can believe it."

About to take a sip, Byron paused. "Poetry?"

The barman nodded. "Word is he put up some of the money to have the Poetry House built."

"The what?"

"It's around the corner and to the left. Poets come and read their works or sometimes the words of dead poets. I've never gone, but my sister has."

Byron downed the Scotch in two swallows, paid, and scooped up the bag and his rifle.

"Why the rush?" the man asked.

How could Byron explain? He practically ran, he was so excited. And there it was, a three-story edifice with a large sign emblazoned with THE POETRY HOUSE in cursive letters. A marquee informed him that a local poetess was giving a reading that very night.

On an impulse, Byron tried one of the doors. It wasn't

locked. He entered and found himself in a cool foyer. A thin young man with curly blond hair was over behind a counter thumbing through a book. He looked up as Byron approached and offered a friendly smile.

"I'm sorry, but we're closed. We don't open until six this evening for the readings, but there's always the café."

"The what?" Byron said.

The man pointed at a side door. "We serve European-style coffee and light fare. Our local poets like to come and mingle and share their poetry."

"God," Byron said.

The man's eyes crinkled with amusement and he held out his hand. "I'm Myron Hobbs, by the way. I run this establishment."

"Byron Carter."

"Myron and Byron?" Myron said, and laughed. "We almost sound like brothers."

Byron gazed beyond the foyer where rows of chairs were set up before a stage. "A place devoted to poetry!" he marveled. "I must be dreaming."

"You enjoy poems, do you?"

"You have no idea."

"Perhaps I do," Myron said good-naturedly. "Shelley is my favorite."

"Mine is my namesake," Byron said.

"Lord Byron? Then you must be aware of their friendship and the time they spent together at Lake Geneva in Switzerland."

"I've read everything on him I've ever come across," Byron said.

Myron suddenly snapped his fingers and straightened. "Say, I know someone you should meet. And by luck, they're here." He came around the counter and beckoned for Byron to follow him to the side door.

The café had an inside and an outside area for tables, and at a table near the curb sat a young woman in a new dress intently reading a book. She was a brunette with a perfect oval face, full lips, and eyes that sparkled. "Myron!" she exclaimed. "Listen to this."

Myron glanced at Byron and grinned and winked.

" 'When all around grew drear and dark, and reason half withheld her ray,' " the young woman read, " 'and hope but shed a dying spark which more misled my way. In that deep midnight of the mind, and that internal strife of heart, when, dreading to be deemed too kind, the weak despair, the cold depart. When fortune changed—and love fled far, and hatred's shafts flew thick and fast, thou wert the solitary star which rose and set not to the last.' "

She looked up, her expression dreamy, and clasped her hands to her bosom. "Isn't that glorious? Isn't it wonderful? Isn't it so very romantic?"

"He's no Shelley," Myron said, and laughed.

"That's from his *Stanzas to Augusta*," Byron said. "One of my favorites."

The young woman seemed to notice him for the first time and blinked as if in surprise. "Oh. Who do we have here?"

With a flourish Myron made the introductions. "Miss Olivia Rabineau, I'd like you to meet Mr. Byron . . . Smith, wasn't it? I brought him over because apparently he loves Lord Byron as much as you do."

"You don't say," Olivia said.

"He's new to town," Myron mentioned. "Perhaps you'd be willing to answer any questions he might have?"

Olivia looked Byron up and down and said softly, "I would be delighted." Catching herself, she coughed and motioned and brightly asked, "What do you think of it so far?"

Byron glanced at the Poetry House and at a theater down the street and the river of well-dressed people and finally at Olivia's lovely face and sparkling eyes. "I think I'm falling in love," he said.

38

For all of ten seconds Asa Delaware thought that Mayor Tom Oliver was joshing. Then he realized the man was in earnest. "You sent for me. Or, rather, your secretary must have."

"I did what now?"

"Here." Asa reached into his slicker and brought out the folded letter. He handed it across the desk, saying, "It caught up to me in Ludlow, Texas."

The mayor went on smiling as he unfolded it. No sooner did he begin to read than his smile faded and he said, "You got this in Texas?"

"I can start right away," Asa said. "I need to know who we are up against. How many guns they have. Who their leader is. Those sorts of things."

"Guns? Leader?" Oliver's brow furrowed. "What is it you do, exactly, Mr. Delaware?"

A feeling of unease came over Asa. "I tame towns, as you well know. It's why you sent for me."

"Tame?" Mayor Oliver said. He looked at the letter and at Asa and blurted, "My God. I think I've heard of you. Don't you kill people for a living?"

"Only those who deserve it," Asa said.

Oliver appeared shocked. He sat back and looked at the letter again and shook his head and muttered.

"I didn't catch that," Asa said.

"This is unbelievable."

"What is?"

"First off," Oliver said, wagging the letter, "I didn't send this. My secretary's name is Rachel, not Cecilia. But I do know Cecilia Preston, and I'm afraid you've been the victim of her diseased mind."

"You say she's ill?" Asa said in confusion.

"By diseased I mean demented. She hates our town. Hates what it has become, rather. I'm afraid her sending for you is merely the latest in her endless ploys to get revenge."

"You didn't send for me?"

"No."

"The offer of five thousand dollars to tame your town isn't genuine?"

"It is not."

"This woman concocted the whole thing?"

"Evidently." Oliver slid the letter across his desk. "I don't blame you for looking so surprised. You've come all this way for nothing. Ordville doesn't need taming, Mr. Delaware. Quite the contrary. We are as happy and prosperous a town as you'll find anywhere. Our citizens are law-abiding. We have no bad men. No gunmen. No rowdy cowboys who ride in every Saturday with their six-shooters blasting, I believe is the custom."

"All this way," Asa said. The full import of it had sunk in and his disbelief was changing to anger.

"It's incredible that she would do something like this," Mayor Oliver said. "I mean, her letters to the *Ordville Gazette* are one thing. As are her rants at our council meetings. To say nothing of how she badgers our poor marshal."

"You have law here?"

"Of course we do. Colorado isn't Texas, after all. We're much more civilized."

"There's that word again."

"Pardon?"

Asa stared at the letter and crumpled it in his fist.

"The woman who sent this. Where do I find her?"

"To what end? I wouldn't blame you if you wanted to slap her silly. But she can't help herself. She honestly can't."

"I want to talk to her," Asa said. "I want to find out why me."

"Ah." Mayor Oliver called out Rachel's name and the secretary was in the office in a twinkling.

"Sir?"

"We have Cecilia Preston's address, do we not?"

"It's on the letters she's sent you in her file," Rachel said.

"Would you write it down for Mr. Delaware here, and give it to him when he leaves?"

"Sir." Rachel bobbed her chin and left.

"Efficient as can be, that girl," Mayor Oliver said. He made a teepee of his hands while giving Asa a close scruitny. "Is there anything else I can do for you? I trust you've heard of our Indian policy. Other towns are laughing at us behind our backs, but Mr. Studevant is quite set on it."

"I'm not—" Asa said, and stopped. "What Indian policy?"

"Indians are welcome here."

Asa waited, and when the mayor didn't go on, he said, "That's it?"

"Indians and blacks and Mexicans and Chinese and any others you can think of. The downtrodden. The neglected. The abused."

Asa still didn't understand. "Welcomed how?"

"To start a new life. You're undoubtedly well aware of the rampant prejudice in this country. Whites hate the redman. Whites hate blacks. Whites hate anyone whose skin color is different."

"There are blacks and redskins who hate whites for the same reason."

"Be that as it may, Mr. Studevant is having none of it. He desires to have Ordville be a shining beacon of tolerance to the entire world."

This was a new one on Asa. He didn't quite know what to say so he stood and announced, "I'll be leaving. Sorry to have imposed on you."

"That's quite all right." Oliver watched Asa pick up the carpetbag and shoulder the leather case. "One last thing, if I may."

Asa waited.

"As I keep pointing out, this isn't Texas. We don't go in for gunplay. The wearing of firearms is strictly prohibited."

Asa opened his slicker. "I don't wear a pistol."

"Good." Oliver smiled broadly. "It was a pleasure to make your acquaintance."

Asa strode out.

"Here you go, sir," Rachel said, rising from her desk and handing him a slip of paper. "Cecilia Preston's address."

"I'm obliged."

Asa crossed the waiting room. He looked back as he was about to step into the hall and saw the secretary in the office doorway, her back to him. He also clearly heard Mayor Tom Oliver give her an order.

"Send for the marshal."

39

Noona seldom had someone as handsome as James Tharber show an interest in her. It was flattering. It also made her suspicious. "I *am* looking for a job," she mentioned, adding, "I mainly do saloon work."

"Saloons? You?" Tharber acted genuinely surprised.

"What do you have against saloons?"

"Not a thing," Tharber said. "But with your looks you could do much better. That hair, your face, you're positively sultry."

"If I am, it's not on purpose."

Tharber laughed. "Before you get the wrong idea, no, I don't mean you should ply your beauty at establishments of ill repute."

"Establishments? My, how you talk," Noona said. "In Texas we call them whorehouses."

Tharber did more laughing. "God, you'd be a natural at it."

"You still haven't said what 'it' is."

"An escort service."

"You've lost me," Noona admitted.

"You're a delightful babe in the woods," Tharber said.

"This baby kicks," Noona told him. *And shoots folks*, she thought in her head.

"It's about money," Tharber said. "Not how much you'll earn but how much other people make. Take saloons. The people who go there are mostly laborers and clerks and the like. Common people, you might call them."

"Is anyone ever common?" Noona asked.

"Now, see? A question like that would please them to no end."

"Please who?"

"I'm getting to that," Tharber said, and continued. "Now take those establishments I was talking about. Some are shabby affairs that draw the dregs. Higher-priced bordellos lure in businessmen and the like with more money to spend. Follow me so far?"

"I've never been accused of being stupid," Noona said.

"Now let's consider the very rich. Normally you wouldn't catch a wealthy gentleman at a saloon or a house of ill repute."

"Perish the notion," Noona said.

"There are quite a number of wealthy men in Ordville, and they prefer to be discreet. More selective, if you will. Which is why they use an escort service."

"A what?"

"Escorts. Women and men who hire themselves out for a night on the town with the well-to-do. Escorts wear the best clothes and are taken to the best restaurants and the theater and the like. And they're paid handsomely for their time."

"Are they expected to go to bed with whoever takes them out?" was the first question that popped into Noona's head.

"I won't lie to you," Tharber said. "Sometimes that happens. But it's completely up to the escort. If they want to, fine. If not, they are dropped off and thanked for a fine evening and that's that."

"You know an awful lot about this escort business."

Tharber's smile was positively dazzling. "I should." He paused. "I run one. Well, sort of."

"I'm plumb shocked," Noona said. "And what do you mean by sort of?"

"The man who owns the escort service is Arthur Studevant. Perhaps you've heard of him? He runs saloons, whore-houses, you name it."

"Sounds like he doesn't miss much."

"If you only knew."

"Would I get to escort him?"

"Mr. Studevant?" Tharber acted surprised by the question. "Don't be ridiculous. He never has to pay for the company of a woman. They fall over themselves to be with him." He lowered his voice. "Besides, it might not be in your best interests."

"Why not?"

"Let's just say he likes it rough and let it go at that."

"By 'it' you mean . . ."

"I do," Tharber said. He sat back. "I'd like to offer you a job. Trust me when I say I don't do this with just any woman. Only special ones."

"You could flatter a skunk out of its stink," Noona said.

Tharber laughed. "Yes, you're absolutely precious. So what do you say?"

"This is sort of sudden."

"I imagine you'd like time to think it over. That's fine. Here." Tharber reached into his jacket and brought out a wallet embossed with silver curlicues. He flipped it open and held out a small card with a flourish. "So you can find me again."

It read THARBER ESCORT SERVICE in gold letters and had an address under it.

"I'll think about it," Noona said. By that she meant she'd talk it over with her pa.

"Please do." Tharber boldly reached across to place his hand on hers. "I trust my instincts, and they tell me you could be one of the best in my stable."

Noona whinnied like a horse.

For a few moments Tharber appeared shocked, then he laughed harder than ever. "Oh my. Yes, you would entertain their socks off."

"So long as it's not their britches," Noona said.

40

The Preston place was on the crest of a foothill. It stood apart from the rest, surrounded by a high fence with iron bars. Asa glimpsed it through the trees as he came up the street.

The gate was open, and he went along a curved gravel carriageway and around some pines, and stopped.

It wasn't a house. It was a mansion. An older structure, a rarity in Ordville. All the other buildings were new. This one showed signs of neglect. The paint was chipping. Pine needles and leaves were everywhere on the portico. Two of the shutters were at a cant, the windows in need of washing.

A large brass knocker squeaked when Asa lifted it. He pounded hard, releasing some of his anger. When a long time passed and no one came, he pounded again, even harder.

More minutes elapsed and Asa had about concluded that no one was home when a female voice that crackled with age called out from the other side.

"Who is it? What do you want?"

"My name is Asa Delaware. I'm here to see Cecilia Preston."

A bolt rasped, locks were thrown, and the heavy door opened a couple of inches. A brown eye rimmed by wrinkles peered out. "How do I know you're him and not someone pretending to be?"

"Why would anyone pretend to be me?" Asa asked.

"I wouldn't put anything past him," the woman said.

"Past who?"

Instead of answering, her brown eye roved from his derby to his boots. "You do look like how I read Asa Delaware is supposed to look. It's plain as the nose on your face that you have Injun blood."

"Don't remind me," Asa said.

"You don't like having Injun blood?"

"I'm not here to talk about me," Asa said. "Are you her? Are you the one who sent me a letter claiming it was from the mayor?"

"The mayor?"

"I've just come from him."

"You sound mad."

"I traveled all the way from Texas to find out I was played for a fool. I'd like to know why, lady. I'd like to know what game you're playing."

"Simmer down, Mr. Delaware. In the first place, I never mentioned the mayor in my letter. You must have assumed he had me send it. In the second place, I can explain to your complete satisfaction."

"I doubt that."

She opened the door wider. "Yes, I'm Cecilia Preston. You can hit me if it will make you feel better."

She had white hair and wasn't much over five feet. Her dress was of a kind popular twenty years earlier, her shoes long out of fashion. She needed a cane to get around, and her shoulders were perpetually stooped.

But it was her face that mesmerized Asa. Her eyes were brown, with an uncommon burning intensity that was all the more remarkable for her wrinkles. It was a noble face, the kind you might see in a painting. And there was something else about it, something Asa couldn't quite put his mental finger on, a shadow that came and went.

"So, you're Mrs. Preston."

"It's 'Miss' now," she said, moving aside. "Please come in. I promise everything will be made clear."

The hall smelled of must. The floor hadn't been polished or even swept in a coon's age, and the walls were drab from neglect.

She noticed that he noticed. "I live alone, Mr. Delaware. No maid. No cook. No servants of any kind. Don't mind the dust. It won't kill you."

"This place looks old."

"It was here before Ordville."

"How is that possible?"

"My grandfather made a small fortune in the fur trade. He preferred the wilds to human company, so he lived out here in the middle of nowhere. My father inherited it, and I inherited it from him. Then that prospector and his silly mule came along and discovered silver not two miles from here, and the next thing I knew, I was surrounded by the town."

"I'm told you're an eccentric."

"Our good mayor said that, did he?" she replied with contempt.

"He gives the notion you're a thorn in his side."

"I've tried to be, to him and the rest of them who serve the demon."

"The what?"

"You heard me correctly, Mr. Delaware," Cecilia Preston said. "Ordville is under the sway of a demon from hell. His name is Arthur Studevant, and I'd very much like you to slay him."

41

Byron was taken aback when Olivia Rabineau glanced at a clock on the café wall and said, "Oh, my. I completely lost track of the time. We've been talking for two hours."

"We have?" For Byron, they were two of the best hours of his life. Olivia admired Lord Byron as much as he did, and was as well read on his works. They'd sat in the sun and drunk coffee and talked about *Don Juan* and *Childe Harold's Pilgrimage* and Lord Byron's shorter poems and satires, and it was like drifting on clouds of pleasure. Then she brought him crashing down.

"I'm afraid I must go."

"Oh."

Olivia smiled. "Don't look so glum. I'd very much like to see you again, if you're willing."

Byron had never been more willing about anything in his life.

"It's so rare to meet a fellow worshipper of the one true poet."

"I heard that," Myron Hobbs said, coming up to their table. "And I trust you were referring to Shelley?"

Olivia had the most wonderful laugh. "Myron, I must thank you for introducing us."

"My pleasure," Myron said. "We poets must stick together."

"Which reminds me," Olivia said. "He tells me he's looking for a job. Why don't you hire him?"

"What?" Byron said. His pa expected him to get work at a saloon, as he always did.

"Why not?" Olivia rejoined. "You love poetry as much as we do. And Myron was saying just last week that between the café and the public readings, he's kept so busy he rarely has time to read Shelley anymore. Didn't you, Myron?"

"Indeed I did," Myron said. "And you know, that's not a bad idea. I wouldn't want to hire just any clod off the street."

"Clod?" Byron said.

"Anyone who doesn't appreciate poetry like we do," Olivia said.

"I'll do it," Myron declared, and pulled out the chair next to Byron and sat. "What do you say? You won't get rich, but you'll live, breathe, and eat poetry and poets, and what more is there in life?"

"That's persuading him," Olivia said.

Byron hesitated. His pa was counting on him to learn all he could about whomever they were up against. It could prove crucial.

"What's wrong?" Olivia asked.

"My father . . . ," Byron began.

"He wouldn't approve?" Myron assumed. "I was in the same boat. My father despises poetry and doesn't understand why I love it so much. When I opened the Poetry House, I did so against his express wishes. He's been cold to me ever since."

"Your father, too?" Byron said.

"I don't have that problem," Olivia said. "My father goes along with whatever my mother likes, and she likes poetry almost as much as I do."

"I say stand on your own two legs," Myron said to Byron. "Where else could you get to mingle with those who share your passion? San Francisco, without a doubt. New York City, I'd imagine. But hardly anywhere else."

"Leap at the chance," Olivia urged. "You might never have another like it."

Maybe it was the fact that she wanted him to, or maybe it was his long-simmering resentment that his father placed so little value on the thing that mattered most in his life, or maybe it was just plain stubbornness that caused Byron to say, "You've almost persuaded me. What would you have me doing?"

"You'd help out here at the café, and on nights when we have readings, you can help set up the chairs and help me sweep out the place." Myron laughed. "It doesn't sound very exciting, I know. But hearing the poets and poetesses and getting to know people like Olivia will make it a real treat, I should think."

"Please say yes," Olivia said, and placed her hand on Byron's.

"Yes," Byron said.

Myron clapped him on the back. "You can start tomorrow, if that's agreeable."

"It is." Byron liked that Olivia hadn't removed her hand. The warm feel of her palm made him tingle.

"And if your father is like mine and gives you an earful over it," Myron said, "you're welcome to come stay here. I have some rooms at the back that I let the poets use when they come from out of town."

"I'll keep that in mind."

"How do you think your father will take the news?" Olivia asked.

"I'll be lucky if he doesn't shoot me," Byron said.

42

"A demon, ma'am?" If Asa needed proof that the mayor was right about Cecilia Preston, there it was.

"You think I'm crazy?" Cecilia closed the door and threw the bolt. "But I assure you I'm not. Arthur Studevant is the most wicked man alive."

"If you say so," Asa said. His anger was fading. How could he stay mad at a woman who clearly had lost a few bales out of her hay wagon?

"Come with me, Mr. Delaware. All I ask is an hour of your time to convince you. If I can't, off you go, and no hard feelings."

"And if you do convince me?" Asa humored her.

"I hire you as I've intended all along."

"*You* hire me?"

"You've met our sorry excuse for a mayor. You don't expect him to do it, do you?" She moved down the hall, her cane *tap-tap-tap*ping in front of her. "I was serious about the five thousand. If you take the job, I'll pay you out of my own pocket."

"You will?"

"I just said it, didn't I?"

Asa didn't know what to make of her. One minute she

was talking about demons, the next she acted perfectly reasonable. He decided it wouldn't hurt to hear her out. And if, as he reckoned, he'd turn her down, he might be able to play on her conscience and have her reimburse him for the train tickets. It was the least she could do given that she'd duped him.

The shadowed hall brought them to a sitting room where a single lamp glowed. The room had the same musty smell as everything else. She indicated a sofa with her cane. "Have a seat while I prepare refreshment. Would you like coffee or tea?"

"I'd like to hear you explain yourself," Asa said. "I'm not thirsty at the moment."

"Very well." Cecilia clomped to a settee across from him and eased down. Folding her hands on top of the cane, she leaned on it. "Where to begin?"

"That demon business would do."

"No," Cecilia said. "I should go back to when it started. To when Arthur Studevant bought the mine from Lester Ordville."

"You've met him? Studevant, I mean?"

"I haven't, no. And I hope to God I never do. He'd try to use his demon wiles on me."

Asa sighed.

"I heard that," Cecilia said.

"Get on with it."

Cecilia colored. "Very well. As I was saying, Studevant bought the mine and brought in hundreds of new workers. He bought up all the property he could, too, and built saloons and bawdy houses and had women brought in from all over."

"I don't hear the demon part yet."

"Be patient, Mr. Delaware. I'm getting to that." Cecilia gazed at a curtain-covered window. "Studevant backed Tom Oliver for mayor. But the man running against Oliver was well-liked, and Oliver should have lost. But guess what. He won. Then Studevant backed a man for town marshal, and although there were two others in the running, guess what. Studevant's man won."

"Rich people meddle in politics all the time," Asa said.

"True, true," Cecilia agreed. "But not to the extent Studevant has. You see, it's not that he's civic minded. Or that he's more law-abiding than the next person. He did all that, and more, so he could control the town lock, stock, and everything."

"And that's demonic?" Asa came close to laughing.

"You're not listening. Arthur Studevant has set himself up as God. No one can do anything in this town without his say-so. The few people who spoke out against him have been silenced or left or—"

"You haven't," Asa cut her off.

"He figures he doesn't need to bother, that no one will believe me. I'm just that crazy woman who lives all alone and talks to herself."

"Miss Preston," Asa began.

"I'm still not finished. I'd like to give you a list. It's people you need to talk to. People who can tell you what Studevant is really like. Go see them and hear their stories and then come back and give me your decision."

"I'd just as soon be on the next stage to Denver," Asa said, "but I'll do it on one condition."

"Name it."

"That if I turn you down, you pay me for my time and trouble."

Cecilia surprised him by saying, "That's only fair. Would two hundred dollars do?"

"That's more than enough."

"Then we are in agreement. Let me fetch that list." Bracing herself on the cane, she slowly stood and hobbled off.

Asa took his watch from his vest. It wasn't quite two o'clock. He seemed to recollect that a train to Denver left at six. Plenty of time for him to pay visits to whomever the old woman wanted him to see, get back to get his money, and then collect Byron and Noona and be on the train before it pulled out of the station.

He vowed to never let something like this happen again. A new rule was called for: Check on everyone who wanted to hire him.

In some instances that wouldn't be practical, like in towns that didn't have a telegraph office. But most places it would, and save him a lot of boot leather and aggravation.

The tap of her cane let him know she was coming back. She had a folded sheet of paper, which she tossed to him and he easily caught.

"Seven names?" It was more than he'd figured on. His plan to leave by six might not pan out. "I can't get to all of these today, can I?"

"Probably not. They're scattered all over Ordville. And I need to let them know you're paying them a visit. Do it tomorrow."

"Lady," Asa said, and stopped. He would be damned if he'd waste an entire day hunting all over for seven people who were likely as loco as she was.

"Every one of them is important, or I wouldn't ask," Cecilia said. "If you're the honorable man I think you are, you'll do it. When you've heard them out, you'll understand. And you'll want to kill Arthur Studevant as much as I do."

"I doubt that's possible," Asa said.

43

Asa shook his head in annoyance as he wound down the carriageway to the iron gate. If he'd ever had a more peculiar day in his whole life, he couldn't recollect it.

The old woman really believed Arthur Studevant was some sort of demon. It was ridiculous.

Asa went out the gate and turned to head for the train station as a man with a badge stepped from the shadows and barred his way.

"Been looking for you," the lawman said.

Asa stopped. He was good at reading people. He had to be, in his line of work, or he wouldn't stay alive long. And his initial read of the man in front of him wasn't favorable. "Oh?"

The lawman was of middle height, middle build, and middle just about everything. He had little chin, full cheeks, and eyes that made Asa think of the black-footed ferrets that preyed on prairie dogs. He wore a bowler and a suit with a vest. Pinned to the vest was a badge twice as big as any Asa ever wore. Engraved on it in big letters was TOWN MARSHAL. He wore a gun belt, but his jacket was over his holster and Asa couldn't see what model his revolver was. "I'm Marshal Pollard."

"Hard to miss you're a law dog," Asa said.

"This?" Marshal Pollard said, and tapped his badge. "It helps with drunks who can't hardly see, and so when folks see me coming, they know who I am."

Asa secretly wondered if the oversized badge didn't match the man's opinion of himself. But he kept that to himself. "This a social call?"

"Mayor Oliver asked me to look you up."

"I make him mad?"

"He wanted me to set you straight on a few things."

"Well, now," Asa said.

Marshal Pollard gazed up the hill through the trees at the mansion. "I take it you've been talking to Cecilia Preston?"

"The mayor told you I was coming to see her," Asa reckoned.

"That's why I was waiting," Pollard said. He moved his arm so his jacket moved, and now Asa could see a pearl-handled Smith & Wesson high on the lawman's hip.

"What do I need to be set straight on?"

"I'll get right to it," Pollard said. "I know who you are. I know you used to be a lawman, so you rate a courtesy I wouldn't give others."

"Oh?"

"You've seen the town?"

"I've walked over a good bit of it."

"Then you know it doesn't need taming. Did you see anyone wearing a firearm?"

"The only one I've seen is on you."

"Did you see any hard cases? Anyone at all who struck you as living on the shifty side of the law?"

"I did not."

Marshal Pollard nodded. "And you never will. I run a tight town, Delaware. Arthur Studevant likes things neat and tidy, and that includes Ordville."

"I've heard he backed you to wear that star."

Pollard jerked a thumb at the mansion. "From her? Yes, he brought me in from Wyoming. I was marshal of a town called Benton."

Asa found that interesting. Benton had started as a tent

city for workers when the rail line was being laid along the foothills. Where most tent cities folded away once the rails were in, Benton sprouted into a town thanks to nearby mineral springs. Popular as a cure for every ailment under the sun, the mineral springs drew folks from all over, particularly the well-to-do.

"Mr. Studevant owns a number of businesses in Benton," Pollard was saying. "I did the same for him there as I'm doing here."

"You run a town the way he likes," Asa said.

"Exactly. So let me make it clear. Ordville doesn't have any use for you. We have law and order here." Pollard tapped his badge again. "And we don't abide troublemakers."

"The last thing I'd ever want to do," Asa said, "is make trouble."

"Good to hear that. I don't know what nonsense that crazy woman has been filling your head with, but she's had it in for Mr. Studevant for a long while now. Did she tell you about her husband, about how she blames Studevant for his death?"

"No."

"Ask her. It will explain everything." Pollard looked at the mansion once more. "Damned crazy woman." He consulted a pocket watch and frowned. "I have somewhere to be, so there's only one thing more to say." He locked his ferret eyes on Asa. "It would please me greatly if you don't stick around."

"I was thinking of leaving anyway," Asa said.

"The next train out would be best."

"I will if I can."

Marshal Pollard smiled, but there wasn't any warmth to it. "Nice making your acquaintance." He touched the brim of his derby and headed down the hill.

"Hmmmm," Asa said.

44

Adjacent to the train station was a small restaurant called the Motherlode. Asa had noticed it when they got off the train. He thought it was a peculiar name for an eatery, but it was as good a place as any to meet at six o'clock that evening with his son and daughter.

At quarter to six he was at a booth with his back to the wall so he could see the door and windows. His carpetbag was under the table close to his feet and the shotgun case was in his lap.

Asa sipped the coffee he'd asked for and gazed about him. The restaurant was the same as the rest of Ordville, clean, tidy, and well-run.

A tiny bell over the door tinkled, and in came Noona. Her rifle case was across her shoulder. She set down her bag, leaned the Spencer against the booth, and slid in.

"How did it go?" Asa asked.

"It's been some day, Pa."

"Same here."

The waitress came and Noona asked if they had any juice. The waitress said yes, they had some orange juice left, squeezed fresh that morning.

"You and your juice," Asa said when the waitress

brought the glass. "You've liked it since you were knee-high to a grasshopper."

Noona drank, smiled, and said, "Ahhhh."

"We'll wait for your brother and then share what we've learned," Asa said.

"What I've learned," Noona said, "is that this town isn't like anywhere we've ever been."

"Ain't it, though?" Asa said.

"Part of me felt out of place. There I was, toting a rifle around, and there wasn't another living soul with a gun. It was spooky."

"I met one with a gun," Asa said. "The town law dog. You watch out for him, you hear?"

"Uh-oh," Noona said. "Is he a bad man with a badge?"

"I'm not sure what he is yet," Asa said, "but he raised my hackles."

They sat in silence for a while, both of them sipping and observing the people who came and went.

"I wonder what's keeping that brother of mine," Noona remarked. "He's usually punctual."

Asa grunted. He'd been watching out the front window and saw a man go by from right to left. Not two minutes ago the same man had gone by from left to right—a tall fellow with a pockmarked face and a hooked nose in the usual derby and suit who peered intently into the restaurant both times. This time, Asa caught sight of a bulge on his hip, and when the man turned to peer in, a flash of tin on his vest. "I'll be damned."

Noona started to swivel so she could see out the window.

"Don't," Asa said. "He'll know we know he's been shadowing me."

"Who has?"

"I believe it's a deputy." Asa came to the obvious conclusion. "Sicced on me by Marshal Pollard."

"This Pollard doesn't cotton to town tamers?"

"He thinks town tamers and troublemakers are one and the same."

Noona shrugged. "We've had law wary of us before."

"He'd like if I left as soon as I could."

"Now that's wary," Noona said.

The bell tinkled and in came Byron. He smiled as he came over and was still smiling as he sat next to his sister. "Sorry," he said.

"You're smiling, and you're sorry," Asa said. "Who are you, and where's my real son?"

"Pa," Noona said.

"That's all right," Byron said. "He can poke fun if he wants. I'm immune to his barbs."

"Since when?" Noona asked.

"We'll take turns." Asa got them on track. "Girl, you go first. Did you find a saloon to work at?" He didn't mention that their coming to Ordville was all for naught and they'd likely be gone within twenty-four hours.

"I did not," Noona said. "But I might have other work."

"As an escort?" Asa said when she finished her account. "Never heard of such a thing. And this escort service is run by Studevant like he runs most everything else?" He remembered Cecilia's words: "lock, stock, and everything."

"I didn't know what to do, so I put him off," Noona said. "Told him I'd think it over and get back to him in a day or two."

"How about you?" Asa asked Byron.

"I have a job."

"Which saloon?"

"Someplace different."

"Different how?" Asa wanted to know, and sat speechless as Byron related his day's events. "A house of poetry? I've never heard of the like."

"I've discovered heaven on earth," Byron said. His smile had become a permanent fixture.

"You were supposed to apply at a saloon," Asa reminded him, "so you can find out about the bad men in these parts. Or are all the local variety poets?"

Noona laughed. "Oh, Pa."

"You should see it," Byron said. "It's like a dream come true."

"How about you, Pa?" Noona asked. "What did you find out?"

Asa left nothing out, from his meeting with the mayor to his talk with Cecilia Preston and the tin star.

"So there's no taming to do?" Noona said. "It was a trick on her part."

"How about that," Byron said. "The great Town Tamer, Asa Delaware, played for a fool by an old biddy who isn't in her right mind."

"I'd be careful with talk like that," Asa said. "Anyone else would be eating teeth right now."

"So when do we head back to Texas?" Noona was quick to divert them.

"I promised that old biddy, as your brother calls her, that I'd talk to some folks tomorrow. After, she's to pay me two hundred dollars."

"So tomorrow night or the morning after?"

"More likely the morning," Asa calculated. He had seven people to visit, and they were spread all over town. He'd be lucky to be done by late afternoon. "That's when we'll go."

"No," Byron said.

Asa and Noona looked at him and Noona asked, "You'd like to stay longer?"

"I'd like not to leave." Byron squared his shoulders and sucked in a breath. "I know I said I'd do one last job and then head east. But that was before Ordville. Why go east when everything I want is right here?"

"You've been in this town less than a day," Asa said.

"So? I could stay a week or a month and my mind wouldn't change. You've seen this place, Pa." And for once, Byron didn't exaggerate the "Pa" with a hillbilly twang. "It's incredible. The theaters, the opera house."

"The Poetry House," Asa said.

"That most of all. I doubt there are more than two or three in the whole country." Byron shook his head. "No. I'm sorry. I'm staying. There won't be any last hurrah. It will just be Noona and you from now on. Me, I'm starting a whole new life." And with that, he picked up his rifle case and bag and walked out.

"Well, damn," Asa said.

45

With every step that Byron took, he felt more invigorated. The world seemed awash in the bright light of new adventures and opportunity. He'd finally done it. He was as free as a bird to take wing on his heart's desires.

Byron hadn't felt this happy in he couldn't remember how long. He was his own man. Good-bye to town taming. Good-bye to killing people. Good-bye to blood and spilled guts.

Byron laughed, and a hand fell on his shoulder that brought him up short.

"Hold on there, mister. I'd like a word with you."

Byron turned.

A tall man with pockmarks covering his face and a thin slit for a mouth had one hand hooked in a gun belt. A badge was pinned to his vest. It read DEPUTY.

Byron bristled at being laid a hand on, but he reminded himself that Ordville was to be his new home and that he should get off on the right foot with the local law. "What can I do for you?"

"I'm Deputy Agar. I'd like to know your business with Asa Delaware."

"Why?"

"Just answer the question."

"Is it against the law to talk to somebody?" Byron heard himself say. He knew he should cooperate, but there was something about this Agar that prickled the short hairs at the nape of his neck.

"Look, boy," the deputy said. "I'm just doing my job. Marshal Pollard wants me to keep an eye on the Town Tamer and make sure he doesn't cause trouble."

"My pa isn't a lawbreaker," Byron said. Not normally, anyway.

"Your—" Deputy Agar glanced at the Motherlode. "And that gal who was with you?"

"My sister."

"You don't say."

"We work together. Or we did. I've just parted company with them. They're heading back to Texas in a couple of days, and I'm staying on."

"How come?" Deputy Agar asked suspiciously.

"Do you really need to ask?" Byron gestured. "Look around you. This town is incredible. The culture. The energy. The feel of the very air. I've never been to anywhere as wondrous."

"The culture?" Agar said. "The feel of the air?"

"I like it so much, I'm fixing to live here," Byron revealed. "I've taken a job at the Poetry House and—"

"The Poetry House?"

"Do you know Myron Hobbs?"

"That Nancy boy who gets up onstage and reads poems for a living?"

"I'll be working for him. With any luck, he'll let me do a few readings of my own." Byron recited a few lines to show he could. " 'I love the language, that soft bastard Latin, which melts like kisses from a female mouth.' "

"What the hell was that?"

"It's from *Beppo* by Lord Byron. Isn't it marvelous?"

"Is he one of them poets?"

"One of the most famous ever."

Deputy Agar did a strange thing. He reached up and pinched his cheek.

"Why did you do that?"

"No reason," Agar said. "Are you sure you're Asa Delaware's son?"

"Why would I make it up?"

"It's just—" Deputy Agar stopped. "They say your pa is as tough as can be. That at man-killing he's up there with the likes of Hickok and Hardin."

"He has his moments," Byron said.

"Didn't any of it rub off?"

"How's that again?"

"Nothing," Deputy Agar said, and then, half to himself, "Life can be peculiar sometimes."

"Am I free to go?" Byron asked.

"Sure, boy. You go ahead. I've got to report to the marshal. He'll want to hear this." Agar turned partway. "Where can we find you if the marshal needs to have a talk with you later?"

"Where else?" Byron said. "I'm staying at the Poetry House."

"Of course you are. Behave yourself, poet." Agar snorted and headed up the street.

Byron refused to let anything spoil his mood. A new day had dawned for him, and he bubbled with excitement at the prospects.

A new life. A new job. A new friend in Myron Hobbs. And then there was Olivia.

46

It wasn't widely known but the Rocky Mountains had more than a few glaciers. Which must be why, Noona reckoned, that the owner of the the Glacier Hotel picked the name. It wasn't the most expensive in Ordville, but it was far and away one of the nicest places Noona had ever stayed. Her room had carpet on the floor and a double bed with the softest of quilts and a water closet. That her father splurged for rooms for both of them was a mild surprise. Usually, he'd suggest they sleep off in the woods.

That he knocked on her door about nine was a bigger surprise. That he was holding a brandy bottle was an outright shock.

"Pa? I was just about to turn in."

"I'd like to bend your ear," Asa said, and took a swig.

Noona smothered her worry and motioned at a chair in the corner. He walked over, sat, and took another swallow. "What has you out of sorts? As if I can't guess."

Asa frowned. For an instant his eyes were mirrors of pain. "Pardon my language, but what does he see in that goddamn poetry?"

"He likes it, is all."

"No, he *loves* it. He cares for it more than he cares for you or me."

Noona perched on the edge of the bed and folded her hands. "He's always liked to read. You know that. Ma encouraged him, remember? She bought him books all the time."

"I never thought it would come to this. If I had, I'd have prevented it."

"I don't see how. What, you would have taken a switch to him for liking verse?"

"I never hit either of you once your whole lives."

"I know," Noona said, and smiled. "All it usually took was a glare to get us to do what we should. You have powerful eyes. It's why the bad men squirm in their boots."

"Poetry," Asa said, and bitterly laughed. "Of all the things in the world, sissified words."

Noona frowned. She should have seen this was coming. Her father had been holding in his feelings for so long, the dam was bound to spring a leak. "I don't know as I can explain it to you other than Byron wants a new life. You can't blame him for that."

"We're family."

"Granted. But how many fathers and daughters work together like we do? Very few."

"You're special, gal," Asa said. "You always have been."

Noona felt her ears grow warm. "Thank you. Byron is special, too."

"Byron is a knothead."

"He is not."

Asa stood, swigged, and commenced to pace. "We had a good thing going. Maybe we weren't getting rich, but it was clean, honest work."

"Now, see," Noona said. "Byron saw it different. Not so much clean as blood-drenched. And not so much honest as sanctioned murder."

Asa stopped pacing. "He said that?"

"More than once. And he couldn't take it anymore. Poets have sensitive souls. They're not like the rest of us."

"Hogwash. What you call 'sensitive' I call 'squeamish.'"

It's like those people who can't stand to swat a fly. They never grew up."

"Byron is a grown man."

"On the outside," Asa said. "But inside he never got past that age where boys stand outside a girl's window at night talking mush."

"Oh, Pa," Noona said, and had to laugh.

"What we have to decide," Asa said, "is whether to go on with the taming. Just the two of us."

Noona's shocks were compounding one on another. "What else would you do if you didn't tame? Take up a badge again? Work as a cowhand? Wash dishes?"

Asa moved to the window and stood with his back to her. "I toted a star for years and I was good at it. But I'm a little long in the tooth for that now."

"Nonsense. If you can tame, you can wear tin."

"It's not the same work. The taming, I do when I want. We're in and out and it's over. Being a marshal or a sheriff is a twenty-four-hour job, seven days a week."

"You're nitpicking," Noona said. "Find law work at a quiet town where all you'd have to do is sit at a desk all day and whittle."

"That would shrivel me," Asa said.

Noona walked over to stand next to him. She glanced at his face, and her heart went out to him. This business with Byron had pierced him deep.

"I was raised on a farm, but I couldn't cowboy. I'm no good with a rope or at throwing calves. And being in the saddle all day would kill me."

"You're in the saddle a lot now."

"Not nearly as much as a cowboy is." Asa sipped some brandy. "As for washing dishes or putting on a clerk apron, that would shrivel me, too."

"What are you saying? You're fixing to retire and sit in a rocking chair the rest of your days? That would shrivel you to nothing."

"It'd be best for you."

"Me?"

"You could get on with your life. Live like other gals do.

Find yourself a fella and say, 'I do' and have a home and a family."

"Never said I wanted that."

"All females do."

"Not true, Pa. Not true at all."

"Well, anyway," Asa said. "We have time to hash it out yet. I promised that crazy woman I'd talk to some people tomorrow so she'd pay us two hundred for us coming here. We'll use her money for fare back to Texas and have our minds made up by the time we get there."

"Mine already is," Noona said. "I want to go on taming for as long as we can."

"I don't know, daughter," Asa said. "I truly don't."

Noona didn't know what else to say. They stood in silence staring at the lights of the town, and after a while she took the brandy bottle and enjoyed a sip herself.

"You can keep it," Asa said. Turning, he walked out and quietly closed the door after him.

"Damn you, Byron," Noona said. "I love you. But damn you, anyhow."

47

Byron had settled into a back room at the Poetry House. His clothes hung in the closet and his rifle was under the bed against the wall where no one was likely to find it. And where he could forget it was there.

He wanted a clean break with his old life. A complete break.

Myron told him to take the evening and enjoy himself, that his work would start in the morning. He went to the café and sat outside and watched the well-dressed towns-folk bustle by as the gray of twilight gave way to the blue-black darkness of a high country night.

Byron was hoping against hope that a certain young woman would stop by, and when someone blocked the light from the lamp and a shadow fell across him, he looked up with a smile, thinking it was her.

"I'm Marshal Pollard," one of the two tin stars said. "You've already met Deputy Agar, here."

"That I have," Byron said.

"We need to talk," Marshal Pollard informed him, and without being invited, he pulled out the other chair and sat.

Deputy Agar moved to one side, his hand resting on his revolver.

"Nice night," Byron said.

"So long as it stays peaceful," Marshal Pollard replied, scrutinizing him in that manner lawmen had of taking someone's measure.

"Why wouldn't it?"

"The most notorious Town Tamer in the country is in my town. And you're his son."

"So?" Byron said. "Didn't your deputy tell you that my father and I have parted ways?"

"He did."

"You didn't believe him and came to see for yourself?"

"The thing is," Marshal Pollard said, "Mr. Studevant is concerned by your pa being here. And anything that makes him uneasy I deal with so he can feel easy again."

"You have no cause to feel uneasy about me," Byron said. "I have given up taming. My life will be poetry now."

"Poetry," Marshal Pollard said, and grinned a peculiar grin. "And I'm supposed to believe that?"

"Come to my room and I'll show you my books on Lord Byron. When I send for the rest, you can see them, too."

"See?" Deputy Agar said to Pollard. "I told you, didn't I?"

"Hush," Pollard said. He placed his left forearm on the table but his right stayed close to his six-shooter. "No, boy, I don't entirely believe it."

Byron supposed he shouldn't blame him. A lot of people regarded poetry as womanish and anyone who liked it as having a lot of empty space between their ears. "I give you my word it's true."

"Maybe," Marshal Pollard said. "But I don't know you from Adam. What I do know is that your pa has a reputation for taking the law into his own hands. And it troubles me that he's sticking around a few days instead of taking the next train out as he should have."

"Oh, that," Byron said. He explained about the old woman and the two hundred dollars she had offered his father, thinking that would put the lawman's mind at ease.

Instead, Pollard straightened and scowled.

"He's fixing to talk to people on some list she gave him?"

Byron nodded. "And then collect the two hundred and leave."

Pollard abruptly stood. "You might want to consider taking the next train out yourself."

"I like it here. I'm staying."

"That's not up to you."

Byron felt a burst of anger. "It's a free country. I can do as I please."

"If you think so," Marshal Pollard said. He gestured at Agar, and the pair headed up the street.

Byron noticed that everyone in their path was quick to get out of their way. "It's none of my business," he said to himself. "Not anymore."

"What isn't?"

He came out of his chair so fast, he bumped the table and nearly spilled his coffee. "Olivia," he said, so happy that he almost grasped her hands.

To his delight, she grasped his. "My mother wanted me to stay home tonight but I persuaded her to let me come for a while. I just had to see you."

"You did?" Byron said, and grew warm from head to toe.

"May I sit?"

"You may do anything, anytime." Byron held out a chair for her.

"I thought we should get better acquainted," Olivia said sweetly.

Byron couldn't think of anything he'd like more. He cast a troubled glance up the street and then forgot about the lawmen and concentrated on the beauty across from him.

"What would you like to know?"

48

When Asa emerged from the Glacier Hotel at eight the next morning, the mountain air was crisp and clear and Ordville was awash in the ebb and flow of a new day. The businesses were already open and early shoppers were abroad. Miners from the night shift had been relieved and were homeward bound. A logging wagon rattled by, the bed piled high with logs.

Across the street, a petite woman in a pink outfit and carrying a pink parasol was walking a little dog on a leash. The dog had on an outfit the same color as hers.

"Just when you think you've seen everything," Noona said at his side. "She ought to be ashamed of herself, dressing that poor critter like that."

"Are you sure you want to tag along?" Asa said. "You could take the day to stroll about, maybe do some shopping."

"I have all I need," Noona said. "I'm not one of those females who buys stuff just for the sake of buying it."

Asa took out the list. "Seven names is a lot. And since we don't know the town that well yet, I thought we'd take a carriage."

"My, oh my," Noona said. "You're splurging right and left."

"The sooner we get it done, the sooner I have the two hundred."

Carriages were for hire everywhere. They found one parked half a block away, the driver relaxing on the seat with a pipe in his mouth.

"Are you for use or are you taking the day off?" Asa asked.

The driver removed the pipe from his mouth and chuckled. "If I took the day off, the wife would throttle me. Anywhere you'd like to go, I can take you."

Asa read the first name and the address.

"That's not far. Climb in."

"Just so you know," Asa said, "I'll have need of you when I'm done there, and for quite a while after."

"Maybe you should hire me by my day rate," the driver said. "You'd pay less in the end."

Asa asked how much and the man told him and he nodded. "Deal," he said.

The church sat atop a hill. A small building with a bump for a steeple, by Ordville's standards it was downright humble.

A sign said that services were conducted every Sunday morning and two evenings a week.

Asa tried the door but it wouldn't open, which was unusual. Most churches never locked their doors. He was about to knock when something scraped and the door swung in. "Reverend Wilmer?"

"I am." The parson was stout with ruddy cheeks and warm eyes. He wore black and a white collar. "Who might you be?"

"Cecilia Preston sent me." Asa introduced himself and indicated Noona. "This is my daughter. We'd like—"

Reverend Wilmer held up his hand and looked both ways and down the hill. "Come in so we can talk in private." Once they entered, he quickly shut and locked the door.

"Expecting an Injun attack?" Asa joked.

"There are worse things," Reverend Wilmer said. "Follow me, please."

A dozen pews on either side fronted an altar and a cross. Several candles were burning.

A room at the rear had a desk and a shelf with the Bible and other books and a couple of chairs. Reverend Wilmer waited for them to seat themselves, then closed the door.

"Is it me, Parson," Noona said, "or are you a mite skittish?"

Wilmer sat behind the desk and gave her a halfhearted smile. "If you only knew."

"As I was saying," Asa said to get things rolling. He had six more to visit, and he wanted to get it over with as soon as possible. "Cecilia Preston sent me. It's about Arthur Studevant."

"Lord help us," Reverend Wilmer said.

"She seems to think my talking to you is important. What do you have to do with Studevant?"

"As little as possible, I assure you." Wilmer wrung his hands. "She told me you were coming. I wish she hadn't sent you, but she's determined."

"What has you spooked?" Asa asked.

"He does."

"Studevant? You've met him?"

"No. I wouldn't want to. That man is the devil personified."

"Cecilia Preston calls him a demon."

"She might be right."

Asa sat back. "Are you the one who put that notion into her head?"

"I didn't have to. Not after what happened to her husband."

"She didn't mention him."

The parson bowed his head. When he raised it, the cheer was gone from his face. "Her husband, Charles, was the salt of the earth. They used to come to Denver now and then and always visited my church." He stopped and did more hand wringing.

"I'd like to hear it all," Asa said.

Wilmer bit his lip. "They lived here before the town existed. When that old prospector found silver and people started swarming in, Charles and Cecilia didn't think much of it. The town was a ways off from their house. But then it grew, and before they knew it, all the land around them was overrun. Except for the fifty acres they claimed as their own."

"Had they filed on it?"

"What?" Wilmer said. "I honestly don't know. I doubt it would have made a difference in light of what happened. For you see, when Arthur Studevant took over, he didn't like having fifty acres of woods in the middle of his town. No sir. He asked them to sell, but the Prestons refused."

"That was their right," Noona said.

"Studevant didn't see it that way. He accused them of standing in the way of progress. He invited Charles to one of his saloons to talk it over, and the next morning Cecilia was awakened by the marshal pounding on her door. She had waited up for Charles but fell asleep."

Asa didn't like where this was going. He didn't like it one little bit.

"Marshal Pollard told her that Charles was dead. That he'd had a lot to drink and played cards and got into a fight and was knifed. Cecilia knew better. Charles rarely touched hard liquor and wouldn't have anything to do with games of chance." Wilmer did more lip-biting. "But that wasn't the worst of it. Studevant claimed that Charles agreed to sell him the fifty acres and that they signed a bill of sale, and that he paid Charles and Charles lost the money playing poker."

"Oh my," Noona said.

"On her next visit to Denver she came to see me and poured her heart out. I was incensed. I'd heard about all the saloons and bawdy houses Studevant ran, and I felt moved by the hand of God to do something about it. I came here and started this church to stem his tide of wickedness."

"And?" Asa prompted when the parson didn't go on.

"I had faith in the Lord. He was my buckler and my strength. I preached against the evils of this town, and the man responsible for them."

"And?" Asa again prompted.

Reverend Wilmer blanched and swallowed. "And one day the wickedness came calling at my door."

49

Noona had seen a lot of ugliness in her life. People who had been shot. People who had been stabbed. She'd shot more than a few of them herself but only stabbed a man once. As accustomed as she was to violence, the parson's account had bothered her. "Do you believe him, Pa?"

"No reason for him to lie."

The carriage was winding toward the second address on Cecilia Preston's list. Above them, the driver cracked his whip.

"The marshal and the deputy would do that? They'd beat a man of the cloth within an inch of his life? And threaten him with worse if he didn't stop his sermons on Studevant?"

"You saw how scared he was," Asa said. "He had tears in his eyes."

"God," Noona said.

The carriage wheeled into a side street bordered by homes. It came to a stop and the driver called down, "This is it."

Asa climbed down, held the door for Noona, and they crossed a yard to a porch. He had to knock several times before the door opened a crack and a brown eye peered out at them.

"Yes?"

Asa explained about Cecilia Preston. "She said I was to talk to a Mrs. Florence Grissom. Would that be you?"

"It would," she answered, but she didn't open the door. "Cecilia sent a note you were coming, but I wished she'd asked me first."

Noona stepped closer. She had found that females responded better to her than to her pa or her brother. "Please, ma'am. We won't take much of your time."

"Very well. Although it's against my better judgment."

Florence Grissom wore a homespun dress and had her hair in a bun. She was thickset and square-jawed and looked as if she wouldn't be afraid of anything. Ushering them to the kitchen, she set out cups and saucers and put coffee on to brew. Only then did she take a seat. "How much did Cecilia tell you about what Studevant did?"

"Not a lick," Asa said. "She wanted me to keep an open mind."

"That sounds like her." Florence coughed and shifted. "This will be strictly between us?"

"It will."

"Not even my husband is to know, you hear?"

"I've never met the man."

"I mean it. He's been through so much. He can't find out I spoke to you behind his back."

"We won't tell a soul," Noona said.

"Very well." Florence composed herself. "My husband, Pete, works as a bartender at the Aces Saloon. He used to own it. Then Arthur Studevant came along."

Asa looked at Noona and she took the hint. He wanted her to do the talking. "I passed the Aces yesterday and saw inside. It struck me as grand," she mentioned.

"It is," Florence said with undisguised pride. "You see, we were living in Denver when we heard about the silver strike. Pete thought it was our big chance. We'd scrimped and saved for years so that one day he could have a saloon of his own. We came and built the Aces, and I never saw him so happy."

"How long did he run it?"

Florence's features clouded. "It wasn't hardly a year from the time the Aces opened until Studevant bought out Lester Ordville. That's when the trouble started. Studevant made a tour of the town and stopped at the Aces. He liked it so much, he offered to buy it. Pete told him no. That it was his dream come true. But that wasn't good enough for Studevant."

"Did the marshal and his deputy pay your husband a visit?"

"Them and a few others. They came here, not to the saloon. It was late one night. We hadn't bolted the door, and they walked right in." Florence shuddered and her eyes moistened.

"No need to go on if it upsets you," Noona said.

Florence didn't seem to hear her. "They beat him," she continued, barely above a whisper. "Two of them held me and the rest hit and kicked Pete until he was near senseless. Then the marshal told Pete that if he didn't sell, they'd come back and do the same to me."

"The scum," Noona said.

"And then the marshal said—" Florence shook, and uttered a tiny moan. "The marshal said that Arthur Studevant would take it kindly if Pete stayed on and ran the Aces for him." She looked at each of them, tears trickling down her face. "Can you imagine? What sort of man can do such a thing?"

"A demon," Asa said.

50

And so it went.

Their third stop was at a cabin on the outskirts. A man by the name of Halsey Finch lived there. Finch told them that he had owned the best hotel in Ordville. Then Arthur Studevant came, and he was told that he should sell out and leave. When he refused, he was paid a visit in the dead of night by five men wearing badges. Four pinned his arms and legs while the fifth went to work on him with a hammer.

"Do you see this?" Finch asked, holding up his mangled left hand. "I can't even use it anymore."

Next was a woman who had run a thriving restaurant.

Studevant decided he wanted it for himself. The marshal and his deputy paid her a visit, and while she absolutely refused to say what they did to her, the very next day she'd signed the restaurant over to Ordville's leading citizen.

Asa and Noona were quiet as the carriage rattled toward the fifth stop.

It was Noona who broke their silence by clearing her throat and saying, "He's worse than Weldon Knox ever was."

"Worse than anyone," Asa said.

"It wouldn't be like any of the other towns we've done."

"No," Asa agreed, "it wouldn't."

"How can we, when he's so rich and has the law to back him?"

"I don't know."

"But you're fixing to?"

"I haven't made up my mind."

Noona fixed him with those piercing eyes of hers. "I know you, Pa."

They pulled up in front of a quaint cottage shaded by tall spruce. Asa let Noona go first, and after she used the brass knocker, the door was jerked open by a solid block of a woman with an expression as friendly as an Apache's. She had wisps of gray in her hair and she was holding a carving knife and wearing an apron.

"What do you two want?"

Noona explained about Cecilia Preston, and some of the unfriendliness faded from the woman's face. Some, but not all. "She got word to me that a man was coming, but she said nothing about a girl. I can guess what she wants, but I'm not sure it's wise."

"What isn't?" Asa asked.

She glared at him and said out of the blue, "Men are scum. My husband never amounted to much, and now this."

"Now what, ma'am?" Noona asked.

"I'm Cornice Baker," the wrathful block of ire said. "It's my daughter she wants you to talk to. But stirring that up again will only make it worse."

"Why don't *you* tell us what happened?" Noona suggested. "We can leave your daughter out of it."

Cornice gnawed on her lip, then said, "No. You need to see and hear for yourself." She moved aside. "Come in. But don't say anything until I say you can. I can't predict how she'll be."

She set the knife down on a lamp stand and led them down a short hall to a bedroom.

In a chair by a shaded window sat a young woman in a pretty dress. She was quite striking, with lustrous flaxen hair and an ethereal beauty that almost made her seem angelic. She didn't look around when they entered. She went on staring out the window, her face as blank as if she were lifeless.

"My daughter," Cornice whispered, her voice breaking, "Laura." She went to the chair, squatted, and placed a hand on her daughter's arm. "Laura, darling. It's mother."

The young woman didn't reply or move.

"Can you hear me? There are some people here to talk to you."

Laura slowly turned her head and smiled at Cornice. "Mother," she said in a sort of dreamy way.

"Yes, dear. It's me. Did you hear me about the people who'd like to talk to you? It's important they hear about that night."

Laura's expression changed. Horror crept into her eyes, her face contorted, and she opened her mouth as if to scream.

"It's all right," Cornice said, patting her daughter's hand and stroking her hair. "It's over, remember? They'll never hurt you again. Not while I draw breath."

"Oh, Mother," Laura said plaintively. She burst into tears and buried her face in Cornice's shoulder and wept.

Noona cleared her throat. "We can come back another time, Mrs. Baker."

"No," Cornice said almost harshly. "You'll hear her out, by God."

Cornice patted and comforted her daughter until Laura stopped crying and sat up and sniffled. "Let me fetch a handkerchief," she said, and left the room and came back with one she used to dab at Laura's nose and cheeks.

Laura sat back and stared out the window.

"Can you tell them, sweetheart?" Cornice said. "Do you have it in you?"

Laura shuddered. "We were walking down the street one day, Mother and I," she began, "and this man saw us and came over. He said his name was Studevant, and he asked Mother if it would be all right if I was his supper guest."

"God help me," Cornice said bleakly. "I said yes."

"He seemed so nice," Laura went on, still staring out the window. "And Mother said he was important, and a rich gentleman."

"God help me," Cornice said.

"A carriage came for me, and I was admitted to the

man's suite, and everything was so nice. The man showed me around and we ate a wonderful meal and sat talking. Then I said it was getting late and I had to go."

Cornice was a study in misery.

"And the man said no, I couldn't, and he took hold of me and pulled me. I tried not to go with him, but he was so much stronger than me and he forced me into a bedroom and—" Laura stopped.

Noona let out a low hiss.

"Afterward, I asked him why," Laura said bleakly. "When he could buy any woman he wanted, why did he do that to me? Do you know what he said?"

"No," Noona said, her voice rasping.

"He laughed and said he likes it that way. Likes it rough, as he put it. Likes it with sweet young things, as he called me. He said . . ."

"That's enough, dear," Cornice said, patting her hand. "That's more than enough." She glanced over her shoulder. "It is, isn't it?"

"Yes," Asa said. "We're sorry to have disturbed you. We'll let ourselves out."

"Thank you for your time," Noona said.

They were almost to the carriage when they stopped and looked at one another.

"I don't care how different it is," Noona said. "There has to be a way."

Asa didn't answer, but his eyes were molten fire.

51

The fifth person on the list had, apparently unknown to Cecilia Preston, left town. He'd been staying at a boardinghouse. The woman who ran it said that the man had a great fear of Arthur Studevant but had never told her why. She suspected it had something to do with the time he came back beaten bloody. She was sorry, but that was all she knew.

As the carriage rattled toward the sixth stop, Noona fingered the dagger she always had strapped up her sleeve.

"I bet those tin stars of Studevant's were to blame."

"Yep," Asa said.

"You're not saying much today."

"Do I need to?"

"No," Noona said. "You don't."

Bedelia Huttingcot was a Southern belle who lived in an apartment over a general store where she now worked.

Bedelia was in her twenties and had been employed at one of Studevant's bawdy houses until one night she decided she didn't want to anymore. She made the mistake of telling the madam who ran the house for Studevant, and the next morning Marshal Pollard and Deputy Agar showed up at her door.

"They told me I couldn't quit until Studevant said I could, and I told them to go to hell. That's when the marshal pulled out a folding knife and did this to me." Bedelia touched the jagged scar that had made a ruin of her left cheek.

Their seventh stop turned out to be the cemetery.

Asa turned to the driver. "Are you sure this is the right address?"

"It's the one you gave me."

Asa looked at the sheet of paper. Cecilia had written a name next to the address. "We're looking for Annie Spencer."

The cemetery barely had a hundred graves, the town was so new, and the headstone was easy to find.

"Annie Spencer, sure enough," Noona read the inscription. "Born November first, 1877. Died June twentieth, 1887." She paused. "About a year ago."

"She was ten," Asa said.

"How does a little girl tie into this?"

"Let's go ask."

Cecilia Preston must have been watching out her window, because she opened the door before the carriage came to a stop in front of the mansion. "Well?" she said, beckoning them in.

"That was some list," Asa said.

"That last one," Noona said, "Annie Spencer. Why was she on it?"

"Her father worked at the mine. He was one of the few who spoke out against Studevant when Studevant took it over. One night someone set fire to their cabin. Her father and mother were horribly burned, and the girl died. They've since left town."

"Only ten years old," Noona said.

Cecilia ushered them to the parlor and bid them sit while she brought refreshments.

"I don't want any, thanks," Asa said.

"Me, neither," Noona said.

Cecilia sat across from them and clasped her hands.

"Was it enough? Will you do it?"

"I'm pondering on it," Asa said.

"Is it the money? Five thousand isn't enough? I was told that a thousand is your usual fee, but if five thousand isn't enough, I'll pay more."

"It's not the money."

"Then what?"

"When I said I was pondering on it," Asa clarified, "I meant I was pondering how to go about it."

"What's to ponder? Taming towns is what you do. It's why I sent for you."

"This wouldn't be a usual taming. The town didn't send for us. You did. Arthur Studevant is looked up to as its leading citizen. He has the law in his pocket, and more power than God."

"He's mortal like everybody else," Cecilia said. "All you have to do is walk up to him and point that shotgun of yours at his face, and it's over."

"And spend the rest of my days behind bars," Asa said. "No thank you."

"Are you saying it can't be done?"

"It can be done, but it has to be done right."

"Just right," Noona said. "Or we'll both be wearing prison stripes."

"You'll do it, though?" Cecilia anxiously asked. "You'll bring an end to all this horror?"

Asa looked at Noona and Noona nodded. "Or die trying," he said.

52

---·---

Asa and Noona no sooner walked into the Glacier Hotel than Marshal Pollard came upon them from the right and Deputy Agar from the left. Two other men wearing deputy badges were over by the front desk.

"Been waiting for you," Marshal Pollard said.

"Wasn't here," Asa said.

"You've been gone all day. Mind telling me where you've been?"

Noona said, "We were seeing the sights. Your town is the kind a body's not likely to forget."

"It is scenic," Marshal Pollard said. He reached inside his jacket. "Have something for you." Holding them out, he said, "Can you guess what they are?"

"I don't need to guess. I can see them," Asa said. "They're train tickets."

"That they are," Pollard said, "first class all the way to Texas. The train leaves at eight in the morning, and we expect you to be on it."

"We?"

"Some of my deputies and me will be here at seven-thirty to take you to the station."

"We know where the train station is," Noona said.

"We wouldn't want you to get lost getting there," Marshal Pollard said, and Deputy Agar snickered. Pollard reached out and gripped Asa's wrist, turned Asa's arm so his hand was palm up, and slapped the tickets into it. "Here you go."

"You shouldn't ought to touch people unless they want you to," Asa said.

"Just doing my job," Marshal Pollard said.

Asa raised the tickets. "You pay for these your own self?"

"I did not," Pollard said. "They're a gift from the big man, himself. Arthur Studevant bought them for you. To show there's no hard feelings over you coming all this way to tame a town that doesn't need taming."

"Is that why?" Noona said.

Marshal Pollard gestured at Agar and the other deputies, and they moved to the glass doors. Pollard looked back. "Be sure to be ready by seven-thirty. If you're not, we'll have to help you along."

"So this is what being run out of a town feels like?" Asa said.

Pollard laughed. "You're not being run out so much as being invited out. And you have to admit, those tickets are damned decent of Mr. Studevant."

"It's nice to know he can be decent," Asa said.

Noona waited for the glass doors to close to remark, "I can't get over how brazen they are about it."

"They wear the badges," Asa said.

"And they work for God Almighty."

Asa smiled a cold smile. "They figure they can get away with just about anything, and have been for a good long while."

"Nothing lasts forever, Pa. You taught me that."

Asa slid the tickets into his slicker. "It's almost suppertime. Are you hungry?"

"Not at the moment."

"Do you know what I'd like to do?"

"I'd like to do it, too."

They took their time, strolling along as if they didn't have a care in the world. Noona looked in a few shop windows and Asa bought tobacco for his pipe. By the time they reached the Poetry House, the sun was relinquishing its reign to the fading gray of twilight.

They were about to go in when Asa glanced at the café and said, "I'll be switched."

Byron was waiting on a table. He wore an apron, carried a wooden tray, and was setting glasses of water down. He gave a bow to the customers and went in.

"From serving whiskey to serving soup," Noona said. "Is that a step up or a step down?"

"Be nice."

"Listen to the kettle," Noona said.

They settled into a corner table, and it wasn't a minute later that Byron hustled out and approached the table, smiling. When he saw them, his smile faded.

"You two haven't left yet?"

"It's a pleasure to see you, too, son," Asa said.

"If you've come to talk me into going back to Texas with you, you've wasted your time. I like it here, and I'm staying."

"May we see a menu?" Noona asked. "We haven't eaten yet, and I'm hungry."

Byron placed a menu in front of each of them and stood back. "What are you up to?"

"Wanted to see you, is all," Asa said.

"As loco as it sounds," Noona said, "I miss you."

"I refuse to go back."

"No interest in one last job?" Noona asked.

"Didn't you just hear me? I'm staying, and that's final."

"That's good. Because the job isn't in Texas or anywhere else," Noona said. "It's right here."

Clearly startled, Byron came around the table and crouched. "What in God's name are you talking about? Ordville doesn't need taming."

"If you only knew," Asa said.

"What I know," Byron said, "is that the marshal didn't send for you, and there isn't a bad man to be found anywhere in town."

"If you only knew," Asa repeated himself.

"We can use your help, brother," Noona said. "We have to do it smart, and you're better at smart than both of us."

"You *are* loco," Byron said. "The both of you. You can't tame a town that doesn't need to be tamed."

"They've given us until morning to get out of Dodge," Asa said. "You have until then to make up your mind."

"There's nothing to make. I don't want any part of this. They haven't asked me to leave."

"We need you," Noona said. "We're staying at the Glacier Hotel if you change your mind."

"Consarn you both, no." Byron stood. "I'll be back to take your order, but that's all. Not another word about town taming. I'm through with that for good." He walked off in a huff.

Asa sighed and his shoulders sagged. "About what I expected."

"We do it our own selves, then?" Noona asked.

"We do," Asa said.

53

Byron was incensed by their gall. After he'd made it as plain as he could possibly make it that he was done with town taming for now and forever, they showed up to persuade him different.

He worked the rest of his shift in a funk. He tried not to think of it; he tried to dwell on the slice of heaven his life would be after they were gone.

And on Olivia.

Byron was off at seven, and she was to meet him there. They were attending the theater together at eight, a production of Shakespeare's *Romeo and Juliet*, the first of what he hoped would be endless nights in her company.

He couldn't think of a more fitting play. He'd only known her a short while but he was, as poets liked to say, smitten. He imagined himself on his knee, reciting poetry to her. How romantic that would be.

At five minutes to eight, Byron came out to clean the tables, only to have his way barred by a pair of badges.

"Remember me, boy?" Marshal Pollard said. "And Deputy Agar, here?"

"I don't forget much," Byron said.

Pollard slid a hand into his jacket and held something out. "Take it."

"What's this?" Byron said, even though he could see what it was.

"A train ticket. I gave one to your father and your sister. All three of you are to be on the one that's leaving at eight in the morning."

"But I don't want to go. I like it here. I told you that, remember?"

"You did."

"Then why the ticket?"

Marshal Pollard hooked a thumb in his gun belt. "It could be I don't believe you about that poetry business. It could be I think your pa is up to something or he wouldn't have spent all day nosing around town."

"He did what?"

"Things get back to me," Pollard said.

Byron smiled and began, "I can assure you—"

Pollard poked Byron in the chest. "I'm not finished. It could be that even if you were telling us the truth, it doesn't matter. Someone wants you to leave, so you're leaving."

"I'm free to do as I please."

"Think so? Then don't be on that train tomorrow, and see what happens."

"You can't go around threatening people."

The marshal tapped his badge. "See this? I can do any goddamn thing I please. It would please me at the moment to pistol-whip you but there are people around."

Boiling with anger, Byron was about to say, "I'd like to see you try." But he held his tongue.

"Be on that train, boy," Pollard said, and he and his deputy wheeled around and stalked off.

"Well, hell," Byron said. He stared at the ticket and went to rip it up but didn't.

"What's that you're holding, handsome?"

Byron turned so fast, he nearly tripped. "Olivia," he blurted. "You're early." He shoved the ticket into a pants pocket. "It's nothing."

Her dress was gorgeous, the height of evening fashion for young ladies. Lace at her throat and in the trim on her sleeves lent a touch of elegance. "Are you all right? You look rattled."

"No, no," Byron said. "Just hurrying to get done on time."

"Wasn't that the marshal and one of his deputies you were just talking to?"

"They had some coffee," Byron lied.

Olivia smiled and touched his chin. "I'll be right here when you're done."

Byron experienced the oddest sensation. As he went about turning in his apron and hastening to his room at the back so he could change, he felt as if he were floating on air.

Olivia Rabineau was the kind of woman he'd only ever dared to dream about being with. The kind he imagined himself reading poetry to. The kind he imagined holding in his arms and lavishing ardent kisses on.

He supposed he was making much more of it than there was. It was only their first time out. But he took meeting her as an omen. Perhaps, just perhaps, more would come of it.

"Damn my romantic soul anyhow," Byron said with a grin as he rushed out.

Myron happened to be coming around the corner and nearly bumped into him. "Look at you," he exclaimed with a smile. "Off for a night on the town with the fair maiden."

"Fair doesn't do her justice," Byron said.

"As Shelley put it," Myron said, and quoted his favorite poet, " 'Spirit of beauty, thou dost consecrate with thine own hues all thou dost shine upon.' "

"That's her," Byron said, and not to be outdone, he quoted Lord Byron, " 'She walks in beauty, like the night of cloudless climes and starry skies. And all that's best of dark and light meet in her aspect and her eyes.' "

Myron laughed. "I can't tell you how wonderful it is to meet a kindred spirit."

Byron smoothed his jacket. "I hope she finds me as wonderful."

Clapping Byron on the arm, Myron said, "Off you go, my friend. And may she be taken by you to her very heart."

It was the most heavenly night of Byron's existence. Olivia was bright and dazzling and warm. They discussed poets and poetry and sat close in the theater and listened to one of the greatest works of one of the greatest geniuses in the English language, and life couldn't be any more perfect.

Afterward, Byron walked her home. Arm in arm, they traveled the quiet streets, and if they passed another human being, Byron was blind to their existence. All he saw was Olivia. All he heard was Olivia.

And when at last they came to the gate to her house, parting truly was sweet sorrow.

"I had the most marvelous time," Olivia said, taking her hand in his. "I can't thank you enough."

"It's I who should thank you," Byron said. "You've given me a memory I'll treasure forever."

Olivia glanced at the house and then quickly rose onto the tips of her toes and kissed him fleetingly on the mouth. "Until the next time."

Byron watched until the door closed behind her. As he turned and headed up the street, he felt that for the first time in his life, everything was right with the world.

Then he came to a corner lit by a streetlight, and out of the darkness around him came Marshal Pollard and Deputy Agar.

54

To say Byron was shocked was putting it mildly. He realized they must have followed him from the theater. Suddenly his perfect night was tainted. "You again," he said.

"Us again," Marshal Pollard replied. "And we've brought friends." He snapped his fingers, and two more deputies materialized from different directions.

A spike of alarm filled Byron. They had him surrounded. "What's the meaning of this?"

"I've had my men keeping an eye on you," Marshal Pollard said. "And it's obvious you didn't get the message."

"Which?" Byron said, although he knew full well.

"About leaving on the morning train. I have a feeling you don't aim to."

Byron looked up and down the street, but no one else was in sight. At that hour in this part of town, most people were abed. "What makes you say that?"

"Boy, don't take me for a fool," Marshal Pollard growled. "I saw you courting Miss Rabineau. I can't say much for her taste in men, but I can say something about your taste in females. You're overreaching, boy."

"Stop calling me that," Byron said. "And what do you mean by overreaching?"

"Because, *boy*, she's too good for you. She comes from a good family. You come from trash. You have redskin in your blood even though it doesn't show."

Deputy Agar growled, "You're not fit to be with a lady like her."

"The fact that you were," Marshal Pollard said, "tells me you're not fixing to take the train. And I can't have that."

"You can't make me leave," Byron declared.

Marshal Pollard smiled the sort of smile a mountain lion might right before it pounced on a deer. "You keep forgetting. I'm the law. I can do any damn thing I like."

"Damn upstart," Deputy Agar said. "You need to be reminded of your proper place."

"My what?"

Marshal Pollard nodded at the other two, and they lunged.

Byron came crashing down from the clouds of romance to the reality of being seized and held fast. He struggled, but he'd reacted too late. "Now just you hold on."

Pollard nodded at Agar, and the deputy drove his fist into Byron's gut.

Pain exploded, so much pain that the world burst in bright light and Byron would have doubled over and collapsed if not for the pair holding him.

"Bring him," Marshal Pollard said.

Awash in agony, Byron was aware of being carried with his feet dragging, down the street and into a vacant lot. He was hauled over by a fence and shoved so his back was to it.

The four lawmen formed a half-ring in front of him.

"You brought this on yourself, boy," Marshal Pollard said.

The pain had eased enough that Byron found his voice. "You don't want to do this."

"There you go again," Pollard said. "Telling me what I should and shouldn't do."

"Some jackasses never learn," Deputy Agar spat.

"Especially breeds," one of the others said.

Byron thought of his rifle and his knife and the revolver

he hardly ever used, all back in his room at the Poetry House. "This isn't right."

Marshal Pollard snorted.

"It isn't legal."

"I have a town to look after, boy. Now and then I have to stretch the law a mite. Like I'm stretching it now to make damn sure that three troublemakers take their trouble somewhere else."

"But I told you," Byron said, "I have nothing to do with my father anymore."

"So you claim."

"Why would I lie? All I want is to be left alone to live my life as I see fit."

"At the Poetry House."

"I love it there."

"A Texan who likes poetry," Marshal Pollard said. "You must take me for an idiot."

"I'm being honest with you."

"Sure, boy," Marshal Pollard scoffed. "Sure." To the others he said, "I've listened to enough of his malarky. Get on with it."

Just like that, Agar and the other two deputies waded in.

Byron got his fists up with his arms low to protect his belly. He blocked a punch to the ribs and countered an uppercut to his jaw, but there were three of them and he couldn't avoid all their punches. His jaw was jarred and his ribs flared, and then a blow caught him on the side of the head and his legs buckled.

The blow nearly blacked him out. No fist could do that. One of them had resorted to a blackjack, and he found out which when Deputy Agar struck him again across the top of his head.

Byron struggled to stay conscious, to rise. He clawed at the ground but couldn't find the strength.

"Look at him," Deputy Agar said. "No more sense than a tree stump."

"Finish it," Marshal Pollard said. "But remember. Not the face or anywhere it will show."

A rain of pain fell on Byron—kicks and punches that

seemed without end—to his chest and stomach and sides and back and even his arms and legs. He felt himself sliding into a black well and desperately clung to the brink.

Then a hand gripped his chin, and Marshal Pollard said, "Be on that damn train."

There was a last blow, and Byron pitched into the well.

55

Noona was a light sleeper. Since she had been little, the slightest sound would wake her.

So it was that in the still hour before dawn her eyes snapped open, and she lay listening and wondering what woke her up.

The Spencer was on the bed beside her. She had set it there as a precaution. Given the horrible things that Marshal Pollard had done to the people she and her father talked to, she wouldn't put anything past him.

A minute went by and the stillness was unbroken, so Noona closed her eyes to catch a few more winks before she had to be up.

A faint rap on her door brought her off the bed in a bound with the rifle at her hip. It wasn't a knock so much as a scrape, as if someone had run their hand over it.

Noona had thrown the bolt so they'd have to bust the door down to reach her. She crept over and put her ear to it but heard nothing.

Moving to one side in case someone started shooting, she called out, "Is someone there?"

"Sis, it's me."

"Byron!" Noona exclaimed in delight. She leaned the

Spencer against the wall, threw the bolt, and spread her arms to welcome her brother with a hug. "You changed your mind, after all."

Byron sagged against the jamb, his body half folded over, his bag and rifle case on the floor at his feet. "Sis," he said weakly.

To Noona's astonishment, he started to collapse. Quickly, she caught him and wrapped her arm around his waist. "I've got you."

He was god-awful heavy, and it took some doing for her to steer him to the bed. The moment she let go, he fell onto his back and groaned. "Byron?"

"My things," he said weakly, his eyes closed. "Don't leave them in the hall."

Noona brought them in and bolted the door. She lit the lamp, then sat on the bed and asked, "What's wrong? What happened?"

"The marshal," Byron said, and plucked at his shirt, trying to unbutton it.

Noona helped, saying, "Do you want it off?"

"You need to see."

Noona didn't understand until the last button was undone and his shirt fell open. "God in heaven," she gasped. "He did *this*?"

"He had help," Byron said.

Nearly every square inch, from Byron's belt to his neck, was covered with bruises. Dark and light bruises. Big and small bruises. One of the worst was low on his ribs.

"Is your back the same?" Noon asked, aghast.

Byron nodded, and swallowed. "Back, arms, legs, everywhere but my face. They beat the living tar out of me."

"What did you do to provoke them?"

"It's so I'll be sure to be on the train."

"I'll go fetch Pa," Noona offered, and turned to go.

"No. Please," Byron said. "He'd only say I told you so, or give me a look that says the same thing."

"We have to tell him."

"Let me rest a bit." Byron closed his eyes and rolled onto his side. "I hurt so much, sis."

Tears filled Noona's eyes. She placed her hand on his

head, and swallowed. "Rest as long as you want. I'll fetch him when you—" She stopped.

Byron was breathing so loud, it was obvious he had passed out.

Noona coughed and stood. She was shaking, she was so mad. She grabbed her rifle and went out and down the hall to the next room. She knocked three times, lightly, and was about to knock again when it opened. "You're up already?"

Asa was fully dressed. He even had his slicker and derby on. "Never got to bed," he said, and nodded at the Spencer. "You fixing to shoot somebody?"

"You need to see," Noona echoed her brother.

"See what?" Asa asked.

"But not a word, you understand? He's not to know I showed you." Noona crooked a finger.

"Who? And show me what?"

Noona put a finger to her lips and ushered him into her room and over to the bed. She pulled Byron's shirt wide and let the beating speak for itself.

Asa swayed and his face drained of color. When he spoke, his voice didn't sound like him. "Who did this to my son?"

"Who do you think? They want him on the train with us."

"Do we need a sawbones?"

"He made it here under his own power, and he's not spitting blood."

Asa touched the blackest and bluest of the bruises. "This was done by a boot. They must have stomped on him when he was down."

"Just like they did to all those others."

"Those others weren't my boy." Asa gently placed his hand on Byron's head. "I was the first to hold him when the midwife pulled him out. She cut the cord and gave him to me. Your mother was too weak. I was the first to hold you, too."

"I think I remember that." Noona tried to make light, but neither of them smiled.

"It was bad enough, those other folks we heard about," Asa said quietly. "But this—" The color returned to his face and darkened until he was as red as blood.

"He still might not help us."

"Doesn't matter if he does or doesn't," Asa said. "This goes beyond taming. This is personal. I'd do it alone if I had to."

"You're not alone. You have me."

"And me," Byron said. Wincing, he rose onto an elbow. "I'll do this last one and then no more."

"I'm sorry I brought Pa against your wishes," Noona said.

"You don't hear me complaining." Byron struggled to sit up, and they had to help him. "Thanks," he said, and grimaced in pain. "I seem to recall sis saying that we need to do this one smart. Smart how?"

"So they can't link it to us," Noona said. "So the law won't be after us."

"And it would please me mightily if we could do it so they suffered," Asa said.

"I gave it some thought on the way over," Byron said. "We can start by making them laughingstocks and work our way up to putting windows in their skulls."

"That's my boy," Asa said.

Part Five

56

The Express locomotive idled just past the station, chugging slowly. Smoke puffed from its stack but not nearly as much as would spew out once the train was under way. The engineer had leaned out to talk to some kids who were fascinated by the metal behemoth.

Marshal Abel Pollard checked his pocket watch for the fifth or sixth time. "I swear, if they don't show, I'll have them run out of town on a rail."

"Here they come now," Deputy Agar said. "And look at the one we beat on. He can hardly stand."

At a signal from Pollard, the three extra deputies he'd brought converged from three points of the compass. "Morning, you Delawares," he said.

Asa had his carpetbag in his hand and his shotgun under his arm. He set the bag down but not the gun case.

"You almost didn't make it," Marshal Pollard said. "The train leaves in five minutes."

"We were delayed."

"It's my fault," Byron said. "They had to help me into different clothes, and I am mighty slow at things today."

"I wonder why," Deputy Agar said, and snickered.

"I reckon I bit off more than I can chew," Byron said. "Congratulations. You have prevailed."

"At last some sense out of this family," Marshal Pollard said. He stepped up so he was practically nose to nose with Asa. "He has more sense than you. You can give me all the free country guff you want, but the fact of the matter is, it's not free. It's whatever the law says it is. And since I'm the law—" He shrugged.

"Us leaving," Asa said. "Is it your idea or Arthur Studevant's?"

"Does it matter?"

"That tells me right there. I must have gotten him mad and not known it."

"Over what? Talking to that old biddy, Cecilia Preston? Or those others you went to see? They're nuisances at best."

"I would have liked to meet this Studevant," Asa said.

"There's no one I admire more in this world."

Noona had been uncharacteristically quiet but now she heatedly asked, "Is it admirable of him to force himself on young women?"

"My deputy told me that Cornice and Laura Baker were two of those you visited," Pollard replied. "Flat-out liars, the pair of them."

"Laura seemed believable to me," Noona said.

"Think about it," Marshal Pollard said. "Arthur Studevant can have any female he wants. Hell, women are always throwing themselves at him on account of his money. Do you honestly think he needs to force himself on a no-account girl like Laura?"

"Maybe he does it for the thrill," Noona said.

"Some people are perverse that way," Byron said, staring at Pollard.

"All right. That's enough." The lawman straightened. "Agar, get them on the damn train. And make sure they stay on until it pulls out."

"I'll remember you for this," Asa said.

"Just so you do your remembering in Texas."

Deputy Agar placed his hand on his six-shooter. "You heard the marshal. Pick up your bags and climb on board."

Noona went first. Byron second. Asa paused on the step to look down at Pollard. "Give Studevant a message for me."

"I'm not your errand boy," the marshal said gruffly. "Write him a letter."

"Tell him I've never seen an uglier town."

"Ugly?" Marshal Pollard repeated, and gestured. "Did you look around while you were here? Ordville is about the most—what's that word—picturesque town you'll find. What with the mountains and the new buildings and the clean streets and the tony way everybody dresses, it's downright pretty."

"The ugliness I mean is a cancer that has spread all through Ordville, but most folks don't realize it."

"What's he talking about?" Deputy Agar asked. "Who is it has cancer?"

"Damn me if I don't think he's talking about Mr. Studevant and us," Marshal Pollard said.

"He's what?"

"Like all cancers," Asa went on, "it has to be cut out."

Pollard came to the step. "Forget about Ordville. Forget about this cancer you think it has. Go back to Texas and find another town to tame. Because so help me, if you show your half-breed face here ever again, the moment I set eyes on it, I'll shoot you dead."

57

Asa made it a point to sit by a window on the station side so the marshal and his deputies could see him, Noona, and Byron.

"I hate slinking off with my tail between my legs," Noona complained.

"You don't have a tail, sis," Byron said. "I do."

"Enough about tails," Asa said. He stared out at the law dogs, and Marshal Pollard glared back.

"You sure made him mad, Pa," Noona said.

"I aim to make him a lot madder."

Other passengers filed on and presently the whistle sounded and the conductor started down the aisle collecting tickets. The locomotive chugged, spewing a thick column of smoke, and the wheels began to turn.

"At last," Noona said.

Asa shifted and stared back at Pollard as the train got under way. He kept on staring until a bend hid the station.

"You did that on purpose, didn't you?" Byron said. "To get his goat."

"Temper is a weapon," Asa said. "You make a bad man mad, he gets careless. And when he's careless, he's easier to kill."

"I never thought of it like that."

"I think of everything like that," Asa said. He settled back and folded his arms. "Now we wait for Denver."

"Our tickets say we're supposed to switch to another train," Noona mentioned. "What if they check and find out we didn't?"

"I doubt they're that thorough," Asa said. "Pollard reckons he's scared us off. But even if he does, he'll have no idea where we got to."

"He might suspect later on," Byron said.

"Let him. Suspicion isn't proof. He'll have to catch us or kill us to have that, and we're not about to let him." Asa cocked his head. "This plan of yours, son. I honestly don't know if it's brilliant or insane."

"I do," Noona said. "It promises to be great fun."

"Don't make the mistake of not taking this seriously," Asa warned.

"You know me, Pa," Noona said. "I'm always serious except when I'm not."

"I've never been more serious about anything," Byron said grimly. "I never thought of myself as vengeful, but I guess I am."

"Revenge, son," Asa said, "is another word for justice."

"Is what we're doing really just? Or are we deluding ourselves?"

"You saw how it is there. Or didn't that beating teach you anything?"

"I'm here, aren't I?"

"Please don't start, you two," Noona said. "We're together on this one, aren't we?"

"Yes," Byron said, "we are."

In silence they watched the scenery roll by. In the distance, peaks reared miles high into the bright sky, a few gleaming white with snow. Closer, the mountain slopes were thick with forests of pine and spruce and ranks of tall fir, sprinkled here and there with stands of aspens that in the autumn would display spectacular colors.

The train passed through valleys green with life. In some cattle grazed, a ranch sprawled, and in other valleys the soil had been tilled and a red or white farmhouse was basked in sunshine.

Wildlife was everywhere. They saw elk higher up and deer lower down. Eagles and hawks soared. Ravens and jays and a host of songbirds did what birds do.

"This sure beats Texas," Noona said at one point.

"Texas has nice parts, too," Asa said.

"Not as nice as this."

"I like the Poetry House," Byron said wistfully. "When this is over I'm going back. I wrote Myron a note so he wouldn't think I deserted him."

"You did what?" Asa said.

"All I told him was that I had to leave, and I'd explain when I saw him again."

"Damn."

"What's wrong?"

"If Pollard finds out, he might suspect."

"Myron's not about to show it to him. Relax. Our plan will work just fine."

"It better," Asa said, "or we're liable to find ourselves gurgling at the end of a rope."

"No rope for me, thanks," Noona said. "Or prison, for that matter. I couldn't stand being caged like some poor critter. I'd shoot myself first."

"Let's hope it doesn't come to that," Asa said.

58

The Express rolled into Denver on time, as it nearly always did when the weather cooperated.

In the thirty years since a gold rush saw its founding, the city had prospered. The largest city along the front range of the Rockies, with a population of over thirty-five thousand, each year the number climbed.

"It's a regular beehive," Noona commented as they started their search.

The buildings weren't as new as in Ordville. The people didn't dress as fashionably. Despite its size, Denver had a frontier atmosphere—and a reputation for violence and some of the sassiest whores this side of anywhere.

No one paid any attention to the Delawares, which suited Asa fine. No one would remember them should Marshal Pollard or one of his deputies come to Denver and ask around.

They roved along various streets until they came upon a clothing store.

"This should do us," Asa said.

It did. They each bought new clothes.

For Asa, it was a wide-brimmed black hat, a black Macintosh, and black pants.

For Byron, it was a checkered shirt, bib overalls, and a straw hat. When Noona looked at him and raised her eyebrows, he said, "They'll think I'm a farmer gone bad."

"You look as if you have plows on the brain," she teased.

"Why, thank you," Byron said.

For her part, Noona chose a man's shirt and pants, both too big, which made them baggy like she wanted them. She also selected a high-crowned hat into which she could tuck her hair. "So they'll mistake me for a man," she said when Byron gave her the same look she'd given him.

"The clothes aren't all we need," Asa reminded them, and led the way to the feed and grain.

They found a bin of grain sacks, and each of them picked one up and fingered it.

"I don't know about this, Pa," Noona said. "It's too rough and thick. It'd scratch our skin and we'd half-suffocate."

"Not to mention we won't be able to see a thing, even with eyeholes," Byron said.

"I'm afraid you're right," Asa agreed. "Let's keep looking."

Two blocks down, a mercantile bustled with customers. Asa found some burlap sacks for sale, but they were as rough as the grain sacks. He considered pillowcases. It would be easy to cut the holes, but when they were sweaty the cotton would cling and he didn't want that. He was still searching when Noona came up holding a roll of white material. "What have you got there, daughter?"

"Muslin," she said. "Feel it and hold it up to your face."

It had a loose weave so air would pass through. And when Asa placed it over his eyes, he could see through it.

"This would work wonderful for the masks," Noona was saying. "The holes will be easy to cut, and if they shift on our face somehow, as you just saw we can still see through it."

"I don't like the white," Asa said.

"They sell bottles of dye. I figure we color the masks black."

"This will work fine," Asa complimented her. He looked around. "Where did your brother get to?"

"Where do you think?"

The books were at the very back. Byron was paging through one and didn't realize Asa was there until Asa nudged him.

"More poetry?"

"I wish. It's not as popular as in Lord Byron's day."

"I wonder why."

"Pa, please. I thought we agreed to a truce."

"I'm sorry, son. I've tried and I've tried and I just can't get used to it."

"Well, once this is over, you won't have to worry about it anymore."

"It's not the verse, it's you."

"Have I ever failed to do what needs doing? Have I ever not squeezed the trigger for you?"

"For that I'm grateful." Asa turned. "Come on. Your sister has found what we need."

Byron touched his sleeve. "Hold on. Something is starting to bother me."

"Uh-oh," Asa said.

"We didn't talk this out when I brought it up before, and we should."

Asa looked around to be sure no one was listening. "All right. Air your lungs."

"This won't be a typical taming. Some might say all we're doing is taking the law into our own hands."

"Taming is always taking the law into our own hands."

"But that's wrong, isn't it?"

"Here we go again."

"Please. I'm serious."

Asa looked around again. "If you're going to back out, now is the time to do it."

"Who said anything about backing out? I told you I'd see it through and I will."

"Then quit bellyaching," Asa said. "No, we're not duly sworn law officers, or knights in shining armor or any of that poetical nonsense you like."

"Then what are we, exactly?"

"Killers," Asa said.

59

The Overland stage rumbled into Ordville nearly an hour late. The stationmaster wasn't worried when it didn't show on time. The stage was often late. Rockslides, fallen trees, and steep grades were common causes. But on this particular day the cause was something else.

Cockeyed Jack was on the box, and he commenced bellowing at the outskirts. He cracked his whip and bawled over and ·over, "The stage was robbed! The stage was robbed!"

By the time the stagecoach reached the Overland building, a considerable crowd was trailing along.

The stationmaster, Harvey Spence, heard the ruckus from blocks away and was out under the overhang when the stage came to a stop. Harvey swiped at the cloud of dust it raised, and coughed. "What are you hollering about up there?" he asked even though he'd heard clearly.

Cockeyed Jack sprang down, a remarkable feat given his years, and seized Harvey by the shirt. "We was held up! And it was the strangest damn holdup you ever did see."

Harvey noted the presence of women and children among the onlookers and exercised his authority with, "Watch your language. There are ladies and whatnot."

"What?" Jack said. He glanced around, his left eye looking one way and his right eye looking another. "What?" he said again.

"The holdup," Harvey Spence said. "Let me hear about the holdup."

"Hold on," a voice commanded, and through the throng shouldered Marshal Abel Pollard. As nearly always, Deputy Agar was a second shadow.

The stage door opened and a woman in her fifties poked her head out. "Marshal! You should have been there. A man pointed a gun at me and everything."

Another passenger, a pasty-faced man in a rumpled suit, vigorously bobbed his chin and declared, "I thought I was a goner."

"Oh, posh," the woman said. "They were polite as could be."

Marshal Pollard held up a hand. "Quiet down, all of you. I'll take your statements in a minute." He turned to the driver. "Let me hear your account."

Cockeyed Jack licked his dry lips. One of his eyes appeared to be looking at Pollard while the other was fixed on Agar. "We were comin' up the last of the bad grades. You know the one, Marshal, about a mile down."

Pollard nodded.

"Well, it slowed us, of course, and the team was at a walk by the time we reached the top. And there they were!" Cockeyed Jack exclaimed.

"Who?"

"Why, the robbers. Or highwaymen, I reckon they're called nowadays."

"How many? And what did they look like?"

The woman had climbed down and was fluffing the hair that hung from under her hat. "There were three. They were on horseback, and they held guns on us."

"Are you tellin' this, or am I?" Cockeyed Jack said.

"No need to be huffy," she said.

"Keep telling," Marshal Pollard instructed Jack.

"Well, anyhow, they pointed long guns at us and one of them said, 'Would you be so kind as to come to a stop?'"

Marshal Polllard blinked. "He said what?"

"'Would you be so kind as to come to a stop?'" Cock-eyed Jack repeated.

"I told you before they were as polite as anything," the woman said. "I don't think I've ever heard of bandits so polite."

"Consarn you, Maude Adams," Cockeyed Jack said. "He wants me to tell it, not you."

"She'll get her turn," Marshal Pollard said. "What happened next?"

Cockeyed Jack rubbed the stubble on his chin. "Well, with three long guns pointed at me, I wasn't about to say no. I stopped and the farmer came up close and said—"

"Wait," Marshal Pollard said. "The farmer?"

"That's what I call him on account of how he was dressed," Cockeyed Jack said. "He had overalls and a straw hat and looked just like a farmer except for the mask."

"Hold on, hold on," Marshal Pollard said. "Let's back up a bit. What did the other two look like?"

"One was wearin' one of those raincoats. Macintoshes, I think they're called. He was all in black."

"I took him for the mean one," Maude Adams said. "Outlaws always have a mean one in the bunch."

"Damn it, Maude," Jack said, and continued. "Him and the farmer were middling sized. The third man was shorter, and didn't speak once. The farmer said, 'Would all of you inside please step down' —"

"Gosh, he was mannered," Maude said. "I bet if you invited him to supper, he'd say 'please' each time he wanted the salt."

"Mrs. Adams, please," Marshal Pollard said.

"Now she's got you doin' it," Cockeyed Jack said.

Pollard glared.

"Anyway, as I was sayin', the farmer asked for everyone to climb down and Mrs. Adams and the other four passengers obliged. And the farmer pointed his gun at them and asked if they had any biscuits."

"He what?"

"You heard me," Cockeyed Jack said. "The robber said, as nice as could be, 'Would any of you fine people happen to have fresh biscuits? I am enormously hungry.'"

"Enormously?"

Cockeyed Jack nodded. "His exact word. You don't think I'd sling a ten-pounder like that around myself, do you?"

"And then what?"

"Well, the passengers all said as how they didn't have any biscuits and he said they could climb back in. And once they did, he said to me, 'Thank you for stopping. You can go now. But I do ask a favor of you.'"

"A favor? What kind of favor?"

Cockeyed Jack looked at Maude Adams with his right eye and Jack and Maude looked at the other passengers, and all of them looked at Marshal Pollard.

"I don't know as I should tell you," Jack said.

"Why in hell not?"

"It's liable to make you mad."

"Goddamn it, Jack."

"All right, all right." Cockeyed Jack took a deep breath. "The farmer said to give you his love."

A great hush fell. The onlookers who had been whispering stopped and stood stock-still and stared at the marshal. The passengers and Jack stared at the marshal, too.

Pollard's mouth had dropped open. For all of ten seconds he appeared stupefied. Then the scarlet tinge of anger crept up his neck and face, and he put a hand on his six-shooter. "Was that your notion of a joke?"

Cockeyed Jack thrust out his hands. "He said it! As God is my witness, he did."

"We all heard him," Maude Adams said. "That nice outlaw sent our town marshal his love." And she tittered merrily.

More than a few of the onlookers laughed.

Deputy Agar was a study in confusion. "What in tarnation is going on, Abel?"

Marshal Pollard stared down the mountain. "I wish to hell I knew."

60

The marshal formed a posse, and they thundered down to the grade and searched for tracks. They promptly found some and almost as promptly lost them when the tracks led to a stream. They split and followed the stream in both directions but couldn't find where the outlaws left it.

In Ordville, word spread like a prairie fire.

When Marshal Pollard and the posse returned, they were pointed at and grinned at.

"Had any biscuits lately?" a man shouted from a saloon doorway.

Not a block later another man called out, "Give our love to the farmer."

"I don't much like being laughed at," Deputy Agar grumbled.

"It's me they're laughing at, you jackass," Marshal Pollard said, "and I like it even less."

"Someone was playing a prank," Agar said. "It has to be."

"They picked the wrong hombre to play it on," Pollard said.

Pollard visited every saloon in town. He let it be known that he would pay a hundred dollars out of his own pocket for information that led him to the identities of the three stage robbers.

No one came forward. In a few days the townsfolk stopped joking about it. They had something new to gossip about.

Cornice Baker's daughter, Laura, had hung herself.

The next Friday, Cockeyed Jack was on his usual Denver-to-Ordville run. He was climbing the last steep grade and came to the top and was astounded to see the same three highwaymen. He brought the stage to a stop without being told to and declared, "Not you three again!"

The passengers peered out. None of the men resorted to a firearm, not with what they took to be three rifles trained on them.

The farmer gigged his horse close to the stage and said to Cockeyed Jack as politely as anything, "How do you do?"

"I am plumb surprised that you're back," Jack confessed. "We didn't have any biscuits last time, and we don't have any now."

"Do you happen to have any sugar?"

"Sugar?"

"We would be happy as anything if you did. I didn't buy enough, and we have run out for our coffee."

"You put on those masks and hold us up for sugar?"

"I would do it for beans if we were out of beans."

"Don't this beat all." Cockeyed Jack shook his head. "You are as loco as anything. The three of you. No, I ain't got no sugar, and I doubt my passengers do, either."

The farmer bandit, as Jack liked to think of him, looked at the heads poking out of the stage. "Sugar, anyone?"

"No, sir."

"Why in hell would anyone bring sugar on a stage?"

"Maybe you ought to visit a general store. They have sugar galore."

"I'm terribly disappointed," the farmer bandit said. "The vagaries of life are truly fickle."

"The what?" Jack said.

"Would you do me another favor?" the farmer bandit asked.

"Not again. What is it this time? Send your love to the marshal like before?"

"No," the farmer bandit said. And he told them what it was.

One of the male passengers cackled, and a female passenger said, "I never!"

"First it was love and now this," Cockeyed Jack said. "What is the matter with you?"

"I'd be ever so grateful." The farmer bandit wagged his rifle. "Off you go. I trust all of you will have the nicest of days."

"Mister," Cockeyed Jack said as he raised the reins, "when they passed out brains, you were off in the outhouse."

"Now, now," the farmer bandit said. "If it's stink we're talking about, let's stick to the marshal."

Cockeyed Jack muttered, flicked the reins, and the team broke into motion. The stage gained speed on the flat, and he held them to their top speed for the rest of the distance to town.

Jack didn't whoop and holler like he did the last time. He brought the stage to a halt in front of the stage office and said to Harvey Spence, who was waiting as usual, "You won't believe it. Those three did it again."

"You were held up?"

A couple of kids were rolling a hoop with a stick and overheard. Lickety-split, they ran up the street hollering, "The stage was robbed! The stage was robbed!"

In no time a crowd collected and hurled questions at Cockeyed Jack, but he refused to say a word. He climbed down and was holding the door for the passengers when Marshal Pollard and Deputy Agar arrived.

"Did I hear right?" the marshal asked.

"You did," Jack said.

"What did they want this time?" Deputy Agar asked with a smirk. "More biscuits?"

"Sugar," Cockeyed Jack said, and looked at the marshal. "And for me to ask you to do something."

"Do I want to hear it?" Marshal Pollard.

"No."

"Tell me anyway."

"Do you give your word that you won't hit me?"

"You have my word. What the hell is it this time?"

Cockeyed Jack raised his voice so everyone in the crowd would hear him. "The farmer bandit wants you to give Arthur Studevant a kiss."

Thanks to the guffaws and peals of mirth from the good citizens of Ordville, only Cockeyed Jack and Deputy Agar heard Marshal Pollard reply.

"I will by-God kill them."

61

The whites called it Shoshone Mountain. A family of sheep-eater Shoshones once lived on it. The sheep weren't the kind whites raised. They were mountain sheep. It took considerable skill to stalk the high crags and bring a mountain sheep down with an arrow.

Then the whites came along and hunters picked the sheep off from a distance with rifles, and the Shoshones found it increasingly harder to fill their hungry stomachs.

So they left.

In a meadow high on a south slope, nestled at the base of a bluff where they were out of the wind, the three town tamers had made camp.

A fire crackled, and coffee was on to brew.

Byron touched the top of the pot and jerked his finger back. "It will be ready soon," he announced.

Across the fire, seated cross-legged, Noona grinned and said, "I thought that business about the sugar was a nice touch."

"Thank you."

Asa finished picketing the horses and came over with his Winchester shotgun cradled in the crook of an elbow. "Tell me again how this is smart."

"It's smart in so many ways, I'm amazed at my own brilliance," Byron said.

"The love and the kiss parts don't sit well with me," Asa said. "It's not dignified."

"You wanted them to be laughingstocks," Byron reminded him.

"From what Cornice told me," Noona said, "everyone is laughing at that no-good law dog and at Studevant behind their backs. And some laugh to their faces."

Byron chuckled. "You hear that, Pa?" he asked without the hillbilly twang. "You wanted to get everyone's attention. Well, we have. You saw the newspaper that Mrs. Baker gave sis. We were the talk of the town the first time. This time we're the talk of the territory."

Asa grunted.

"We have drawn attention to the cancers, as you call them. Exactly as you asked me to."

Asa grunted.

"You didn't want to stir up the townsfolk by actually robbing the stages and having posses out combing the countryside, and here we sit, with no posses to worry about."

Noona laughed. "They don't take us serious, is why. If we'd stolen their money and valuables, they'd be fit to lynch us."

"What I'd like to know," Byron said, "is how much more of this we have to do before we bed those cancers down, permanent?"

"Listen to you," Asa said. "Since when did you become bloodthirsty?"

"Since I was beaten within an inch of my life," Byron said.

"Paitence, son," Asa said. "As I keep having to remind you, we have to do this so that when we get to the bedding down, no one puts the blame on us."

"And no one *knows* it was us," Noona amended.

"How many more stages do we pretend to rob, then?" Byron asked.

"We're done with stages," Asa said. "They were to get jaws wagging."

"It's too bad we can't tame all our towns this way," Noona said. "This is fun."

"I'm happy you're amused, daughter. But never forget that the opposition is taking this serious."

"Don't worry, Pa," Noona said. "I'm fond of breathing."

62

Everyone knew the carriage on sight. The grandest in Ord-ville, Arthur Studevant had imported it from Paris, France. Gossip had it that it was a popular model with the European rich.

The driver wore a purple uniform complete with a high hat. He sat straight and proud and handled the six horses in their fine livery with expert ease.

Marshal Pollard happened to be at his desk thumbing through circulars when the carriage came to a halt outside his office. He looked out the window and said, "Oh, hell."

The driver scrambled down to lower the step and opened the door and even bowed slightly in the manner of a court retainer.

Arthur Studevant had a stately air about him. His slicked black hair with gray at the temples, his immaculate clothes tailored in the European style, his polished shoes and his cane with its gold knob set him apart from common humanity. He alighted and took a couple of steps and stopped so that the two men who emerged after him could flank him on either side.

Deputy Agar had gone to the window when the marshal swore, and he remarked, "His bodyguards are with him."

"When aren't they?" Pollard said.

"They're spooky, those two."

Rumor had it the bodyguards were cousins. They certainly looked enough alike. Both were tall and broadshouldered and had a pantherish aspect when they moved. Both had mustaches and gray eyes, which was fitting since they both always dressed in gray. Gray short-brimmed hats. Gray suits. Gray slickers on occasion. Even gray gun belts and gray holsters. Two holsters apiece, for the cousins were a rarity. Both were two-gun men. They were equally proficient with either hand.

People liked to bestow nicknames, so it wasn't unusual that the bodyguards had acquired a nickname of their own.

They were called the Gray Ghosts.

Arthur Studevant entered the jail and gave Deputy Agar a look that made Agar swallow.

The Gray Ghosts followed, each moving as silently as their namesakes. Their boots were made of soft leather with soft soles, and they never wore spurs. They made no more sound than Apaches.

Studevant had a folded newspaper under his arm. Opening it, he placed it on the marshal's desk and said, "Where's my kiss?" He wasn't smiling. His blue eyes were ice and his jaw was granite.

Pollard stared at the *Ordville Gazette* in disgust. "I asked Fiske not to print that, but he said it was too newsworthy to pass up."

"I'll have a talk with our so-called journalist," Arthur Studevant declared, and his tone implied Fiske wouldn't like what he said. Leaning on his cane, Studevant regarded Pollard with his piercing blue eyes. "I was out of town when the first incident occurred. I heard about it, naturally, since it was all anyone was talking about when I returned."

"Those damned outlaws," the marshal said.

"I'm beginning to worry about you, Abel," Studevant said.

Pollard sat up. "What for? I've always been ready and willing to do anything you want me to."

"That's not the issue here," Studevant said. "The issue is outlaws who aren't outlaws."

"How's that again?"

Studevant sat on the edge of the desk and rested the cane with the gold knob across his shoulder. "Yes, I definitely have need to be concerned. I took you for sharper."

"I'm as sharp as the next hombre," Pollard angrily replied.

"Then explain why you didn't come see me after the first incident."

Flushing, Pollard spat, "Because it was damned embarrassing, that's why. Folks were laughing at me behind my back. That farmer outlaw sending his love. He made a fool of me."

"There is no farmer outlaw. There are no outlaws, period."

"How can you say that? The driver and the passengers saw the highwaymen with their own eyes."

Studevant bent down so they were almost face-to-face. "*Outlaws* don't send their love to marshals. *Outlaws* don't ask marshals to give a town's leading citizen a kiss." He paused, and his voice vibrated with suppressed fury. "*Outlaws* don't stop a stage to hold it up and then not take anything."

Deputy Agar chimed in with, "They were fixing to rob it. The first time they wanted biscuits and the second time it was sugar."

Arthur Studevant said without looking at him, "If you open your mouth again, Deputy, I'll have Dray and Cray take you into a cell and pistol-whip you until you spit out teeth."

Agar glanced at the Gray Ghosts, and shivered.

"Now, then," Studevant said to Pollard, "I admit that when I heard about the first incident, I, too, assumed it was someone out to humiliate you. But this latest"—he tapped the newspaper—"is intended to humiliate both of us."

"Why these jackasses are going to so much trouble to annoy us has me stumped."

"Are you puzzled?" Studevant asked.

"I am."

"Are you confused?"

"I reckon I'm that, too."

"Are you mystified?"

"I'm not rightly sure what that means, but if it has anything to do with puzzled and confused, I am."

Arthur Studevant stood and moved to the window and stared out. "In Wyoming you showed great promise, Abel. It's why I sent for you when I needed someone to carry out my wishes here in Ordville."

"I'm obliged," Pollard said.

"You should be. But if you desire to go on serving me, you mustn't be as stupid as everyone else."

"Sorry?"

"There is more going on here than meets our eyes. Whoever these men are, they're up to something. Their purpose isn't clear yet. But what to do about it is."

"I'm listening," Pollard said.

"Twice now they've stopped the stage from Denver at the last grade. It's likely, if not certain, that they'll stop it a third time. You must have men lying in wait for them."

"But the stage comes four times a week, and we don't know which day they'll pick."

Studevant turned. "So send out deputies each and every time until these outlaws who aren't outlaws show up."

"I suppose I could," Pollard said.

"No, you *will*. And once you have them behind bars, you're to send for me and I'll question them personally. And Abel?"

"Mr. Studevant?"

"I don't like having to solve your problems for you. Especially a problem as simple as this. Use your head as well as your revolver and your fists. Prove to me that my trust in you is justified, or I'll find someone else to wear that badge."

"Don't you worry," Pollard said. "I'll catch those three if it's the last thing I do."

63

It was common knowledge that every Friday night Arthur Studevant attended the theater. Just as it was that the Gray Ghosts always went with him, and that he always had a new pretty lady on his arm.

Studevant had a mansion on the outskirts of Ordville, but he spent more time at the Studevant Hotel. His suite comprised the entire top floor.

On this particular Friday, three figures stood in the shadows of a recessed doorway and watched Studevant's fancy carriage clatter off down the street.

"There he goes," Noona said. "It's too bad we can't just shoot him and be done with it."

"And wind up at the end of a rope?" Asa said. "No thank you, girl." He moved out of the doorway, the Winchester at his side, hidden by the Macintosh.

Byron came last, saying, "We might be recognized without our masks."

"You took off your straw hat and have a jacket on," Asa said. "Keep your chin down and your head low until we get there."

They crossed where the street was darkest and walked

around to the rear of the hotel. The back door had a sign that read STAFF ONLY.

The desk clerk was reading and didn't hear them start up the stairs. They encountered no one until the fourth floor, when a man dressed for a night on the town hurried past without so much as a glance.

Two lamps lit the top floor hallway. Asa had Noona extinguish one while Byron blew out the other.

"Masks," Asa said, and they donned them.

"Remember, gal," Asa said to Noona. "Not a word out of you or they'll know you're not male."

"I know what to do, Pa."

Asa knocked, and when a balding gent in a starched black uniform answered, Asa pointed the shotgun at his face.

"One yell, and you're dead."

"My word," the man blurted.

"You are?"

"The butler, sir. Jeems is my name."

"Back up," Asa said. "Arms high."

Jeems dutifully obeyed. "You've only just missed Mr. Studevant. I'm afraid if you're here to rob him, you won't find much of value."

"Liar," Asa said. He pressed the muzzle against Jeems's chest and forced him back until he bumped into a chair. "Sit."

Jeems sat.

"You know what to do," Asa said to the others. "I'll keep our friend company."

Byron and Noona each drew knives from hip sheaths and went into different rooms. Shortly, from out of the rooms came ripping and tearing sounds.

"What are you up to, if I might inquire?" Jeems asked.

"You'll find out soon enough," Asa said.

"You're those highwaymen I read about, aren't you?" Jeems said. "The ones Mr. Studevant has taken a personal interest in."

"Has he, now?"

"I should point out he'll be incensed by this intrusion. I've been in his employ for fifteen years and know him well."

"You might want to go to work for someone else."

"I couldn't do that. No one else would pay as handsomely."

"Were you here the night he raped that girl?"

"I'm aware of her accusation, and he did no such thing," Jeems said indignantly. "But no, I wasn't. He'd given me the night off."

"Wonder why," Asa said.

"It's a shame about the young lady," Jeems continued. "Doing herself in like that."

"She did what?"

"It was in the newspaper." Jeems motioned at several on a polished mahogany stand. "That Miss Baker hanged herself. Tied a rope to a rafter in her house. Her poor mother found the body."

Asa sidled to the stand. Covering the butler, he picked up the top *Gazette*. He didn't have to look any farther than the first page.

"Did you know her?" Jeems asked.

Without thinking, Asa answered, "Met her once."

He folded the newspaper and slid it into a pocket.

Byron emerged, laughing. "Done with this room," he said. "It's too bad we can't burn the whole hotel to the ground."

"A lot of other people stay here," Asa said.

"We could go door to door and warn them to leave."

"No."

Byron gestured at the room he'd just vacated. "This doesn't hardly seem enough."

"There'll be more," Asa said. He had partly turned and wasn't covering the butler.

"Might I interject a comment, sir?" Jeems asked.

"What is it?" Asa said. He'd just as soon the man be quiet.

"I'd very much like both of you to drop your guns," Jeems said, "or else."

The "or else" became apparent when Asa glanced over his shoulder and discovered a derringer trained on him.

64

Asa wanted to kick himself. He'd been careless, and now look.

"I'd put that down were I you," Byron said. "You'll only get one of us before the other gets you."

Jeems kept the derringer pointed on Asa. "But who is to die and who is to live? That's the question."

"You're a butler, not a gun hand," Byron said. "Why are you doing this?"

Asa slowly slid his right foot along the floor. If his son could keep Jeems talking, he might get close enough to club him with the shotgun. Better that than a shot, which would bring the management and others on the run.

Jeems surprised him by noticing. "Stand perfectly still, sir. I'm an able shot."

"Why die for an animal like Studevant?" Byron asked.

Jeems didn't answer. Instead he stood and said, "I'll have to ask the two of you to place your rifles to the floor. Nice and easy, if you please."

"Don't do this," Asa said.

"I'm afraid I have to," Jeems said. "Mr. Studevant might fire me if I do nothing, and I do so like this job."

Asa looked past the butler and gave the slightest of nods.

He tried one more time. "We have no wish to harm you. It's Mr. High-and-Mighty who has a reckoning coming."

"Is that why you're doing this? It's part of some vendetta?"

"The derringer," Asa said. "Hand it over."

"Not in a million years."

"Very well," Asa said. "Do it."

"Do what?" Jeems asked.

By then Noona was behind him. She'd crept out of the other room unnoticed and as silently as a Comanche slunk up. Now, without any warning, she raised her Spencer over Jeems' head and brought it crashing down.

The butler stiffened and gasped as his eyelids fluttered. The derringer fell from fingers gone limp, and a moment later Jeems lay on the floor next to it.

"You did good," Asa said.

"I felt sort of sorry doing it," Noona said. "It's not him we're after."

"He made his choice." Asa helped himself to the derringer. "Now let's finish up. Destroy everything you can without making much noise."

Noona stepped to a painting of an aristocratic woman from perhaps a century ago. Drawing her knife, she slashed the canvas from top to bottom and side to side. "I'd sure like to see his face when he sees what we've done."

"He'll be fit to be tied," Asa predicted.

They spent the next fifteen minutes cutting and ripping. More paintings, the furniture, even the huge four-poster bed that Arthur Studevant slept in. Byron took particular delight in slashing the canopy to ribbons.

In one room Asa found a writing desk and paper and ink. It gave him an idea. He sat down and called Byron over. Together they crafted a short letter that began with, *Dear Editor.*

A groan from Jeems prompted Asa to bind and gag him, and they were done.

They stepped to the door and admired their handiwork, with Noona saying, "He'll take this like a bear takes being poked with a stick."

"We want him to," Asa said.

"The important thing now is that the rest of the town finds out," Byron said.

"Let's skedaddle," Asa said. "Masks off." He removed his and poked his head out. The hallway was empty. Holding the shotgun under his Macintosh, he hurried to the stairs.

On the third floor they encountered a couple going up, but the man and woman were arm in arm, fondling, and only had eyes for each other.

Once outside, they hugged the shadows. Half a dozen side streets and two alleys brought them to their next stop.

The *Ordville Gazette* operated out of a brick building that fronted on Main Street. The press was on the bottom floor, the offices above.

"Look at him," Noona said when they peered in the wide window. "He sure is dedicated."

Richard Fiske was setting type. He wore an apron and a visor and his fingers were stained with ink.

"Preparing tomorrow's edition," Byron guessed.

"Let's give him something for the front page." Asa had cut a slit in the note he'd written so that all he had to do was slide the paper over the knob and it would hang there. He knocked and quickly retreated around the corner.

They heard the door open and a voice call out, "Yes? Who's out here?"

A few heartbeats more, and, "What's this?"

Asa grinned, and he and his pride and joys melted into the night.

65

Marshal Abel Pollard was summoned to the Studevant Hotel the next morning shortly before eight. He had barely settled into his desk with his usual cup of coffee, when one of the Gray Ghosts showed up and said that Arthur Studevant demanded to see him *now*. He took Agar along.

Pollard could never tell the Gray Ghosts apart and asked, "Are you Dray or Cray?"

"Cray."

"In all the time you've been working for Mr. Studevant," Marshal Pollard mentioned, "I never did hear where you two are from."

All Cray said was, "Didn't you?"

Pollard simmered. First the summons, now this. The Ghosts never showed him any respect. For that matter, they never showed anyone any respect except Arthur Studevant.

"I bet you're from the South," Deputy Agar said. "That accent you have."

"Do we?"

"And those names of yours," Agar said. "They're Southern, ain't they?"

"Are they?"

"You'd think it was a secret or something," Agar said testily.

A lot of shops and stores had just opened or were about to. Boardwalks were being swept and a haberdashery owner was washing his front window. Newspapers were being hawked on street corners by boys no older than twelve, a little army of them that Richard Fiske hired at pennies a day.

"Did you hear that?" Deputy Agar said. "It's a special edition."

No, Pollard hadn't. He was fuming about the Gray Ghosts and Studevant and hadn't been paying attention to what the boys were bawling about. They always yelled exactly what Fiske told them to, no more, no less.

The boy on the next corner was hollering, "Special edition! Read all about it! Revenge for death of Laura Baker!"

Marshal Pollard stopped, fished out a coin, and bought one. He didn't care that Cray gave him an impatient glance. Unfolding the paper, he couldn't believe the headline: *Raid On Studevant Hotel! Suicide Claimed As Motive!*

Deputy Agar was looking over his shoulder and said, "Oh, my. A raid?"

"That bastard Fiske likes to stir things up to sell his papers," Pollard growled. "Sensationalize" was how Arthur Studevant once put it.

"He'll stir up a lot with that," Agar said.

A small crowd had gathered at the hotel and were staring up at the top floor. A hush fell over them as they parted for the Gray Ghost without them having to say or do a thing.

"They sure are scared of him," Deputy Agar whispered.

"They should be." By Pollard's tally, the pair had killed seven men at Studevant's bidding that he knew of. He suspected the total was a lot higher.

The hotel staff was bustling about like so many agitated bees.

Cray conducted the marshal and his deputy to the top floor where the other Gray Ghost stood guard outside the suite. Without comment, Dray opened the door for them and motioned for them to go in.

"Oh, hell," Pollard said on setting eyes on the shambles. It looked like a madman had swept through the suite with a scythe.

Arthur Studevant was standing in front of a slashed painting, his hands clasped behind his back.

"I came right away," Marshal Pollard said.

For maybe half a minute Studevant just stood there. Then he said, "I was out for the evening. I took a young lady to the theater and then we went to her place where I stayed the night. Normally I would have brought her here, but she didn't want rumors to start."

"It's good you didn't," Deputy Agar said. "You might have run into the vandals who did this."

"Vandals, my ass," Studevant said. "Have you two seen the paper?"

"We have," Marshal Pollard said, and wagged the one he'd bought.

"Read the letter to the editor out loud."

"Beg pardon?"

"You heard me."

Pollard unfolded the newspaper and cleared his throat. "'Dear Editor,'" he began. "'We are outraged citizens who say enough is enough. There is a serpent in your midst, and his name is Arthur Studevant. A young woman has hung herself because of him. She said that he raped her. Why was he not arrested for his foul deed? Why was he not put on trial? Her soul cries for vengeance. Who hears her besides us?'"

"That's some letter," Agar said.

"What do you make of it, Abel?" Studevant asked.

Pollard hated being put on the spot. "Suppose you tell me what to make of it."

Studevant turned and took the paper and glared at it.

"The writer is educated. He uses 'serpent' instead of 'snake' or 'sidewinder.' He has a sense of drama. Notice his questions at the end to appeal to the emotions of his readers? And he's not working alone."

"The 'us,'" Marshal Pollard said.

"Do you know what I think?" Studevant asked, and didn't wait for an answer. "I think we're seeing the handiwork of our so-called highwaymen."

"That farmer bandit in overalls?"

"Who was always so polite and well-mannered, and didn't talk like any farmer."

"I never thought of that," Deputy Agar said. "I wish I was as smart as you, Mr. Studevant."

"I wish you were smarter than a stump," Studevant said, "but no matter." He crumpled the newspaper and gestured at the slashed painting. "Do you see that? It was by a French master. I paid five thousand dollars for it. The total for everything they've destroyed will be fifty thousand or more."

Agar whistled.

"This is a deliberate campaign, Abel. Those sham stage robberies, and now this."

"To stir up people against you?" Pollard said.

"I suspect there's far more to it than that," Studevant said. "The trouble they've gone to. The planning they must have done. No, I suspect that they are out to destroy us. And I very much want them dead before they achieve their goal."

"I'd shoot them for you if I knew where to find them," Pollard said.

"Do what you can. In the meantime, I'll be using my own resources. I'm bringing in a specialist."

"A what?" Agar said.

"His name is Cyrus Temple. Perhaps you've heard of him."

"Isn't he the hombre folks call the Tracker?" Pollard recollected.

"He is. I'm paying him a great deal of money to track down the farmer-bandit and his companions so I can rip their hearts from their bodies."

66

The morning sun rose stupendous and bright over the prairie to the east and gradually spread its radiant glow over the foothills and higher slopes of the Rocky Mountains.

Asa sat at the campfire and sipped his first cup of coffee of the day. He was always up before the others. It came with age. He needed less sleep than they did.

Which was just as well, since he had a lot of pondering to do.

So far things had gone well. They'd pointed an accusing finger at Arthur Studevant without drawing the town's ire on themselves. Their stagecoach antics and their visit to the hotel had set Ordville abuzz.

What it hadn't done—which was the whole purpose—was set posses after them. If they'd killed someone or wounded a stage passenger, people would be outraged. As it was, the good folks of Ordville were more amused than angry—those who weren't incensed at Studevant over Laura Baker.

Yes, things were going well.

Asa admired the sunrise and listened to the warbling of the songbirds and the cry of a magpie off down the meadow. He'd grown fond of the Rockies in the short time they'd been there. The lofty spires thrusting at the sky, the sea of forest, the magnificent vistas. It was no wonder so many folks flocked there.

Noona's blankets moved and her head poked out. "Morning, Pa."

"Daughter," Asa said. "You and your brother have become layabouts."

She grinned and laid her head back down. "It's your fault. We never have much to do."

"That's about to change," Asa said. "It's been a week since the hotel."

Her head popped out again. "What do you have in mind?"

"Your brother came up with another brainstorm last night after you turned in."

"What is it this time? We burn down one of Studevant's saloons? Or better yet, one of his whorehouses?"

"Your brother calls it a list of injustices against humanity."

"Another note to the newspaper?"

"Why not? We want to keep them agitated. And keep Studevant mad. Did you know he had that fancy team of his brought all the way from New York?"

"I did not," Noona said.

"He's very fond of them, folks say."

"I like horses, Pa. You're not fixing to harm them, are you?"

"You know me better than that, girl. But they are pawns in the chess game, as your brother likes to think of this."

"Just so we don't hurt them."

From under the blanket on the other side of the fire came a grunt of annoyance. "Talk a little louder, why don't you? So what if someone is trying to sleep."

"Rise and shine," Asa said. "We'll do those horses today like you suggested, and it's a long ride to town."

"Me and my brilliance," Byron said.

Noona sat up and ruffled her hair and yawned. "I can't wait to get back to Texas. I miss home."

"It'll be a while yet," Asa said. "Remember, we have to do this slow and careful."

"More's the pity," Byron said.

"I should stop and visit with Cornice," Noona said. "She always has newspapers and grub for us."

"We should go together," Byron said. "She baked an apple pie last time."

"It's riskier with the both of you," Asa said. "Your sister can slip in and out with no one catching on."

Noona got up and fixed breakfast, eggs over easy and bacon sizzling with juicy fat. "We're running low on butter," she mentioned.

"We'll ask Cornice to buy us some," Asa said.

Byron forked a piece of bacon into his mouth and chewed lustily. "How long do you intend to stay at this? When will enough be enough and we send Arthur Studevant to hell where he belongs?"

"I haven't set a date."

"Are we talking days? Weeks? Months? I'd like to get on with my life and don't appreciate the delay."

"You mean you'd like to get on with that Olivia gal," Noona teased.

Asa lowered his tin cup and scowled. "I warned you to stay away from her. You better listen. They know you were with her that night and might put a watch on her, thinking you'll pay her a visit."

"I'm not that stupid," Byron said.

"I hope not," Asa said, "for all our sakes."

67

The man who got off the train was big and wide—so big he towered head and shoulders above the tallest of other men, so wide his shoulders brushed the compartments on either side when he moved down the aisle.

His attire added to his size. Even though it was summer, he wore a long-sleeved bear-hide coat that reached to his knees. Made from a black bearskin, it smelled like bear, too. Bear and sweat.

His hat was a stocking-cap fashioned from buckskin that hung to his shoulder and swung with every stride.

His moccasins were the knee-high kind Apaches were partial to.

He carried an old Sharps and had a cartridge belt and a large bone-handled knife around his waist.

Marshal Pollard and Deputy Agar were waiting when the big man got off.

"Cyrus Temple?" Agar said. "Mr. Studevant sent us to fetch you."

Cyrus Temple scanned him from head to boots and then looked at Pollard and said, "At least one of you ain't worthless."

"Hey, now," Agar said. "I've hardly spoken ten words to you."

"It was enough."

"We're on the same side," Pollard said. "You'd do well to remember that."

"I don't kiss law dog ass," Temple said. "You'd do well to remember that."

"You're not very nice," Deputy Agar said.

"No," Cyrus Temple said, "I'm not."

Studevant had also sent his carriage. They rode in silence to the hotel. Temple drew a lot of stares as he crossed the lobby to the stairs.

The Gray Ghosts were at their usual post. Temple stopped on seeing them, then said, "These two are more like it."

"Like what?" Agar asked.

"Not like you," Temple said.

Arthur Studevant was seated on a wood settee, one of the few items of furniture to escape the wrath of the intruders since it didn't have cushions or upholstery.

He rose and offered his hand.

Shaking, Cyrus Temple regarded the destruction. "Twisters strike indoors now?"

Studevant told him about the three bandits and the invasion of his suite.

"It was a week ago and you haven't cleaned the mess up yet?"

"I'm keeping it like this as a reminder," Studevant said, "of how much I want them dead. I'll have it cleaned up when they've breathed their last, and not before."

"That's why you sent for me, I reckon," Temple said.

"I appreciate you coming so quickly."

Temple cradled his Sharps. "I was between jobs when your telegram reached me in Cheyenne. I took the next train, and here I am."

"Have a seat. I'll have refreshments brought and explain my situation."

"All I need to know is who I'm after and where I can pick up their trail."

"I can give you their descriptions but not their names. As for a trail, we'll have to wait for them to strike again."

"That's all right. I'm a patient man. Have to be, in my line of work."

"I'm not except when it suits my purpose," Arthur Studevant said. "And it doesn't suit my purpose to have them continue to belittle me and mock me and try to turn the people of Ordville against me."

"Strange bunch of bandits," Cyrus Temple said.

"As soon as you can, I want them to be a dead bunch of bandits."

"About that," Temple said. "I'm a tracker. I don't kill unless the law will look the other way." He glanced at Pollard. "What way will your law look?"

"Need you ask?" Studevant said. "They do what I tell them to do. But even so, I'd prefer that you take this trio alive if you can. I want them dead, yes. But I want to do the deed myself."

"So I find them and bring them here, or I come fetch you and take you to where they are?"

"It's better if they're not seen in town. When you find them, make damn certain they can't go anywhere while you come get me."

"You're makin' it harder than it needs to be," Temple said.

"In my telegram I offered to pay you twice your going rate. For that much I can make it as difficult as I damn well want."

"So long as I get to do the tracking my way." Temple looked about him and walked over to a chair cushion that lay on the floor. It had been hacked almost to pieces. He nudged it with the toe of his moccasin and said, "You know this is personal, don't you?"

"I know they're out to bring me down," Studevant said. "I suspect they're out to bury me."

"If all they wanted was to have you dead, they'd do like I do and sit off somewhere and pick you off with a rifle."

"Perhaps they're building up to that."

"Could be." Temple gestured at the destruction. "But whoever did it hates you, mister. Hates you somethin' fierce." He added, almost as an afterthought, "Or maybe they're like me and were hired by someone who hates you."

Arthur Studevant gave a slight start.

"Somethin'?" Temple said.

"I may need to thank you twice over," Studevant said. "You've just given me food for deep thought."

"Do you have many enemies?"

"I've made a great many of them."

"That's where I'd start lookin'. I take it you hope they strike again soon so you can get this over with."

"The sooner, the better," Studevant said.

68

The stable was only a few blocks from the Studevant Hotel. Studevant liked his team handy for when he needed to go somewhere on short notice.

Once it was a public stable, but Studevant bought out the owner and now it housed his six carriage horses and no others.

The horses were Clydesdales. Originally bred in the Clyde River Valley in Scotland, Clydesdales proved so popular as draft animals that soon they were being bred in Europe and the United States.

Studevant, though, insisted on owning only those of the purest blood. He imported his team from Scotland.

They were tremendous animals. Each weighed close to two thousand pounds and stood nearly seventy inches at the shoulders. When fitted with their trappings, they presented an imposing spectacle with their rapid gait, long strides, and the hair around their ankles.

The stableman, appropriately enough, was a Scotsman by the name of MacDougal. Studevant imported him from Scotland, too. He had no wife and no children and lived in a room at the back of the stable so he could be close to "his babies," as he liked to refer to the Clydesdales.

On this particular night, MacDougal had tended to their needs and given each an affectionate pat, and then turned in, as he always did, about ten. He didn't bar the front doors. He never did. Horse theft was unknown in Ordville, and besides, no one in their right mind would steal horses that belonged to Arthur Studevant.

The first inkling MacDougal had that this wasn't going to be an ordinary night occurred when he awoke with a start to find a hard object gouging his cheek. Someone had lit his lamp but turned it low, and he saw that the object gouging him was a rifle barrel. Then he looked up. "Sure and by God, what's the meaning of this?"

A man in a straw hat and overalls smiled. "Good evening, sir," he said politely. "I'm afraid we're going to have to impose on you."

"Impose how?" MacDougal asked, struggling to collect his wits. He noticed two other men holding rifles on him and suddenly he remembered the newspaper accounts. "You're those outlaws, by God. The ones who held up the stage and made a mess of Mr. Studevant's suite."

"As a matter of fact," the polite outlaw in overalls said, "we never held up anything. As for the other, we've only just begun to make a mess of his life."

"What did poor Mr. Studevant ever do to you?" MacDougal asked indignantly.

"Poor?" the polite one said, and laughed. "Of all the ways to describe him, that fits least. Bastard fits best."

"I won't speak ill of the man. He paid for my passage to America and gives me a good wage to take care of his team."

"You don't care that he rapes women and has people beaten and murdered?"

"That rape was never proved. And the idea of him killing is ridiculous."

"There are none so blind," the polite bandit said, "as those who will not see."

"You have your nerve," MacDougal said.

The outlaw in a Macintosh broke in with, "Enough. You're wasting time. Get it over with."

The shortest of the bandits came over and covered

MacDougal while the polite one tied his wrists and ankles.

"Those aren't too tight, are they?" the polite one asked when he was done.

"No," MacDougal said.

"Good. Wouldn't want them cutting off your circulation."

"You are damned odd bandits, and that's no lie."

"Would you happen to have a clean handkerchief anywhere?"

"I would not," MacDougal said. "I hardly ever use one."

"How about a clean sock then?"

"For God's sake," the outlaw in the Macintosh said. "Just do it."

The polite one turned to him. "Would you want a used handkerchief or dirty sock in your mouth?"

"Find something clean, then," the outlaw in the Macintosh said.

"I have a washcloth," MacDougal said, and nodded at a wash basin and a pitcher over on a small table.

"That will do. Thank you."

MacDougal noticed that the polite one took particular care not to cause him discomfort as he placed the gag in his mouth and then tied a strip of towel around his head so he couldn't spit it out.

"Remember to breathe through your nose, and you'll be fine," the polite one said.

The outlaw in the Macintosh mumbled something and the three of them departed.

They left the door to MacDougal's room open.

Sliding off the bed, MacDougal eased onto his shoulder and wriggled to where he could look down the center aisle.

The outlaws were leading the Clydesdales from their stalls.

MacDougal was bewildered when the short one produced paint and brushes they had obviously brought with them. He couldn't imagine what they would use it for, and was astounded when they began to paint yellow stripes on each of the Clydesdales.

MacDougal thought he must be dreaming.

The Clydesdales were well trained, and while several fidgeted and stamped when the paint was applied, none kicked or shied.

Then the man in the Macintosh opened the stable doors, and the outlaws led each Clydesdale outside and gave it a swat that sent it trotting off.

That accomplished, the three slipped off into the night.

The polite one in the straw hat left last, and he looked back and grinned and waved.

MacDougal had never seen the like. It occurred to him that these three weren't outlaws.

They were lunatics.

69

Cyrus Temple didn't laugh a lot. He didn't find much in life amusing. But he laughed like hell at the Clydesdales.

It was a little past eight when knocks on his hotel door roused him. Ordinarily he was up at the crack of day but it wasn't often he got to stay in a luxurious hotel like the Studevant, let alone stay in it for free. Since he'd only arrived the day before and reckoned it would be a while before Studevant called on his services, he decided to sleep in.

He always slept fully clothed. That included his bearskin coat. All he had to do was pull his stocking hat on and grab his Sharps and answer the door.

Deputy Agar looked fit to burst. "Mr. Studevant sent me. He needs you right away. They've struck again."

"So soon?" Temple said, both surprised and pleased. He could finish the job that much sooner and collect his small fortune. "What did they do this time?"

"You have to see. We've spent the past two hours running around collecting them."

Temple followed him down the stairs and out the front of the hotel. And there, tied to the hitch rail, were the biggest horses Temple ever saw. Fine animals, four of them bays and two brown, all with white markings on their faces and feet.

And all with bright yellow painted stripes down their sides. "Now there's somethin' you don't see every day."

Arthur Studevant was at the hitch rail arguing with a small man with a Scottish brogue. Nearby hovered the Gray Ghosts.

Out in the street, Marshal Pollard swept an arm at a crowd that had gathered. "I told you to disperse. Go on about your own business."

"It's a free country," a man hollered.

"Will you look at them stripes?" another said, provoking laughs.

Temple laughed, too. He'd never been hired for a job like this one was shaping up to be.

For years he'd scouted for the army until one day he and two other scouts were ambushed by the Sioux. A war party of Minniconjou caught them in the open and chased them until they sought cover in a dry wash. They had to. Their horses were played out.

One of the other scouts had taken an arrow in the back but managed to stay on his horse. They got him off and made their stand.

Temple thought he was a goner. There were eleven warriors and two had rifles, old single-shots they weren't much good with.

All that day he and the other scouts held the war party at bay. The wounded man grew so weak, he couldn't raise his rifle.

Then night fell.

They knew the Sioux would close in. They got the wounded man on his animal and climbed on their own, preparing to light a shuck, when over the sides spilled the warriors. Uttering bloodcurdling whoops, they let fly with arrows and lances and bullets.

His companions went down in the first volley. Temple took a shaft in the shoulder, but battling fiercely he somehow made it out of the wash and fled across the prairie.

The Sioux only chased him a short way.

Temple spent a month at Fort Laramie recovering, and made a decision. No more Injun-fighting. He offered his services as a tracker to anyone who would hire him, not knowing if he'd get a lick of work, and damned if he didn't end up making more money than he ever did scouting.

Now, Temple stopped laughing as Arthur Studevant approached.

"Do you see what they did?"

"I'm right here," Temple said.

"They've made me a laughingstock, yet again." Studevant swore luridly. "My stableman let them waltz in and do as they pleased with my team."

"Is your stableman a gun hand?"

"You're suggesting I shouldn't hold it against him that he didn't put up a fight? Hell, he didn't even have the stable doors barred."

"You sent the deputy to fetch me so I can listen to you bitch?"

Studevant practically had steam coming out his ears. "I expect to be treated with a little more respect."

"Do you want these bandits found or not?"

"Don't ask stupid questions. But a hundred people have gone by since they played their prank. Their tracks have been obliterated."

"You let me worry about the tracks." Temple turned. "Show me where your stable is. You'll see me again when I have news."

"Agar, here, will take you."

Temple didn't much care for the dim-witted deputy. Stupid people always raised his hackles. He reminded himself that this was just another job and soon enough he would be shed of him.

"Yellow stripes," Agar said, hustling along. "I don't savvy it, I tell you. I don't savvy any of it."

Despite himself, Temple said, "Someone doesn't like your boss."

"But the things they've done. It makes no kind of sense that I can see."

"Maybe that's the sense it makes."

Agar glanced at Temple. "You'll have to explain that. It's over my head."

Temple's dislike of the man fell a notch. At least he was honest enough to admit he wasn't the sharpest axe in the tool shed. "They want to make him mad so he'll get careless, would be my guess."

"And then what?"

"They get serious."

Agar shook his head. "It still doesn't make any damn sense." He pointed at a building ahead. "That there is the stable."

"You can go back."

"You sure? You don't want my help?"

"Can you track?"

"No."

"Can you shoot the eye out of a buck at a hundred yards?"

"I wish."

"Then you can go back."

"Good luck," Deputy Agar said, and wheeled.

Temple wasn't superstitious. He didn't believe that four-leaf clovers brought good fortune or that if a black cat crossed his path, he'd have a run of calamities. He believed a man made his own luck, and he made his now by going to the corner of the stable and sinking to a knee to examine the ground.

The outlaws wouldn't have ridden to the stable. Men on horseback were too conspicuous. They'd have left their mounts elsewhere and walked, and stuck to the shadows on the off chance someone might have been out and about and seen them. They'd have come up on the side of the stable and listened and looked before going in. When they left, they'd have gone the same way they came.

All he needed to find was three sets of prints coming and going. The ground was hardpacked, but there was a lot of dust. And there, faint and only partial in some instances, were the three sets he was looking for.

Temple touched a finger to a heel print. "Got you," he said.

70

Noona hummed to herself as she carried the cooking pot to the stream. Things were going wonderfully. Of all the town taming she'd done, this was the most fun.

Noona didn't delude herself, though. It would get ugly right quick as soon as her pa made up his mind to end it. That he hadn't yet told her he wanted Arthur Studevant to suffer some more.

All the other tamings, her pa had got in, done what he was hired to do, and got out again. He'd never toyed with bad men as he was toying with Studevant. He shot them and got it over with.

Studevant was a special case. Based on what Noona had heard, he was snake-mean, through and through. He liked power and money like some gents like whiskey.

All those businesses he took over, silencing anyone who objected, that poor gal he forced himself on . . .

Noona felt sorry about Laura Baker. Or as sorry as she could about someone she'd only known a short while.

She didn't mind making Arthur Studevant suffer. She didn't mind at all.

The sight of a ribbon of blue brought Noona out of herself. The stream wasn't more than a yard wide and not five inches deep but it sufficed for their needs. Squatting, she dipped the bucket and waited for it to fill.

She had left her Spencer back at camp. Her hat, too, so she could let her hair down. She went on humming, and when the bucket was full, she stood and raised it with both hands and turned.

"Holler and you die," said a big man in a bearskin coat. He had come up behind her as silently as anything, and was pointing a Sharps at her.

"Oh, my," Noona said.

"Cyrus Temple," the man said. "You might have heard of me."

"No."

"My name has been in the newspapers."

"So has my pa's," Noona said, and knew she shouldn't have.

"You don't say. What's his handle?"

"I've plumb forgot."

"Suit yourself. I'll trouble you to set down that bucket and turn around."

Noona bent to obey. As she lowered the bucket, she slid one hand under it. When she almost had it on the ground, she whipped up and flung the water at the big man's face.

He did what any man would do. He blinked as the water struck him, and retreated a step.

Noona was on him in a bound. She swung the bucket by the rope handle and it caught him on the jaw. He staggered and waved his arms, his Sharps momentarily forgotten.

Noona hadn't forgotten about it. She swatted at the barrel and knocked the rifle from his hands. Before he could set himself, she slammed the bucket against his knee. She was trying to break it but his legs were as thick as tree trunks. He opened his mouth to cry out but didn't. A shout would bring her pa and her brother.

Noona swung again, at his other knee. Her hope to bring him crashing down was foiled when arms like iron bands wrapped around her, pinning her arms to her sides. She was lifted as if she were weightless.

Struggling mightily, Noona rammed her forehead into

his chin. She thought it might force him to let go, but it was her own head that was swimming.

"Damn, girl," he growled, and threw himself at the ground with her under him.

Noona went to shout to warn her kin, but the world exploded in pain even as a great weight threatened to stave in her chest. She blacked out.

The next Noona knew, she was on her belly with a knee like an anvil in the small of her back and her arms were being pulled behind her. "No," she said, and heaved, or tried to. He weighed a ton.

Noona could still yell a warning. She raised her head and opened her mouth, and a huge hand clamped over her lips, smothering her yell to a gurgle.

A blow to the back of her head ended her struggles.

She revived the second time with a start. She had been gagged and her wrists had been tied, and he was in the act of doing the same with her ankles. She kicked and shifted and drove her foot at his face, but he swatted her leg and put all his weight on both and finished.

Rising, Cyrus Temple cupped her chin and turned her head from side to side, looking puzzled. He stepped back, favoring his hurt leg, and touched his chin and winced.

"Damn, girl," he said. "You're a hellion, and that's no lie."

He picked up his Sharps.

"Now for your menfolk."

71

Byron was cross-legged at the fire, reading. Today it was *Don Juan*. He'd read it when he was younger, back in Texas. It was the first of Lord Byron's poems that he came across, and he'd loved it from the first stanza. It was as if his namesake called to him, a joining of their souls in a way his father could never, ever comprehend.

With so little to do in camp, he had plenty of time lately to read. The past two days he'd enjoyed miscellaneous poems, but now it was time for an epic.

He never ceased to marvel at Lord Byron's insights. Some accused Byron of being too cynical. Not him. The poet had seen through the shams of his day to present the real and the true. And when people were stripped of their pretensions, there was a lot to be cynical about.

He also loved Lord Byron's humor. No one could make him laugh like he did.

Byron was so engrossed in his book that he didn't realize someone had come up until they coughed to get his attention.

An enormous man in a bearskin coat and holding a Sharps on him was studying him as if he were peculiar. "What in hell are you doin', boy?"

"Reading," Byron said, and showed him the cover. "Lord Byron. I do so love his poetry. Don't you?"

"God in heaven," the man said. "First a girl and now this."

"A girl?" Byron said in alarm. He started to rise but the Sharps' muzzle was trained on his chest, and the man said a single word.

"Don't."

Byron sat back down. "Did you hurt her?"

"We had a tussle," the man said. "She's a scrapper, that one. The gent who hired me wants all of you alive so he can kill you himself, so all I did was conk her and tie her."

"Good," Byron said. "But she'll be awful mad. If she gets free, I wouldn't want to be you." He smiled. "Who are you, by the way?"

"Cyrus Temple."

"The Tracker."

"You've heard of me?"

"I read everything I can get my hands on. Books. Newspapers. Penny dreadfuls. You name it. Have you ever read *Sweeny Todd*? It's one of my favorites. But of course I don't love all those anywhere near as much as I love Lord Byron."

Temple's eyebrows tried to meet over his nose. "You wear that straw hat and those overalls and you look like a farmer. But you read poetry and books and talk like no dirt-tiller ever talks."

"I do all of that," Byron said.

"You're play-actin', boy. Who are you really and what in hell are you up to?"

"What we're up to," Byron said, "is hoping to draw Arthur Studevant out of his lair where we can do what should have been done a long time ago."

"So I was right. This is personal."

"Partly," Byron said. "Partly it's what we do for a living."

"Which is?"

"Town taming."

Cyrus Temple digested that. "There aren't many town tamers."

"It's a dangerous profession. No one in their right mind would take it up. My sister and I help our pa."

"A name, boy. I want your name."

"Byron Carter."

"Never heard of you."

Byron set the book in his lap. "We use a different name for taming. Pa says it's to protect sis and me. Personally, I think he does it to rub their noses in the fact he's not what they think he is."

"I've lost your trail."

"He looks Indian but he's not. Our grandmother's doing, and he hates it."

"So what handle does he go by?"

"Asa Delaware."

Temple reacted as if Byron had poked him in the eyes. "The hell you say."

"The hell I do," Byron said, and laughed.

"Someone hired *him* to do in Studevant?"

"They did. He was going to decline, but then he learned what Studevant is like and Studevant's law dogs beat me black-and-blue. And here we are."

"Studevant never told me any of that. Asa Delaware, by God. And Studevant thinks it's just some idiots out to make him look like a fool."

"Oh, that, too."

Temple looked across the meadow and then to the right and the left. "It occurs to me this is suddenly damn serious. Where's that pa of yours, anyway?"

"Right behind you," Byron said.

Temple started to turn, and Asa pressed the muzzle of the Winchester shotgun to the back of his head.

"I wouldn't."

"Hell," Temple said.

"I heard you say you hurt my girl."

"She started it."

"No. You did by coming after us. Who else has Studevant brought in, or did he figure you were enough?"

"I am all I know about."

"Well, then," Asa said.

"I'd like to strike a deal," Temple said quickly. "I lower my rifle and you lower yours and let me walk away. I leave Colorado, and you finish your vendetta or whatever this is."

"No," Asa said.

"I won't tell Studevant about you. Hell, I won't even talk to him. I'll get on my horse and head straight for Wyoming. What do you say?"

"I've already said it."

Temple's voice hardened. "My Sharps is pointed at your boy. I squeeze this trigger, it'll blow a hole in him the size of a pie plate."

"Not quite that big."

"You might get me, but I'll kill him."

"How many have you?" Asa asked.

"Have I what?"

"Killed."

"What the hell does that have to do with anything?"

"I like to know the tally."

"I've never counted them."

"Sure you have. Everybody counts them. Some brag on it, but even the ones who don't brag have counted."

Temple was quiet a bit and then said, "Twenty-two, damn you."

"I heard about that sheepherder and his family. Ranchers hired you to get the sheep off their range."

"Nothing was ever proved. I was set free."

"But you did it."

Temple was angry and went to turn but caught himself.

"Who are you to judge me? You're not God Almighty."

"True. I'm just a man."

"You heard me about your boy. Lower your weapon or he's a goner."

"One last question. Where did you tie your horse?"

"My horse? What do you want him for?"

"I wouldn't want him to starve if he can't get loose."

"Damn you, Delaware. I've tried to be reasonable."

"Some do at the end. They think they can talk their way out of it. I usually let them have their say because they relax a little and that slows them a hair when we get to it."

Asa took a quick step to one side and fired at Cyrus Temple's hands. The buckshot blew the Sharps from Temple's grasp, and blew off his left hand at the wrist.

Temple screamed and staggered and held up the stump.

Blood spurted in large drops, splattering his face and his bearskin coat. "No!" he cried.

"Yes," Asa said, and shot him in the face.

Byron came over holding his book and looked down at the convulsing hulk. "You can see his brains."

"What's left of them." Asa worked the Winchester's lever. "Let's go find your sister and that horse."

"What if he'd squeezed that trigger?"

"He didn't."

As they hurried, Asa glanced back and said, "He was right about one thing though."

"Which is?"

"It's time we got serious."

72

Arthur Studevant was eating breakfast at the finest restaurant in Ordville. He should know. He owned it.

A pair of waiters fawned over him. They'd brought his poached eggs and toast with a glass of orange juice on a silver tray and laid it out for him as if laying it out for a king.

That pleased Studevant mightily. He liked being treated as befit his status.

The trappings of power, was how he liked to think of them. And he loved power more than anything. The power to rule others' lives. The power to control them, to bend them to his every whim.

He loved power more than he'd ever loved another human being. It was his passion, his tonic, his everything.

Studevant couldn't say exactly when he fell in love with it. The oldest of eleven children, he'd been put in charge of their day-to-day chores and whatnot because his father was always off conducting business and his mother flitted about like a hummingbird to keep all the appointments on her social calendar.

He'd gotten used to telling the others what to do and when to do it. He treated them decent but expected them to obey, and he supposed he'd carried some of that with him into his adult life.

Not that he cared where his lust for power came from. The important thing was to have it, to exercise it, to have control.

Now, as he spooned poached eggs into his mouth and chewed with relish, Studevant closed his eyes and for a few moments all was right with the world. He was literally tasting the delicious trappings of the power he loved so much.

Then Studevant opened his eyes and Marshal Pollard and Deputy Agar were entering the restaurant.

Cray and Dray glanced at him, and Studevant nodded.

Agar, always tactless, spoke before he was addressed. "Mr. Studevant, sir, you're not going to believe it."

The taste of the eggs grew bitter in Studevant's mouth. "Such a nice start to the day, too."

"Sir?" Agar said.

"Shut up." Studevant set down his spoon and focused on Pollard. "Let me hear it."

"That tracker fella," Pollard said.

Studevant brightened. Evidently he'd jumped to the wrong conclusion. "He's found them?"

"Somebody found somebody."

"What the hell does that mean?"

"You need to come see."

Reluctantly, Studevant rose and snatched his cane from where he had leaned it against the wall. Not that he needed a cane to get around. The gold knob was so heavy, he could crush a skull with it. "My first instincts were right. You bear bad tidings."

"You have to see," Pollard reiterated.

"How far?"

"The end of town. A crowd is already there. I have some of my deputies keeping them back."

"We'll take my carriage, then."

Studevant didn't demand the full details. While Pollard wasn't always as sharp as he would wish, Pollard was a genius compared to Agar. And if Pollard said he had to see it for himself, then see it he would.

The Gray Ghosts sat on either side of him. To his amusement, Agar kept glancing at one and then the other and nervously licking his lips.

Studevant had often imagined the pleasure he would derive from using his cane on the deputy's skull. He did so now. It lightened his foreboding a little.

Then they turned the last corner, and ahead were a few lots and the fringe of woodland that stretched for miles up into the high country.

An old oak reared higher than the rest, its mighty branches a testament to its endurance. And there, hanging by his ankles from a rope tied to a limb, was Cyrus Temple. The lower half of his bearskin coat had folded out on itself and hung down over his shoulders and head.

Already dozens of citizens had gathered to gawk. Several deputies ensured the curious didn't come too close.

All eyes swung toward the carriage as Studevant alighted. Keeping his features impassive, he strode to the crowd, and it parted like the Red Sea before Moses.

Studevant placed the end of his cane on the ground, leaned on the gold knob, and sighed. "So much for the Tracker. How long would you say he's been dead?"

"I'm no doc, but my guess would be he was killed yesterday and brought here last night," Marshal Pollard replied. "He must have bled out before they brought him."

"What makes you say that?"

"Lift the coat and hold on to your breakfast."

"The breakfast I didn't get to eat?" Nonetheless, Studevant used his cane to raise the bottom of the coat high enough to see Temple's head. Or what little was left of it.

"Shotgun," Pollard said. "Has to be."

A stirring at the back of Studevant's mind gave him pause. He sought for the cause, but it proved elusive. Shrugging, he let the coat drop.

"There's more," Pollard said.

"When it rains, it pours. What else?"

"It's pinned to his back."

"To his backside, actually," Deputy Agar said, and tittered as if it were a great joke.

Studevant rested his cane on his shoulder as he walked around. A sheet of yellow lined paper had been tacked to

Temple's britches. He read the first line out loud: "'To the coward Arthur Studevant.'" A burning started at the nape of his neck and spread up his neck and face. "Those sons of bitches."

Studevant ripped the note free and read the rest, growing hotter by the moment.

> To the coward Arthur Studevant,
>   We send your tracker back to you with our regards and our contempt. We had hoped you would come yourself but that requires courage of an order you don't possess. Only a yellow cur rapes women and terrorizes the elderly. Do you hear that barking? That's you.

Studevant smothered a violent oath. The note was signed, *A Friendly Farmer*. He crumpled it and glowered at the world and everyone in it. "How many have seen this?"

"I don't know. There were twenty people or more here when we arrived."

"Did Fiske see it?"

"I haven't seen him. If he was here, he left before we were sent for."

"I'll bet he has," Studevant said. "I'll bet he rushed back to put out another of his damnable special editions." Shaking his cane in fury, he made for his carriage. "Come with me, all of you."

"What about the body?" Pollard asked.

"Have it cut down and dropped in a hole."

Studevant boiled all the way to the *Ordville Gazette*. He was out of the carriage before it came to a stop. When he shoved open the door, a tiny bell tinkled.

Richard Fiske was at his press, excitedly changing the type. An owlish man who wore spectacles, he half-turned and frowned. "To what do I owe this dubious honor?"

Ignoring Fiske's two employees, Studevant walked over and gave the printing press a hard rap with his cane. "No," he said.

"Freedom of the press, by God," Fiske said. "Or haven't you heard of the First Amendment?"

"Until all this started, I thought you were on my side," Studevant said.

"I'm a newspaperman. I report the news. I don't take sides one way or another."

"I won't be publicly disgraced."

Fiske motioned with the box of letters in his hand. "I'm not the only one who read the note. By now it's spreading all over town. My printing it won't make a difference."

The hell of it was, Studevant thought to himself, the man was right. He could beat Fiske's face in and it wouldn't prevent the inevitable.

"Do you want my advice, Arthur?"

Studevant didn't respond.

"We've shared more than a few drinks together at the club. I happen to believe you didn't rape that girl. And I think that old biddy with her wild accusations is half out of her mind."

"You're making a point?"

"It can't keep on like this. No one will blame you if you go out after them. You have to end it or everyone in town will look down their nose at you. You'll lose all respect."

Studevant had a troubling thought. Without respect he'd lose something else. His power. "Perhaps you are my friend, after all."

"What will you do?"

"What do you think?" Studevant rejoined. "I'm going out after them and bury the bastards."

Part Six

73

The town tamers hadn't gone back to the meadow after they hung Cyrus Temple from the oak tree. They had climbed to a ridge that overlooked the west end of town and dismounted.

Overhead, stars sparkled. A crescent moon added its pale light. To the north, a coyote yipped and was answered by another.

A patch of rock offered a convenient spot to sit. Asa made himself comfortable and placed the Winchester shotgun across his legs.

Noona and Byron joined him.

"Get some sleep if you'd like," Asa said.

"What about you?" Noona asked.

"I reckon I'll sit here a spell."

Byron chuckled. "Our tree apple should cause quite a stir come morning."

"For a poet, you're awful bloodthirsty these days," Noona teased.

"I just want it over with," Byron said. "I want to get on with my new life."

Noona stared down the mountain at the few lights that speckled the town at that hour of the night. "Do you reckon it will work, Pa? Will it goad him enough to draw him out?"

"We'll know come daylight or soon after," Asa predicted.

"I'm sorry about that Tracker getting the better of me," Noona said. "I didn't hear him sneak up, and I should have."

"He got his," Byron said. "He thought he was so slick, but Pa was slicker."

Asa looked at him. "Never gloat over killing a man, son, no matter how much he deserves it."

Byron tilted his straw hat back on his head. "You know, now that I think about it, I've never once heard you gloat over all those you've sent into eternity."

"When you put an end to a man, you end him permanent," Asa said. "It's not a thing to take lightly."

"You've never expressed this sentiment before," Byron said. "I'd never have guessed you felt this way."

"What? You reckoned I enjoy blowing out brains?"

"More or less," Byron said.

"Hell, boy. How can you have lived with me for so long and know me so little? And me your own father."

"Don't start up again, please," Noona said. "We've been getting along pretty well and I'd hate to have it spoiled."

"Don't look at me," Byron said. "I'm being as friendly as I know how."

"All I have on my mind," Asa said, "is whether Studevant will come, and how many he'll bring."

"Those gray fellas for sure," Noona said. "And the marshal and four or five deputies."

"Eight or nine," Byron said. "We've faced worse odds."

"Doesn't matter if there's two or twenty," Asa said. "We have a job to do."

"But is it, though?" Byron said. "The town didn't ask us to come. That Preston woman did. And the town isn't paying us. She is."

"You worry it like a dog worries a bone," Asa said.

"I don't care who hired us. We're doing the right thing," Noona said.

"Yes, we are," Asa said.

"Arthur Studevant isn't on a Wanted circular," Byron said. "He doesn't have the law after him. He's not a bad man, as such."

"He's worse than any bad man we've ever come across," Asa said. "We need a whole new word for him. Cecilia Preston calls him a demon and that fits."

"Weldon Knox was wicked as could be," Byron reminded him. "And devious, too."

"Knox can't hold a candle to Studevant. Knox lorded it over a ranch. Studevant lords it over Ordville and Bentonville and God knows where else. He has the law in his pocket and is friends with the governor and senators and the like. If he ever goes into politics, he could run the whole country."

"Can you imagine what that would be like?" Noona said.

"This country would be a living hell." Asa paused. "You were with me when I talked to those people. Arthur Studevant is the most evil son of a bitch we've ever come across."

"Watch your language, Pa," Byron said. "There's a lady present." He put on a show of glancing every which way. "Somewhere."

"I should kick you," Noona said, but instead she laughed and swatted his arm.

Silence fell until Asa stirred and said quietly, "I couldn't walk away from this, you two. Not and be able to look at myself in a mirror."

"You haven't heard me complain once, have you?" Noona said.

"I have," Byron admitted. "I was dead set against it until they beat me and I learned better."

"I learned something important this time, too," Asa remarked. "Bad men don't always look like bad men. They don't always wear pistols and tote rifles and beat people in the open or gun them down in the street. Some bad men wear suits and tote canes and have others do their beating and shooting."

"I wonder who he's talking about," Byron said.

"Hush," Noona said.

"Evil doesn't have a black E stamped on its forehead," Asa said. "It doesn't always wear its black heart on its sleeve for all to see. Sometimes it pretends to be good. Sometimes it hides its black heart under expensive duds and you have to look deep to find it."

"Why, Pa, that was almost poetical," Byron said.

"Go to hell, boy."

"Pa," Noona said.

"I meant it," Byron said.

"Get some sleep. Tomorrow the killing might commence and you want to be well rested."

"True," Byron said. "The only thing worse than shooting a man when you're half-asleep is shooting him on an empty stomach."

"Honestly, boy," Asa said. "You can be plumb ridiculous at times."

"I take after my pa," Byron said.

74

At the crack of day, Ordville was astir.

The sky had brightened when a milk wagon came up the street and the driver got out to place bottles on doorsteps. He was returning to his wagon when he happened to glance toward the oak tree.

Asa imagined the man's shock.

The driver took a few steps toward the oak, then turned and ran to the nearest house. He pounded on the door and when a man in a robe came out, he pointed at the tree and they exchanged words.

Asa had to imagine what was said, too, since he was too far away to hear them. Something like, "Come see! There's a man hanging on that tree!"

The milkman scurried off to spread the word.

Asa nodded in satisfaction. It wouldn't be long before the demon appeared, he hoped.

The sun rose and Byron and Noona were both awake when the fancy carriage appeared.

"At last," Byron said.

"I wish I was down there," Noona said. "I wish I could see his face."

They saw the great man climb out, saw the marshal and

the deputy and the Gray Ghosts. Even from that high up, they could tell how mad Studevant was by his posture and how he stomped to the carriage like a mad bull after he read Byron's note.

"I do believe we've done it," Byron said.

"We'll see," Asa said.

The carriage went back into town. They lost track of it amid the hills and winding streets. Over an hour went by and it didn't reappear.

"I spoke too soon," Byron said.

"Patience," Asa said.

His was rewarded about the middle of the morning when a large group of riders came from the direction of the Studevant Hotel.

"What have we here?" Byron said.

"I count eleven," Noona said. "And look at the last one. He's leading a packhorse. They aim to stay at it a while."

Asa was more interested in the first rider. "We've done it, by God. His Highness is with them."

"Hark," Byron said. " 'Tis the great man himself, astride a fine chestnut."

"Hark?" Noona said.

The posse came to the oak tree and drew rein. The body had been cut down but the rope still hung from the limb.

Studevant said something and one of the Gray Ghosts climbed down, walked over to the oak, and his right hand flashed. The next instant, the rope fell to earth.

The distant crack of the shot rolled up over the forested slopes and was echoed by the crags far above.

"Did you see that?" Byron exclaimed. "He shot the rope in two."

"That was some shooting," Noona agreed.

"They'll be the ones to watch out for," Asa said. "Those gray fellas."

"How do they expect to find us with their tracker dead?" Byron wondered.

"We help them," Asa said. He stood and bent and unbent each of his legs a few times to restore the circulation. "I'm getting too old for this."

"I'm too young," Byron said.

They climbed on their mounts, wheeled to the west, and rode half a mile deeper into the mountains. A switchback took them to the tree line. Above spread boulder fields and talus with precious little vegetation.

"Do you have a plan or is this make it up as we go?" Byron asked.

"Pa always has a plan," Noona said. "It's what makes him Pa."

"Thank you, daughter," Asa said.

"Then you do have one?" Byron said.

"I do," Asa confirmed, "and it starts with you and your sister gathering up all the downed branches you can find."

"What will you be doing?"

"Pruning my toenails."

"Pa told a joke," Noona said, and laughed.

"Miracles do happen," Byron said.

Asa liked seeing them so lighthearted for a change. He climbed down, let the reins dangle, and climbed to a flat spot that was to his liking. When his son and daughter came out of the trees with armfuls of branches, he said, "Pile it here."

"We're making a fire," Noona guessed the obvious.

"We are."

"A beacon to lure the wicked to their doom," Byron intoned, and gazed gravely down the mountain. "Or to put us in an early grave."

75

Marshal Abel Pollard didn't like it one bit.

He didn't like leaving town. In town he had an edge. He knew Ordville like he knew the back of his hand, and he was the law.

He didn't like charging off into the wilds. He was city born and bred, not a country boy. The wilds were as alien to him as the moon. Oh, he could live off the land when he had to, but he wasn't any great shakes when it came to the kind of skills Cyrus Temple had, and look at what happened to Temple.

Pollard especially didn't like that Arthur Studevant had thrown common sense to the wind and was letting his pride rule his actions. He'd tried to talk Studevant out of it. He pointed out that he suspected the outlaws or whoever they were wanted Studevant to do exactly what he was doing. "You're playing right into their hands," Pollard had warned, but it did no good.

Now Pollard glanced at Agar on his left and then at the six other deputies behind them. Every deputy he had, including two who only worked part-time but were the same as the full-time deputies in that they had no qualms about beating and killing.

Suddenly Pollard realized Deputy Agar was talking to him.

"Psssst, Abel. Didn't you hear me? The big man wants you."

Sure enough, Arthur Studevant was beckoning.

Pollard tapped his spurs and passed the Gray Ghosts to ride alongside Studevant. "Have you changed your mind and want to go back?"

"We've been all through that," Studevant said gruffly. "I'm going to end this one way or the other."

"It's the 'or other' that worries me."

"Once again you disappoint me," Studevant said. "I expected you to be as eager to see that justice is done as I am."

"I thought we're fixing to kill the bastard," Pollard said. "Justice has nothing to do with it."

"Your sarcasm is duly noted. But it's just as far as I'm concerned."

"Just, maybe, but not smart," Pollard said. "Maybe we should make them come to us and not go to them."

"Not that again. Have no fear. We will prevail."

Pollard bit off an angry reply. Studevant was next to the only person he knew who used words like "prevail." The only other one had been that damned nuisance of a poet they had sent packing along with—

Startled, Pollard hauled on the reins and brought his sorrel to a stop. "It can't be!"

Arthur Studevant drew rein, too, raising his arm so the others knew to stop. Shifting in the saddle, he snapped, "What is the matter with you, Abel? Are you losing your nerve?"

"Prevail," Pollard said. "He used the same damn word."

"Who did?"

"And Temple had half his face blown off. Why didn't I see it sooner?"

"What the hell are you babbling about?"

Pollard was tired of being talked down to. "You haven't figured it out, have you? The great Arthur Studevant, as dumb as everyone else. And you keep saying *I'm* a disappointment."

"Have a care, Abel."

Pollard refused to be intimidated. "Tell me, great one. Who do we know who always kills with a shotgun?"

Studevant's confusion was rare. "You do, on occasion. So do a lot of lawmen. And shotgun messengers on a stage rely on them."

"I said always. As in they are half famous for it."

"I've never heard of anyone who *always* uses a—" Studevant froze.

"Think about it," Pollard said. "There were three of them and there are three of these masked outlaws. And one of the outlaws talks fancy and writes fancy. And one of them used a shotgun to take off the top of Cyrus Temple's head."

"How could I have been so blind?" Studevant said, more to himself than to Pollard.

"It has to be them," Pollard said. "All the evidence fits."

"My God," Studevant exclaimed. "It all makes sense now."

"Then we go back?" Pollard hoped.

"Like hell we do." Studevant laughed and smacked his thigh in delight. "Don't you see? Now that we know, *we* have the advantage. They're bound to lay a trap for us, and we'll turn it against them."

"What kind of trap?"

"We'll know it when we see it."

Just then Deputy Agar hollered. "Mr. Studevant! Marshal! Look yonder at all that smoke."

Arthur Studevant glanced up the mountain and bared his teeth like a wolf about to take a bite. "We have them, by God."

76

Asa was glad to be getting it over with.

Their games of cat and mouse weren't to his liking. He preferred to go in, gun down those he was hired to gun down, and go home.

He'd never encountered a situation like this before. Where the bad man was the leading citizen and the other citizens had no idea he was bad. Where through fear and force, a vicious cat lorded it over a bunch of blind mice.

Now, hidden in pines no more than a stone's throw from the bonfire that crackled noisily and spewed a thick column of spiraling smoke into the sky, he stared down the mountain.

The posse should appear soon, Asa reckoned. They would come fast when they saw the smoke.

He'd been lying there over half an hour now.

Noona and Byron were hidden at different points, well away from the fire where they could use their rifles to best effect. Asa was proud of the fact they were sharpshooters, the both of them, able to drop man or beast at a hundred yards as easily as Asa did at close range with his shotgun.

The minutes added one on another and still the posse didn't appear.

Asa grew uneasy. Studevant and his lapdogs should have been in sight by now. Could it be they hadn't seen the smoke? he wondered. But they'd have to be truly blind to miss it.

The bonfire crackled less, and the smoke diminished. The column became snakes and the snakes became threads and the threads became puffs, and in a little while it would be out entirely.

Asa stood. It was plain his plan had gone wrong. The only conclusion he could come to was that Studevant must suspect it was a trap and hadn't taken the bait.

"Damn," Asa said.

He walked out into the open where Noona and Byron could see him and raised his left arm and waved it back and forth until both of them rose from hiding and began to make their way toward him.

Asa went to collect their horses.

This was going to be harder than he thought. He needed to come up with another way to lure the posse within range of their guns.

The fire was nearly out when Noona and Byron got there.

"Wonder what went wrong?" Noona said.

Byron, naturally, had more to say. "This is a bad omen. They should have fallen for it. That they haven't shown tells me they could be onto us."

"I don't see how," Noona said.

"You're taking it for granted they're stupid. They're not, or they wouldn't have pulled the wool over everyone's eyes for so long."

"It could be anything," Noona said.

"Or it could be they've figured out who we are," Byron insisted.

Asa ended their argument with, "Jabber doesn't solve our problem. Namely, how to bring them into our sights, whether they know it's us or not."

"If the bonfire didn't work, what will?" Noona asked.

"I vote we wait a day and ride into town and finish it there," Byron proposed.

"Have a gun battle in the middle of town? With all those bystanders around?" Noona said.

Byron shrugged. "We pick off Studevant and Pollard and it's over."

Asa had been thinking about his previous comment. "Let's say you're right and they've figured out it's us. The important thing then is how many have they told?"

"Hopefully, no one," Noona said.

"We have to find out," Asa said. "The last thing we want is our likeness on Wanted circulars."

"How about if one of us sneaks into town and asks around among our friends," Noona suggested. "I'm least likely to be noticed so it should be me."

"If it comes to that we will," Asa said. "First we go find the posse."

They headed down the mountain with Asa in the lead and Byron coming last.

Noona didn't stay in the middle long. She brought her mount up next to Asa's.

"I don't like this, Pa."

"Me, neither."

"I have a bad feeling."

"Me, too."

"Maybe we'd be smarter to swing wide of Ordville and not stop until we reach Texas."

"Cut tail and run?"

"I'm willing if you are."

Asa looked at her. "No, you're not, and neither am I. You're saying that because you're worried your brother and me will come to harm."

"Well, you maybe," Noona said, and grinned.

"You're a good daughter, gal."

"And he's a good son."

"Some days."

"Oh, Pa."

"As for turning tail, it's not in me. When I was your age I made a decision. I looked around me and saw all the wickedness in this world. I saw evil men and women, doing evil things to others. Killers, robbers, and worse. And I made up my mind to do something about it. I became an officer of the law to do my small part to make this world a better place. A place where it's safe for peaceful folks to get out of bed in the morning and go about their day without fear of being shot or knifed. When I took to town taming, it was for the same reason. To put the bad men of this world six feet under so they can't be bad anymore."

"Gosh," Noona said.

Asa wasn't finished. "There are some who'd say I'm playing at being God Almighty. That no one has the right to be judge, jury, and executioner. I say hogwash. I say that if the good don't stand up for themselves, then the bad have won. That we might as well dig holes in the ground and stick our heads in them like those big birds down in wherever it is."

"Ostriches," Noona said.

"That's not for me, gal. I won't wear blinders and I won't run scared and I won't tuck tail. I will stand up for myself and for those who can't stand up for themselves and I will exterminate the vermin of this world until I breathe my dying breath."

"Land sakes," Noona said.

"What are you on about?"

"That's the most you've said to me since I can remember. Why, it must have been a hundred words or better."

"Quit your teasing."

"Who's teasing?" Noona replied, laughing. Then she sobered and said, "But you know what?"

"You want me to stick to ten words or less?"

"I agree with every word you said. And I'll be at your side until my dying breath, too."

"Let's hope it doesn't come to that," Asa said.

77

The sun was golden in an azure sky, the forest alive with songbirds and the little creatures, like squirrels and chipmunks and an occasional rabbit.

It was so scenic and serene that Asa let his mind wander. He thought about how it would pierce him to the quick if anything ever did happen to Noona or Byron. He thought about the risks they took on his account, and how his wife, God rest her soul, wouldn't have let them.

There were days when Asa missed Mary something awful. Days when her face floated in front of him and seemed so real, he wanted to reach out and touch her.

Some people liked to say that life was hell on earth, and in one respect they were right. It was hell to lose a loved one. Hell to lose someone you cared for with all your heart. Hell to suffer torment the rest of your born days.

If Asa could, he'd turn back time and relive those days with Mary. They were the happiest of his life, her love for him the sweetest savor on God's green earth.

He never could get enough of it. He never could stop marveling that she cared so much. It was the first and only true miracle he experienced in his life. As ordinary and as plain as he was, she had loved him above all others.

Asa was thinking that when a jay squawked and the woods went completely still.

Asa drew rein. He was holding the Winchester shotgun across the pommel and firmed his grip.

"What is it, Pa?" Noona whispered from behind him.

Asa shook his head and motioned for quiet. His short hairs were prickling and he didn't know why. On an impulse he reined to the right toward the cover of a thick stand of aspens, and no sooner did he move his head than a rifle spanged and lead buzzed within a whisker's width of his ear. "Ambush!" he hollered, and used his spurs.

Suddenly rifles were blasting everywhere—six, seven, eight or more.

It was the entire posse, Asa realized, and bent low over his saddle horn. He glanced back and saw Byron doing the same. Noona had slipped onto the side of her mount as the Comanches were noted for doing, hanging by a forearm and an ankle and presenting no target whatsoever.

She was something, that girl of his.

A spruce loomed and Asa reined around it, putting it between him and the riflemen. Slugs tore at the branches and sent slivers and needles raining down.

A horse whinnied stridently. Asa hoped it hadn't been hit. They couldn't afford to lose one. Not now, of all times.

He made it to the aspens but didn't stop. He rode on, checked to be certain Noona and Byron were still behind him, and didn't stop until he burst out the other side.

Asa drew rein. The shooting had stopped. He swung his horse around and relief washed over him. The second miracle of his life had just taken place. Neither Noona nor Byron appeared to have been hit. "Are you all right?"

Noona nodded.

Byron said, "They shot my hat off." Twisting, he pointed at a red furrow inches from his mount's tail. "And nicked my animal."

Beyond the aspens the woods exploded in crackling and crashing.

"They're after us," Noona said.

"Ride like the wind," Asa told them, and suited his own actions to his words.

They were skilled riders, all of them. It was one of the things Asa had insisted on when they were small. Learn to shoot and learn to ride and don't fully trust another living soul except your own family.

But mountain riding wasn't prairie riding or even like hill riding. The slopes were steeper, obstacles more plentiful, low limbs a constant menace.

It took every ounce of concentration Asa possessed to hold to a gallop. He glanced back often. He wouldn't admit it to Noona or Byron, but he was worried. Some posses couldn't be shaken. Some stuck on your trail until they ran you into the ground or killed you, and he had no illusions about which Studevant was out to do.

They had a fair lead, though, and held to it for half a mile or more.

Asa glimpsed a few of the posse now and then. The Gray Ghosts were out in front of the rest. Which figured, given he'd heard they were Confederate cavalrymen once. They'd ridden with Jeb Stuart, or some such.

Asa grew anxious to lose them. But how, when there was nowhere to hide? He didn't want to make a stand. Not yet. Not when there were so many of them.

Ahead, the trees thinned. Asa caught sight of a valley below. On open ground they could fly faster, but they would be riding ducks for their pursuers and their rifles.

Asa was about to veer and avoid the valley when a desperate gambit occurred to him. It was rash and might not work. They might be overwhelmed and slain. But if it did work it would buy them time.

He rode straight for the valley floor. Behind him pounded Noona and Byron, riding side by side now, brother and sister joined in spirit in this direst of perils.

With a jerk of his head and a sharp motion of an arm, Asa caught their eye. They realized he was about to do something.

The valley floor wasn't thirty yards lower when Asa brought his mount to a sliding halt. He was out of the saddle before it stopped. Darting to a fir, he sank to one knee.

Noona and Byron were quick to follow his example. They ran to trees on either side.

"I can hear them," Noona said. "They'll be on us any moment."

"We want them to," Asa said. That was his gambit. The posse would think they were making for the valley floor, and would come on without slowing. "Wait for me. Let them get close." Close enough for him to use the shotgun.

Byron pointed. "Here they come!"

78

The Gray Ghosts rode as one. It was uncanny how they sat their saddles the same and moved the same. They hadn't jerked their pistols yet.

Marshal Pollard and a deputy were next, and both held rifles. Pollard narrowly missed a tree and lost a little ground.

Above them flitted the figures and silhouettes of the rest of the manhunters.

Asa looked for Arthur Studevant but didn't see him. That was too bad. Drop Studevant, and it might break the spirit of the rest.

Noona and Byron were looking at him, waiting for his signal.

Asa rose partway and banged off a shot at one of the Gray Ghosts. Dray or Cray, he couldn't tell. Asa thought he couldn't miss but at the first movement on his part, both of the Ghosts swung onto the offsides of their mounts as Noona had done while simultaneously reining sharply aside, one to the right and the other to the left. The buckshot passed harmlessly over the one Ghost's animal.

The deputy coming on hard after them hadn't spotted Asa, and when Dray and Cray swung wide, he glanced at one and then the other in confusion. By then he was barely ten yards from the tree Asa was behind.

Asa let him have a blast of buckshot in the chest and worked the Winchester's lever to fire again.

Byron and Asa opened up, their rifles banging in a peal of thunder.

Farther up the mountain, Marshal Pollard hastened for cover. So did those behind him.

"Damn," Asa fumed. He'd hoped to drop more than one of them. Rising, he shouted to his son and daughter and sprinted after their horses.

The animals had gone a short way and stopped. The gunfire had made them skittish, and when Asa reached his, he had to snatch at the reins several times before he caught hold and could swing on.

"Only ten now," Noona crowed. "And I think I winged another."

Not enough, Asa thought, and relied on his spurs again. He quickly gained the valley floor and reined parallel to the forest. The trees and undergrowth provided the cover they needed as they fled around the valley rather than across it.

He was surprised the posse didn't come after them.

Midway around, Asa reined into the woods. He pushed on for another quarter of a mile, then stopped and swung his horse broadside to watch their back trail.

No one appeared.

"We shook the buzzards," Noona crowed.

"Too easily," Byron said. "They wouldn't quit over losing one man."

Asa figured the same thing. "They're up to something."

"What can it be?" Noona asked.

"I don't know," Asa said, and that troubled him.

"We shouldn't stop," Byron said. "They'll be after us and we must make it as hard for them as we can."

Another thing Asa agreed with.

For over an hour they pushed their horses to the limit and finally had to stop to let the animals rest.

A finger of rock afforded Asa a magnificent view of the country below, of slope after rolling slope heavy with timber, of the valley in the distance, of a pair of golden eagles soaring over a snow-clad peak and of several ravens lower down.

But there was no sign of the posse.

"Where can they have gotten to?" Noona wondered.

Asa tried to imagine himself in Arthur Studevant's expensive shoes. Would he return to Ordville for someone to take the place of the man he lost? Not likely. Would he make camp and wait for Asa to come to him? Possibly, but Asa wasn't about to ride into another ambush.

Byron joined them wearing the look he often did when he was deep in thought about poetry. "Care to hear my latest brilliant idea?"

"So long as it's brilliant," Noona said dryly.

"We don't wait around for them to make their move. We make a move of our own." Byron paused. "What is the one thing they'd least expect us to do?"

"Walk up to them with our hands in the air?"

"No, sarcastic sister. The one thing they wouldn't expect is for us to be waiting for them when they return to Ordville."

"You're proposing we get there ahead of them?" Asa said. "And what? Lie in wait for Studevant in his hotel suite?"

"We wait for the posse just outside of town," Byron said. "Their guard will be down, them being so close. We do it right and we can pick all of them off."

Asa liked the idea. Liked it a lot. "That's using your noggin, boy. I reckon all these years of rubbing elbows with me have paid off. You were bound to learn something."

"I learned a lot of things from you, Pa."

"Name one," Asa said, not really expecting him to.

"I learned that a person should stand on their own two feet. I learned we should do what we think is right even if others think it's wrong. I learned that we should do what we're passionate about. Find something we believe in, and live it as truly as we know how. I learned to step aside for no man. To treat all women with respect. And I learned that when I'm beaten black and blue, to get back at the sons of bitches any way I can."

Asa stared in amazement. "You learned all that from me?"

"That and more."

"I learned pretty much the same," Noona said.

Asa looked away. An odd lump in his throat was to blame. He'd never talked to them about this before, never imagined he'd had that much of an effect on their lives.

"Something wrong, Pa?" Noona asked.

"No, daughter," Asa said. He was being honest with her. For the first time in a long time, nothing was wrong at all.

79

"His name was Hanks," Marshal Pollard said. "He worked for me now and then when I was shorthanded. Good with his fists but slow on the brain."

Arthur Studevant stared at the dead man they were about to wrap in a blanket with no more interest than if the man were a bug. "He's not a gun hand, then?"

"Hanks? Hell no." Pollard laughed. "His draw was slow as molasses."

"If that's the case," Studevant said, controlling his temper, "why did you bring him?"

"You said to round up every deputy I have. And it's not like there are gun hands on every street corner."

"Or working for you," Studevant said with a pointed look at Deputy Agar.

"I've killed a few, I'll have you know." Agar defended himself.

"Were they tied and helpless?" Studevant asked.

"That was uncalled for," Agar said.

"Were they?"

"Two of the three."

"Deputy Agar is dependable," Pollard said. "That's more important to me than being able to fan six shots as fast as someone can blink." To spare Agar further embarrassment, he gazed about them and said, "Speaking of which, where did those spooky gray goblins of yours wander off to?"

"The Gray Ghosts are on a mission and will return when they've done my bidding."

"You never mentioned any mission to me."

"I saw no need."

"I see." Pollard wheeled and stalked off.

Studevant sighed. The more time he spent in the marshal's company of late, the more he questioned whether he should let him go on wearing a badge. Maybe he should have one of the Gray Ghosts elected to the post. They could ride better than Pollard and shoot better than Pollard, and best of all, unlike Pollard, they never sassed him when he wanted something done.

"You're being awful hard on Abel," Deputy Agar grumbled.

"Eh?"

"I thought you liked him. Why do you keep treating him like he's no-account?"

"I treat him like he deserves. And who the hell are you to question my reasons for anything I do?"

"I'm Abel's pard," Agar said. "I don't like you putting on airs with him."

"Perhaps you should talk to him, then," Studevant said, "and get him to pull his head out of his ass."

Now it was Agar's turn to huff off but he stopped to glance back and say, "Just because you have money, you reckon you're better than everyone else."

"I am."

Agar went after his friend.

"I swear," Studevant said. "I'm surrounded by simpletons." He spied a log and went over and sat and leaned on his cane.

The man who had been leading their packhorse all morning came and stood in front of him. "My handle is Carnes."

"So?" Studevant said.

Carnes was heftily built, with a bushy walrus mustache. His clothes were cheap store-bought but there was nothing cheap about his leather gun belt or the Smith & Wesson he wore high on his left hip. "So I couldn't help but overhear and I wanted to set you straight on a few things."

"*You*," Studevant said, "want to set *me* straight?"

Carnes nodded. "I'm not like Hanks or Agar. I have six notches on my pistol and it would please me mightily to add six more."

"You're telling me you're a gun hand."

"I'm telling you I'm more than that. I'll kill anyone, and I follow orders real good."

"I see," Studevant said. "This is your idea of a résumé."

"I can do everything those Gray Ghosts can do."

"I doubt that. But I'll take your offer into consideration. Your boldness impresses me. I'm in dire need of bold men."

"Keep me in mind." Carnes touched the brim of his bowler.

Studevant smirked. One of the advantages of being rich was that people were forever coming out of the woodwork to bend over backwards for him. He just might give this Carnes a try. Who knew? Carnes might be everything he claimed, and a man could never have enough killers on his payroll.

80

Asa figured the quickest way was a beeline for Ordville, or as much of a straight line as they could manage with slopes and ravines and canyons and gullies to deal with.

A couple of hours, he reckoned, and they'd be there.

He rode taller in the saddle than had been his wont of late. It stemmed from his talk with his son.

Byron didn't realize it, but he'd given Asa the greatest gift any son could give a father. He'd told Asa that he'd done something right, that his upbringing had instilled in him values Asa held dear.

Asa wouldn't have guessed. The only thing he thought Byron cared about was that silly poetry. Only now maybe it wasn't so silly. Not if Byron could read it and still be more like Asa than Asa ever suspected.

Damn, but Asa was proud of the boy. Noona, too, but then he'd always been proud of her.

A cliff reared on Asa's right. On his left towered a phalanx of pines. He reckoned they were a mile or more from their pursuers, and temporarily safe.

A bend in the cliff brought the trees closer. Asa was looking at the ground for sign and had no reason to expect danger.

Or for Noona to shout, "Pa! Look out!"

Asa snapped his head up. He was riding at a fast walk and drew rein, or tried to. Too late he saw a rope had been strung between a pine and the cliff. It missed the horse's ears and caught him flush in the chest. If he had been riding at a gallop it would have torn him from the saddle. As it was, he was lifted half up on the cantle and lost his hold on his shotgun and nearly on the reins. The pain wasn't bad but the shock rattled him. He clutched at the sliding shotgun at the selfsame instant that the rope was pulled violently taut. His horse passed out from under him and he crashed to earth.

Scrambling to gain his feet, Asa froze when a gun barrel was jammed against his temple and the metallic rasp of a pistol hammer sounded in his ear.

"That was right easy," the man holding the pistol said in a Southern drawl.

Asa felt a shiver of dismay. It was one of the Gray Ghosts, who showed no fear at all when Noona and Byron pointed their rifles at him and Noona hollered, "Drop that six-shooter!"

"Your pa would die before me, girl," the Gray Ghost said calmly.

"And both of you as well," said another voice behind them.

Asa's dismay became the clutch of fear. The other Gray Ghost had appeared to their rear with both his Colts trained on Noona's and Byron's backs.

Byron started to turn.

"Don't you," the Gray Ghost warned. "I can hit an apple on the fly, and neither of you are flyin'."

Byron and Noona looked at Asa. The question in their eyes was plain. Should they try or shouldn't they?

"I wouldn't," Asa said. "These aren't amateurs."

"Smart of you, old man," the one holding the pistol to Asa's head said.

"Drop the rifles," the one behind them commanded.

"Damn our luck," Byron said, and let go of his.

Noona hesitated.

"You can't do us any good dead," Asa said.

With a scowl of contempt, Noona cast hers to the grass.

The Gray Ghost next to Asa moved a couple of steps to one side. "This is how it will be. You do as we say, you live. You don't, you die."

The other Ghost said, "Mr. Studevant wants you breathin', but he said we only have to keep you that way if you cooperate."

"Between us and you," the first Ghost said, "we'd just as soon gun you here and now. So please, feel free to do somethin' stupid."

The other Ghost laughed.

"How could you have known where to lie for us?" was the burning question in Asa's mind.

"We've been followin' you since you shot that useless Hanks," the Gray Ghost said. "It was easy to do. Show him, Dray."

The other Gray Ghost reached into a large pocket on his slicker and brought out a folding brass telescope. "A spyglass always comes in handy."

"Damn," Asa said.

"Now you intend to take us to Arthur Studevant, I expect," Noona said.

"Smart gal," Cray said, and snorted in amusement as if she wasn't smart at all.

"You'll want to tie us," Byron said, holding out his arms.

"Well, ain't you a daisy," Cray said. "But no. You can't ride well tied, and we have a lot of riding to do."

He wagged his twin Colts. "Now let's get to—"

"Hold on," said Dray in a suddenly suspicious tone.

"What?" Cray said.

"Have them climb down and search them. And I mean *search* them. Word is they're damned tricky." Dray gouged his Colt into Asa's temple. "And if either makes a fuss, I splatter their pa's brains."

"Damn you," Asa said.

"Flatter me all you want," Dray said.

Cray backed to the cliff where he had clear shots at Byron and Noona. "You heard my cousin. Off those critters and reach for the clouds."

With obvious reluctance, Byron and Noona did as they were told.

With a lightning flourish, Cray twirled his left Colt into its holster. He expertly patted Byron down and found a pocket pistol inside Byron's overalls. "Yep. You're tricky, all right." He moved to Noona and reached out to pat her.

"I don't want you touching me," Noona said.

"You don't have a say."

"A dagger up my sleeve. It's all I have."

Cray unclasped it and slid it out and tossed it, too. He reached for her again.

"I just told you that's all I have."

"And you expect me to believe you? Be serious, gal."

Noona colored at the intimacy of his groping and glared when he was done. "I told you."

"You're pretty when you're mad."

"I can't wait to kill you."

"Listen to the firebrand," Cray said, and laughed. "Or is it that you like to kill?"

"Sometimes it has to be done and you do it. That's all there is to it."

"Liar. You do like it. I can see it in your eyes." Cray smiled. "Too bad we're on opposite sides. I could go for a she-cat like you."

"Dream all you care to."

Dray's lips were a slit of annoyance. "Are you havin' fun, cousin? Am I interruptin' your courtin' by remindin' you we have a job to do?"

"Don't be so prickly," Cray replied, sounding prickled himself.

"Now it's your turn," Dray said to Asa, and in no time he discovered the derringer up Asa's sleeve. "That's all the hideouts."

"Let's get them to Mr. Studevant, then," Cray said. "He can't wait to beat them to death with that cane of his."

81

Asa racked his brain and came up empty.

They had been riding for half an hour. Dray was in the lead and Cray brought up the rear, with Dray half-twisted in his saddle so he never took his eyes off them.

The pair had gathered up their rifles and the shotgun and short-guns and put the latter in their saddlebags and tied the long guns to their saddles.

They were damned efficient, these two. Asa was mad at himself for the ease with which he'd been captured. Now he and his children were only an hour or so from death's door.

Studevant would take great delight in killing them. Asa imagined that gold-knobbed cane smashing Noona's and Byron's heads to pulp, and resolved not to let that happen. But how to turn the tables?

"So you're Southern boys." Asa broke his silence.

"We are," Dray said. "But we ain't boys."

"You fought for the South?"

"We wear gray, don't we?"

"I fought for the South, too," Asa lied. He would have except he had no truck with slavery and those who thought that folks with black skin were less of a human being than folks with white skin. A person couldn't help how they were born. All his life he'd been looked down on because he'd been born looking like a redskin when actually he was white, and it fostered a keen hate in him for any kind of bigotry whatsoever.

"If you think that will make us get all weepy and let you go," Dray said, "it won't."

"What if we paid you to let us go?" Noona said. "I have a few thousand socked away."

At the rear of their line, Cray laughed. "Girl, you're plumb ridiculous. Mr. Studevant pays us that much a month."

"Five more years of this, and we'll be set for life," Dray said.

"Your boss doesn't have that long left," Asa said.

"Give it a rest, old man," Dray said. "You're licked and it's over except for your screams."

"Were you there when he raped the Baker gal?"

"Shut up, old man," Dray said.

"You were, weren't you? You and your cousin. And you did nothing to help her."

"I told you to shut up."

"Or what? You'll shoot me for talking? I bet Studevant said you're not to kill us unless we resist. And none of us is resisting."

"I can shoot you in an arm or leg and he wouldn't mind."

"True Southern gents, the both of you," Asa spat. "You let a young gal be violated and did nothing."

"I'm losin' my patience with you," Dray warned.

Asa hoped so. He was deliberately trying to provoke them. A desperate plight called for a desperate act and he had one in mind. They were nearing some firs that would do nicely. "Yes, sir," he said over his shoulder to Noona and Byron. "Take a good look. We're in the presence of two noble sons of the South."

Dray drew rein and wheeled his horse. "Not one more word, by God."

"Noble," Asa said with all the scorn he could muster. "Are your mas still alive? If not, they must have rolled over in their graves when they saw that girl raped and you two *gentlemen* did nothing to help her."

In a blur, Dray's right-hand Colt was out and he gigged his horse alongside Asa's. "You don't listen for shucks, old man."

"Go to hell, you worthless gob of spit," Asa defiantly shot back.

It was childish. It was almost silly. Yet the insults worked.

Dray snarled and whipped his Colt at Asa's face. Asa got an arm up and took the blow on his wrist. The Macintosh absorbed most of it although it still hurt like hell. The bone didn't break, but Asa cried out, "My arm!" and went into his act. He threw himself from the saddle in a headlong dive at a fir only a few feet away. Twisting in midair, he contrived to hit the trunk with his shoulder but make it look as if his head bore the brunt. He fell flat and quivered and groaned, then lay still.

"Pa!" Noona cried.

"Don't move, gal," Dray barked.

"You neither, boy," Cray said to Byron.

Asa heard the clomp of slow hooves as Dray brought his animal around.

"Get up, old man."

Asa lay motionless.

"Get the hell up, I said! Your sham doesn't fool me."

Asa stayed put.

"It looked to me as if he struck his head," Cray hollered up.

"Goddamn it," Dray said.

"Don't just sit there," Cray said. "Climb down and see. We're wastin' time."

Asa heard Dray's saddle creak and the crunch of dry pine needles under a heavy foot.

"If you are fakin', I will pistol-whip you."

A hand fell on Asa's shoulder. He kept his eyes closed and stayed limp as he was roughly rolled onto his back.

"Well?" Cray asked.

"I don't see no blood," Dray said.

Asa's chin was gripped and his head turned from side to side.

"Nor any hen's eggs, neither."

"Smack him a few times."

Asa braced himself. The stings were sharp but minor. He rolled his head with each as he had seen unconscious men do when slapped.

"He's out like a snuffed candle," Dray said.

"Try water from your canteen," Cray suggested. "If that don't work, we'll throw him over his horse and take him as he is."

"Stupid old man," Dray grumbled. "Provokin' me like he done."

Asa heard more crunching and cracked his eyelids.

Dray had a six-shooter in his right hand and the strap to the canteen in his left. He came back, sank to a knee, and shoved the six-gun into its holster so he could uncap the canteen.

Asa's moment had come.

82

Asa exploded into motion, ramming his fist into Dray's throat. Dray reacted instantly, dropping the canteen and grabbing at Asa's arm even as his other hand streaked to the Colt. Asa was grabbing for it, too. He got hold of it, but Dray got hold of his hand and clamped it in a vise, preventing him from drawing.

They grappled.

Asa heard the other Gray Ghost yell, heard the bang of a pistol and the whiz of lead.

Dray was nearly purple in the face and gasping for breath. The blow to his throat must have nearly crushed his windpipe, and his struggles were growing weaker.

Noona screamed, and there was another shot. She wailed, "Byron!"

A surge of fury lent Asa a rush of strength. He wrenched and twisted and had the Colt free. Dray clutched at him as he cocked the hammer and shoved the muzzle against Dray's belly.

The blast was muffled but not the result. Dray was knocked back. He stayed on his knees, though. Gurgling and wheezing, pure hate in his eyes, he clawed for his other Colt.

Asa shot him in the face, and swiveled.

Byron was down and there was blood. The other Gray Ghost was standing over him with a Colt half-pointed but couldn't use it because Noona was on him, hitting and raking with her nails.

As Asa looked, Cray backhanded her and sent her sprawling. "Bitch!" he said, and pointed his Colt at her. "Studevant can go to hell. First you and then I finish your brother and then your—" He glanced toward his cousin and Asa, and stiffened. "No."

Asa shot. He wasn't any great shucks with a pistol. He never had been. It was partly why he used a shotgun. He aimed at Cray's chest but he wasn't sure he scored because Cray didn't act like he was hit.

Cray fanned a shot from the hip.

A stinging pain shot up Asa's side. He thumbed back the hammer and fired again, saw Cray's Colt boom and buck.

Then Noona was next to Cray. She was still on the ground, and kicked him in the knee. It must have hurt like hell because his leg gave and he glared down at her and pointed his six-gun.

Holding the Colt two-handed, Asa aimed at Cray's head, thought *Please, God*, and fired.

The heavy slug drilled a hole in the Gray Ghost's temple and smashed out the other side of his skull, spewing a lot of hair and brains. Cray blinked, just once, and pitched forward.

Noona avoided the body and scrambled to her brother. "Byron!" she cried. "Byron!"

Asa pushed to his feet. He touched his side and his palm moistened with blood. Heedless, he ran to his children, his heart close to breaking at the prospect of losing one.

"Oh, Byron," Noona said, tears glistening her cheeks. She had his chin in both hands, and let out a sob.

"Quit making such a fuss. And quit blubbering on me, for God's sake."

The sound of his son's voice was a tonic to Asa's soul. There was a wound high in Byron's left shoulder. He was bleeding but unless the wound became infected, he should live. "Thank God, boy," he said, and coughed.

"He took a slug meant for you, Pa," Noona said, her tears still flowing.

"He did what?"

"This Ghost was fixing to shoot at you and Byron leaped in front of him and took the slug himself."

"I wasn't thinking straight," Byron said.

A hot sensation spread from Asa's chest to the rest of his body. He felt his eyes moisten and didn't care. He tried to speak and couldn't.

"Pa? Are you all right?" Noona asked. She was looking at him in concern.

Asa did more coughing. He placed his hand on Byron's good shoulder and said, "I've been a fool."

Noona came around Byron on her hands and knees and put her hand to Asa's side. "You've been shot, too. Let me have a look-see."

"Pa?" Byron said.

Asa let her part the Macintosh and open his shirt and winced when she probed.

"How is he?" Byron asked.

"He'll have another scar to add to his collection," Noona said. "It took off some flesh and scraped a rib, but he'll live." She smiled and kissed Asa on the cheek. "Don't scare me like that."

"Me, either," Byron said.

Asa bowed his head and cried.

"Pa?" they both said at the same time. Noona clasped one of his hands and Byron, despite his wound, took hold of the other.

"Pa, what is it?" Noona asked.

Asa shook his head.

"Pa, please?"

Byron said, "Damn it, we've never seen you cry, not even when Ma died. What's wrong?"

"Everything is right," Asa got out.

"You're making no sense," Noona said. "Did that conk on the head addle you?"

"No conk," Asa said. "I was faking."

"Then what?"

Asa raised his wet face and kissed her on the cheek and

then astounded them both by bending and kissing Byron on the cheek, as well.

"Pa?" Byron said, sounding strained.

Asa sniffled and swiped at his face with his sleeve. "This is how it's going to be," he said, his self-control returning. "We'll get a fire going and boil water and clean and bandage that wound of yours. You're to rest while your sister watches over you until I get back."

"And where will you be?" Noona asked.

"Ending this once and for all."

83

Finding their camp was easy.

The smoke gave them away. They'd kindled a fire and made themselves comfortable. A log had been pulled up for Studevant and he was drinking coffee and going on about something or other.

Marshal Pollard had hunkered across from him with a tin cup in both hands and was sipping and listening.

Deputy Agar stood nearby, his thumbs hooked in his gun belt.

The other deputies, all five of them, were lounging and talking.

Concealed by the low branches of a spruce, Asa took a deep breath. He was about to do something reckless, and he didn't give a damn.

The Winchester shotgun held one in the chamber and four in the magazine. Five shots weren't enough to drop eight shooters, but he didn't care about that, either.

There sat Arthur Studevant. Who had raped a young woman. Who'd had others beaten. Who had people murdered. Just to further his own ends.

Asa didn't care about that, either.

Not anymore.

All that mattered to Asa was that his son had been beaten and shot and his daughter hurt.

This wasn't about town taming anymore.

This was personal.

Squaring his shoulders, Asa marched into the clearing. They didn't see him right away.

It was the marshal who noticed first. His mouth fell and he sat stock-still with the tin cup halfway to his mouth.

"... should be back by sunset," Studevant was saying. "That's what they told me and they always keep their word."

"It will be something if those Gray fellas of yours bring the Delawares back alive," Deputy Agar said.

By then Asa was close enough and he stopped and said, "They won't be bringing anyone back."

Studevant gaped.

The five deputies looked confounded.

Deputy Agar bawled, "It's him!" and went for his hardware.

Asa shot him in the chest.

At twelve feet the force was enough to hurl Agar off his feet and the spread was enough to blow a hole in him as wide as a watermelon.

Before the body hit, Asa had jacked the lever and pointed the Winchester at the Lord of Ordville. "Guess who is next."

Arthur Studevant took a swallow of coffee and said, "Well, now. This is an unexpected development."

"Your Gray Ghosts send their regards from hell," Asa said.

"You killed both of them? I'm impressed."

"I'm not here to impress you. I'm here to end your days."

"Asa Delaware," Marshal Pollard said. "I was right that it was you and yours. I figured it out after we left town this morning. I should have figured it sooner but you threw me off with those disguises and that kissin' business."

"It was supposed to throw you off." Asa took a couple of steps so the tin star didn't block his view of the deputies.

"What do you want, Delaware?" Studevant said.

"Don't ask stupid questions." Asa was so eager to squeeze the trigger, he had to will himself not to.

"You do me and the others will gun you."

"Count on it," Marshal Pollard said.

"A grown man should know when to keep his mouth shut," Asa said, and curled his finger on the trigger.

Pollard had no chance to react. The blast slammed him off his heels and smashed him flat onto his back with most of his neck missing and his face mangled.

Asa worked the lever and again swung the shotgun at Studevant.

"Here now. You can't shoot me in cold blood."

"Funny words coming from you."

Studevant glanced at the deputies. "Carnes? The rest of you? What are you waiting for? You're five to his one and he can't have more than a few shots left."

A deputy with a walrus mustache stood. "Just so we're clear. If I gun this old goat, I get Pollard's star?"

"The job is yours, Carnes," Studevant said.

"You hear that, boys?" Carnes said to the other deputies. "I'm your new boss. Anyone who wants to keep his job, the ball is about to drop." He squared on Asa and sneered. "You can't kill all five of us, mister."

"I don't know," Asa said. "As bunched together as you are—" He didn't finish. He shot Carnes in the head, pumped the lever, and shot at two deputies who were shoulder to shoulder. The buckshot riddled both, and that left two who were further apart. He charged them as they drew. With a flick of his wrist he fed the last shell into the chamber and took off the top of the quickest's head.

Not breaking stride, Asa drove the stock into the mouth of the last, drove it once, twice, and a third time. The man crumbled, gagging and spitting blood and teeth. Asa kicked him in the neck, and he went limp.

Asa reached for his cartridge belt.

Behind him, a gun hammer clicked. "I wouldn't, were I you."

Asa imitated stone.

"You can turn around," Arthur Studevant said. "I want to see your face when I do it."

"I want the same thing," Asa said as he slowly rotated. He let go of the Winchester and it clattered at his feet.

Crossing his hands in front of him, he stood as if meekly awaiting his fate.

Studevant had risen and held a short-barreled Starr revolver he must have produced from under his jacket. "I can't describe the pleasure this will give me."

"I've noticed you like to hurt folks," Asa said.

"Only those who stand in my way." Studevant's eyes glittered with spite. "I'd love to beat you to death with my cane, but I don't know where your brats are, so I'd better get this over with."

"I would have liked to take my time with you, too," Asa said. "But we don't always get what we want."

"I do," Studevant said. "I always have my way."

"At what cost?" Asa said.

Arthur Studevant laughed. "At no cost to me but at great cost to others. And do you know what? It doesn't bother me a bit, grinding others under my heel. The little people of this world have only themselves to blame for being little. I'm worth more than all of them put together. I'm important. I matter. I'm *somebody*."

"You're dead," Asa said, and in a flash he raised the Remington derringer and shot Studevant smack between his important eyes.

Part Seven

84

They had placed four tables together at one end of the outside café at the Poetry House so that there were enough seats.

They all came.

Cecilia Preston, smiling, at peace with herself for the first time since the murder of her husband.

Cornice Baker, who would never be at peace again, the memory of her daughter searing her every waking hour.

Bedelia Huttingcot, the dove who gave up selling her charms for money at the cost of being scarred the rest of her days.

The miner who had stood up to Studevant and had his house burned down and his little girl along with it.

They all came.

Asa, wearing his derby and slicker and usual clothes, listened to their thanks and shook their hands, some with tears in their eyes. He said little.

Noona had on her everyday clothes. She smiled and told them no thanks was needed, that it was what they did for a living.

Byron didn't say much, either. He sat across from Asa and they stared at each other without hostility for the first time in a very long time.

At last everyone had said their piece and got up to go.

Cecilia Preston put her hand on Asa's shoulder and looked him in the eyes. "What you did was no small thing."

"Like my daughter told you, it's what we do."

"You have saved lives. You have saved God knows how many from suffering as we have."

Cecilia rose onto the tips of her toes and kissed him.

"God be with you, Asa Delaware."

"Carter," Asa said. "It's Asa Carter."

Then the townsfolk were gone and the three of them were alone.

Noona said huskily, "Well." She embraced Byron and kissed him. "I'll miss you, idiot."

Byron managed a lopsided grin. "I'm sorry, sis."

"Don't you ever be," Noona said. "You're happy. You have found peace." She grinned and poked him in the ribs. "Or at least that Olivia gal." She touched his face, and smiled, and turned away.

It was Asa's turn. "There are no words," was all he could say.

"I love you, Pa."

Asa looked down at his boots and had the illusion they were misty as from falling rain. He blinked and recovered enough to say, "I love you, too, son. I wish you the best."

"It's not like we'll never see each other again. I'll come visit you two, and you two better come visit me."

"We will."

Asa started to turn but stopped and opened his arms and they hugged. For a moment, in his mind, Asa was holding a ten-year-old cheerful bundle of vigor, and it was almost more than he could endure.

Asa and Noona shouldered their carpetbags and their weapons and bent their steps toward the train station.

For Asa, sounds seemed to come as if from a great distance, and the street seemed strangely deserted even though it was full of people. "Damn," he said.

"I know," Noona said.

"How about you? You don't have to do this if you don't want to anymore."

"I like killing bad people. I like it a lot."

"Some would say it's not fit work for a female."

"This female doesn't care what other people think. I live as suits me, not as suits anyone else." Noona grinned. "I learned that from my pa."

Asa stood straighter and gave his head a toss, and suddenly the world around him was restored to its usual state.

"I can't wait to get home and relax for a spell," Noona said.

Asa made a strange face and said, "Uh-oh."

"Don't tell me. So soon?"

"I had my mail relayed, and a letter caught up to me from the mayor of a small town called Kimbro."

"Are you sure it's the mayor this time?"

Asa laughed.

"Let me guess. They have some bad men who are giving them problems?"

"They do."

"Then we'll rest up a day when we get home, and get to it. We are the town tamers, after all."

"That we are," Asa said.

Read on for an excerpt from David Robbins's

BLOOD FEUD

Now available from Signet.

Summer green clothed the rugged slopes and deep valleys of the Ozark Mountains. Bears and cougars prowled, coyotes yipped and coons ran, and a wealth of birds warbled and sang. It was a beautiful land, and it was a beautiful girl who came to Harkey Hollow.

The girl was all of eighteen. Tawny of skin, with corn silk hair, she moved with agile grace. She wore a plain homespun dress, green like the world around her, and nothing else. Her feet were bare. They had never known shoes.

Scarlet Shannon was her name, and she was where she should not have been.

Scarlet knew better than to come to Harkey Hollow, but she was fond of blackberries and they grew thick and delicious. She was wary but sure of herself, ready to flee should there be cause. She pricked her ears, and her eyes darted like a doe's on the lookout for wolves.

The vegetation thinned. Scarlet hunkered behind a sugarberry tree and surveyed the hollow. The blackberry bushes were as thick as ever and hung heavy with plump berries.

Save for a few bees and a swallowtail butterfly, nothing moved. The only sound was the tweet of a wren.

Scarlet moved into the open. She hefted the old wooden

pail she'd brought and scooted to the nearest blackberry bush. She plucked a ripe berry and plopped it into her mouth. Closing her eyes, she chewed slowly, swallowed, and grinned. She commenced to pick berries as fast as her fingers could fly. Every so often she glanced about her.

The sun's golden glow splashed the hollow and the surrounding woodland, lending the illusion that all was well.

Scarlet went on picking. For every two she put in the pail, she helped herself to another. She plucked and ate, plucked and ate, moving deeper into the patch as she went. Once she looked up and saw how far she had gone and took a step as if to turn back but shook her head and continued plucking.

The cicadas stopped buzzing.

Somewhere a squirrel chattered as though it was angry and a blue jay screeched noisily.

Scarlet's pail was half full. She came to a bush with some of the biggest blackberries yet and put two in her mouth. She bent to get at those near the bottom and heard the blue jay do more screeching. Belatedly, she realized what it might mean. Her fingers froze midway to a berry.

Just then the forest became completely still.

Scarcely breathing, Scarlet rose high enough to peer over the bushes. She scanned the woods. A goldfinch and its mate took wing and she studied the shadows where the birds had come out of the trees. Her whole body went rigid with dread.

Some of the shadows were moving.

Crouching, Scarlet moved deeper into the patch. She held the pail with one hand and the handle with the other so the handle wouldn't squeak. Rounding a bend, she flattened on her belly as close to the bushes as she could without being pricked by thorns. She folded her arms and rested her chin on her wrist. Time crawled. So did a large black ant, practically under her chin. The temperature climbed. She closed her eyes and fought the tension inside her. The crunch of a twig brought her out of herself.

Harsh laughter pealed and a voice like the rasp of a file on a corn cutter hollered, "You might as well show yourself, girl. We know you're in there."

Scarlet bit her lower lip and felt the blood drain from her face.

"You hear me? We were coming for berries and seen you."

Quietly, Scarlet rose but stayed stooped over. By small fractions she unfurled to where she could see over the bushes.

"We got you surrounded. You ain't going to get past us nohow. Make it easy. Come on out. You don't, you're liable to make us mad."

Scarlet counted seven heads. She dipped low and moved along the path, seeking another way out. But it appeared to be the *only* path, and meandered helter-skelter. Worse, it was taking her deeper into the hollow.

"We know you ain't a Harkey," the voice went on. "That means you're one of *them*. You got grit coming here, girl, but it was awful stupid. What, there ain't no blackberries on your side of the ridge?"

Some of the others thought that was funny. Scarlet almost went past a gap in the bushes. An animal trail, not as wide as she was, but it was better than being cornered. Flattening and holding the pail in front of her, she crawled. Brambles snatched at her dress and scratched her arms.

"I'm patient, missy, but I won't wait forever," the voice warned. "Either you show yourself or we're coming in. And if you make us do it the hard way, there will be hell to pay. We'll take it out of your hide."

Scarlet wasn't overly scared yet. She had confidence in her ability to outrun them if she could find her way out without being spotted. She wriggled along, wincing when she was scratched, until she came to the thicket's edge. A shadow moved across the opening. One of her enemies was out there, pacing back and forth.

"Come on, girl," the voice urged. "Don't be this way. You don't stand a snowball's chance in hell of getting away. Come out and I'll treat you nice. You have my word."

As careful as she could, Scarlet stuck her head out. A stocky block of muscle with no shirt and no shoes had his back to her. She drew her head back before he turned.

"Which one are you?" the voice called. "I don't know all of you by sight. Those I've laid eyes on over to Wareagle won't hardly ever give me the time of day."

Scarlet had a sharp retort on the tip of her tongue, but she swallowed it. She slid the pail to the opening and deliberately moved the handle so it squeaked. Dirty feet appeared and a freckled face lowered and fingers as thick as railroad spikes reached down.

"Rabon! I done found her pail!"

Scarlet exploded into motion. She was out of the gap like a fox-chased cottontail out of a hollow log. Some girls would have scratched or pushed, but she punched him flush on the jaw. He fell onto his backside and grunted, more surprised than anything. It gained her the seconds she needed to wheel and flee into the forest. Her pail and the blackberries were forgotten. She had something more important to think of.

Scarlet flew. Shouts and the thud of pounding feet told her they were after her. She glanced back and her confidence climbed. She had a good lead. There wasn't a boy anywhere who could catch her when she had a good lead. She flew, and she laughed. Her legs were tireless. She had taken part in footraces since she was knee-high to a calf, and could go forever. She needed that stamina now to make it over the crest before they caught her. Once she was on the other side, she was in Shannon territory. They didn't dare follow.

Scarlet's dress whipped about her. Her long legs flashed. The soles of her feet slapped the ground in a rhythmic beat. She glanced back again and laughed louder. She had increased her lead by a good ten yards. She vaulted a log and avoided a boulder and came to a leaf-covered slope where the footing was treacherous. She slipped but recovered and churned higher. Something moved in the leaves, a snake, and she bounded aside.

A rock missed her ear by a whisker.

Startled, Scarlet ran faster. She hadn't thought they would resort to rocks. But then they *were* Harkeys, and as her pa liked to say, the Harkeys were worthless no-accounts. She concentrated on running and only running. A flat clear stretch gave her a chance to put more distance between them. She was almost to a stand of maples when pain flared in her left leg and it buckled under her and the next thing she knew she was tumbling cattywampus. She hit so hard, the breath was knocked from her lungs. She lay dazed, her ears ringing, her vision blurred, struggling against an inner tide of darkness.

Voices and a poke in the ribs brought her back to the here and now.

Scarlet blinked and looked up and felt the way a raccoon must feel when it was ringed by dogs. The seven of them were puffing and sweaty from the chase. Only four wore shirts, and the shirts they wore were little more than rags with buttons. The biggest had a shock of black hair that fell in bangs over bushy brows. His dark eyes regarded her as her little brother used to regard the hard candy in the general store at Wareagle.

"Well, well, well. Ain't you a looker?"

Scarlet realized her dress had hiked halfway to her hips. She sat up and smoothed it and stood straight and tall. Her left leg still hurt and when she put pressure on it, she winced. "Who threw that rock?"

"The one that hit you?" the big one said, and chortled. "That would be me. Good aim, huh?"

Scarlet hit him. She punched him on the jaw as she had punched the other one, but where the other one went down, the big one didn't. His head rocked and he put his hand to his chin and did the last thing she expected; he laughed.

"Not bad. I've been hit harder but only by them that was larger than me, which ain't many."

"What do you want? Who are you, anyhow?"

"As if you don't know. We're Harkeys, all of us. I'm Rabon Harkey and these here are my brothers and my cousins."

"You're a Shannon, ain't you?" one of the others said. "You look like a Shannon with that yellow hair and those blue eyes."

"She's a Shannon," Rabon said. "She can deny it but we know better and now she's in a fix."

Scarlet put her hands on her hips. "I was picking berries. You had no right to come after me like you done."

"You're on Harkey land," Rabon said. "That's all the

right we need." He took a step and poked her, hard, in the shoulder. "What, you reckoned that since you're a girl we'd go easy on you? That you could sneak in and steal our berries and if we caught you we'd let you go?"

"They're not *your* blackberries," Scarlet said. "They're there for anyone who is of a mind to pick them."

Rabon shook his head. "Not if they're on Harkey land. Harkey blackberries are for Harkeys and no one else." He crossed his thick arms across his broad chest. "The question is, what do we do with you?"

"You let me go or there will be trouble," Scarlet warned. "My pa won't take kindly to you mistreating me. I won't tell him if you let me be. I give you my word."

"Is that supposed to scare us?" Rabon snorted, and gestured at the one Scarlet had punched down at the thicket. "Are you scared, Woot?"

"I surely am not, brother," Woot replied. "It'll be a cold day in hell before I'm afeared of a Shannon."

"What do we do with her?" the smallest and the youngest of them asked.

"We can't beat her like we would a feller."

"Why not, Jimbo?" Woot said. "It makes no difference to me. If they're a Shannon they have it coming."

Jimbo turned to Rabon. "It wouldn't be right hitting a female. My ma wouldn't like it. Your ma, neither."

"You ever cut free of those apron strings, you might be a man, cousin," Rabon said. "But you're right. Pa is always saying as how we need to be nice to ladies. So we'll be nice to this one if she's nice to us."

New fear clutched at Scarlet. "How do you mean?"

Rabon stood so they were almost touching. His breath smelled of onions and his teeth were yellow. "You're more than old enough. I bet you have already, plenty of times. A few more won't hardly matter."

"No," Scarlet said.

"It ain't like I'm giving you a choice. It'll be me first and as many of the rest as want, and you can be on your way."

"No," Scarlet said, more forcefully. She went to step around him, but he pushed her back.

"I'm not kidding, neither," Rabon said. "Here or in the shade yonder. I'll let you decide that much."

Scarlet looked at each of them. She saw no pity, no mercy, only resentment of who she was or, rather, *what* she was. The only exception was the young one.

Jimbo; he was troubled. She appealed to him, saying, "Your ma wouldn't like this. It's not decent."

"No, it's not," Jimbo agreed, and turned to Rabon. "All she wanted was some blackberries. You do this, everyone in the hills will be against us."

"She won't ever tell," Rabon said, and took hold of Scarlet's arm. "Will you, girl?"

Before she could respond Jimbo grabbed Rabon's wrist and pulled his big hand off her. "No. I won't stand for it. You hear? She's free to go."

Rabon's features twisted in amazement and then fury. Yet he smiled and patted his much smaller cousin on the head and said, "We'll talk about this later. Right now, the only reason I don't stomp you into the dirt is because you're kin. Remember that when you wake up."

"But I am awake," Jimbo said.

"You were," Rabon said, and punched him. Rabon's knuckles were the size of walnuts, his fist as large as a sledge. His blow lifted Jimbo onto his heels and sent him sprawling in a heap. Rabon rubbed his fist and regarded the rest. "Anyone else object?"

No one did.

Scarlet rammed her shoulder against Woot and drove him back. She was through the ring in a single leap and had taken several more strides when iron fingers locked in her hair and she was jerked off balance and slammed to the ground.

She fought but they were too many and too strong. Her arms and legs were pinned and spread and Rabon reared above her.

"Truth is, girl, I don't care if your kin find out. I'm tired of the stupid truce. My pa and his stories, he had a lot more fun than me. Now I aim to have me some, thanks to you."

And Rabon laughed.

THE LAST OUTLAWS
The Lives and Legends of Butch Cassidy and the Sundance Kid

by Thom Hatch

Butch Cassidy and the Sundance Kid are two of the most celebrated figures of American lore. As leaders of the Wild Bunch, also known as the Hole-in-the-Wall Gang, they planned and executed the most daring bank and train robberies of the day, with an uprecedented professionalism.

The Last Outlaws brilliantly brings to life these thrilling, larger-than-life personalities like never before, placing the legend of Butch and Sundance in the context of a changing—and shrinking—American West, as the rise of 20th century technology brought an end to a remarkable era. Drawing on a wealth of fresh research, Thom Hatch pushes aside the myth and offers up a compelling, fresh look at these icons of the Wild West.

Available wherever books are sold or at
penguin.com

National bestselling author
RALPH COMPTON

"A writer in the tradition of Louis L'Amour and Zane Grey!" —*Huntsville Times*

Penguin Group (USA) Online

What will you be reading tomorrow?

Tom Clancy, Patricia Cornwell, W.E.B. Griffin,
Nora Roberts, William Gibson, Catherine Coulter,
Stephen King, Dean Koontz, Ken Follett, Nick Hornby,
Khaled Hosseini, Kathryn Stockett, Clive Cussler,
John Sandford, Terry McMillan, Sue Monk Kidd,
Amy Tan, J. R. Ward, Laurell K. Hamilton,
Charlaine Harris, Christine Feehan...

You'll find them all at
penguin.com
facebook.com/PenguinGroupUSA
twitter.com/PenguinUSA

*Read excerpts and newsletters, find tour schedules
and reading group guides, and enter contests.*

Subscribe to Penguin Group (USA) newsletters
and get an exclusive inside look
at exciting new titles and the authors you love
long before everyone else does.

PENGUIN GROUP (USA)
us.penguingroup.com

S0151